TROUBLE COMES CALLING

I let myself through the front door and dropped my laundry bags. Before I could flip on the light, a hand grabbed my neck and shoved me to the floor. I rolled over to three masked figures and the unblinking eye of a sleek automatic pistol.

"If you don't move," one of them said, "you won't die."

"How gracious."

"If you mouth off, you won't die, but you also won't like the attention."

In the low light through the windows, I could see the outer office had been tossed. I expected the same was true of mine. I wondered if they'd breached the safe. Then I tried to figure out what I had that was so important it took three guys to retrieve...

EMBER SINS

A C.T. ROBILLARD INVESTIGATION

DOUG LANE

MIDNIGHT-TO-THREE PUBLISHING
2025

ALSO BY DOUG LANE

TWO IN LEFT FIELD
SHADY ACRES AND DARKER PLACES
FROM THE FILES OF THE IRON VANGUARD
THE ROAD WARRIOR LETTERS
HUNDRED ACRE
THE CATNEY AND LANEY COMPANION

This is a work of fiction. The characters, names, places, and incidents are the product of the author's imagination or are used fictitiously. Any resemblance to actual events, locales, or persons, living or dead, past, present, or future, is purely coincidental.

Published by Midnight-to-Three Publishing,
Aloha, OR

ISBN 978-0-9895417-9-4

FIRST PAPERBACK EDITION
9 8 7 6 5 4 3 2 1

For my beautiful bride

PEGGY

Right now, there are 7,164 languages in use
on planet Earth—and yet somehow
there still aren't enough
ways to possibly tell you
how much I love you.

EMBER SINS

Ten-thousand glittering facets to Houston, and I was cashing out next to the ship channel.

There were so many more worthy places to suck a final breath. Inside Co-Cathedral of the Sacred Heart, on the 55th floor of Quadrant Tower overlooking the rocket fields—hells, even the food court at the Art Car Palace would be better. Go quirky or go home.

Not me. I was getting kissed goodnight by the grimy lips of commerce. Dredged and developed from Galveston Bay all the way to the mouth of Buffalo Bayou, the ship channel was industry and diesel and stink for miles. I'd love to know who lost that bet. *Hey Sam! First one to get dragged under by his whiskey has to build a working port in a landlocked city.* Then again, we're down the coast from the city still settling beneath the sea. You find all kinds of outside-the-box thinking along the Gulf Coast.

It wasn't how I wanted to spend a Friday night.

Vetrov punched me again, left temple, and I thought I saw stars. No mean feat with the light pollution from the refineries. Vetrov gloated. "Someone whistled around the house today, I think." Gloating was good. It meant his oyster was ready to shuck.

"I've just about got you figured out," I said. "I know you lure the kids by promising what they need. Money, shelter, food, even plain old love—that's the easy part with a runaway. I know once they get into your car, no one sees them again. I know you drug them, because you toss out your empty anesthetic bottles with the regular trash. Kind of careless, Anatoly. But there's still one thing I'm missing: the how."

The son of a bitch laughed at me. "You're a PI? You've followed me down here at least twice. You must know the 'how' by now." He spread his arm at the waterway beside us, as if introducing the tugboat moored along the concrete apron.

"No, no. The ships, the pay-offs, I get all that. What I'm missing is how someone as stupid as you could have created such an efficient system in the first place."

I braced for the punch I'd invited. Vetrov didn't disappoint. Side of the head again. My equilibrium stuttered. Failed. I landed on my side. Tasted blood. I hate the taste of blood.

"You think you're smarter than me?"

I kept talking. It helped me focus. "I'm not the one who grabbed the under-age daughter of a city councilman. Good reason to flee the country, though. I hear he carries concealed."

"Flee? Please. I come, I go. Not the first time. I get a new name and credentials, I come back in six months."

"A new identity every time you screw up? That's got to get expensive." I pushed up to my knees, slower than I was able. "With that kind of overhead, I can see why you have to kidnap runaways for sex."

He waggled a finger at me. "I don't sex them. It's bad form to mix business and pleasure. I deal in raw material. What the pimps do on the other end, when the boat docks in Saint Petersburg? No matter to me, so long as the deposit is confirmed. You? I kill you for free."

His hand dipped into his sport coat, came back with a gun. No surprise there. I'd sized up the bulge under his arm hours before, when he left his building. He dug in a pocket, came back with a silencer. While he was occupied, I flexed my wrist, felt the collapsed baton drop into my hand from the clip up my sleeve. He was still screwing the silencer in when I popped the riot baton and shattered his wrist with a quick upward swing.

He grunted and lost the gun. It clattered across the concrete, a steel crab that dropped between the tugboat and the dock side with a *plunk* into the water below. Good place for it. I reshaped his knee with a side-swing. He folded hard on the concrete. I hit it again for good measure. A string of Russian invective rattled between the man's teeth. He might as well have had marbles in his mouth.

"If you want to curse at me, speak sailor English. Or French. French worked for Mémé." I stood.

"Fuck you."

"That's better. Where's Leilani Kant?"

Vetrov clutched his leg above the misshapen knee. "You let me go or she dies."

"Not likely. I've been a feather on your tail the last three days. She's not with you. She's not at your place. You don't have an accomplice. That means you hid her until you could sail. You wouldn't deposit her on the ship you're sailing with ahead of time, in case it left without you. You keep coming down here. She's down here." I had some ideas. I'd lost him the day before along this stretch. But there were a hundred squirrel holes along the ship channel, and I had no guarantee he wouldn't burn her if caught, just for the hell of it.

I knew I was right. Being right wasn't enough. I stared down at him. "Where is she?"

"You'll never find her."

The temptation to beat an answer out of him came and went. I had no use for human traffickers, and I was already annoyed about taking a bell-ringing, but so far he'd volunteered everything. I wasn't handing him a Get Out of Jail Free card.

I grabbed him by the broken wrist, not to torture him, though the fresh burst of angry gibberish was a bonus. I looked at his hand. Pulled it close and inhaled. Thought about where I'd lost him and what was down here. There was a faint stink to his suit, a specific, oily reek to his hands.

I let Vetrov fall and pulled my cell. "Barrett."

There was a small chime and she was there. "Go for Barrett."

"There's a spur road off Peninsula. Three maintenance outbuildings. The nearest one to the street has bilge pumping equipment. You'll find her there."

"I'm on it. Leave your channel open."

Vetrov studied me the way one might a magician.

"Process of elimination," I said. "You wouldn't stash her on a private company's parcel. Too easy to be caught where you shouldn't be, or one more criminal mouth to feed with a payoff. Eliminate those, plus all the corporate buildings and docks, and she has to be in one of the port management buildings. Add the piquant bouquet of oily wastewater sucked from between hulls, and the pin drops right into the map. How am I doing?"

Sirens crowded the humid night sky, distant but approaching. Police hoppers. Finally. At least three, bleating like flying sheep in the sky lane.

"She'd better be alive," I told him.

He spat at my feet. Missed. "What if she's not? What can you do then?"

"For starters, I can toss you into the channel to look for your gun."

The police hoppers descended from the ribbon of aerial traffic, angling towards a lot beside the access road. Vetrov knew he was caught. He got a head start on his Miranda rights by shutting up.

Barrett's voice came back over the hand-held. "I've got her, Thib."

"Is she alive?"

"Yeah, but you should get over here."

I didn't ask. I zip-tied Vetrov's wrists behind him and left him awash in red and blue lights.

It was five minutes on foot to the storage building off Peninsula. Barrett met me outside. I followed her through the maze of pump units, compressors, and other equipment. The same smell as on Vetrov permeated the space. The cryo-tube was in the rear corner of the steel-walled storage building. The tarp under which it had been hidden was to the side in a pile.

The tube rested on a workbench. It looked like an oversized bullet and buzzed like cheap neon. The silver finish seemed to glow. I noticed what remained of the red and blue NASA logo on the tube's side.

Barrett shined her flashlight through the glass panel on the side of the unit. Within, I saw the stored form of Leilani Kant. I took a picture with my phone.

"Really, Thib?" Barrett's expression suggested I needed to grow up.

I shrugged. "The cops are going to take a hundred of them. Do they ever offer me any for my case files?"

"I hope you have space for a few more." Barrett pointed under the bench. Another tarp. The second tube held an Asian girl who didn't look older than 14. Two more tubes parked in the space yielded a girl and a boy, faces dirty from life on the street, packed like so much frozen food for a host of ugly appetites.

"Is it too late for you to send him looking for his gun?" You might think the disgust in Barrett's voice was enough for both of us.

You'd be wrong.

"Where was the ship headed?"

The officer taking our statements on his portable glanced up from the transcription screen as if annoyed I was asking questions. He was still young, a few years on the force without a lot of hard turns. Moyer? Mayer? The PD had at least one of each, and I couldn't tell them apart. This one's name tag was hidden under his body armor. "Antarctica. Hell of a place to hide out."

"It was a transfer point," I told him. "His typical M.O. was to switch to a Russian research vessel en route, float for a while, and ship with them back to Saint Petersburg. Eight months for the entire trip."

"Doesn't extended time in cryo mess with the head?"

Barrett nodded. "So far. No one in the space industry has cracked it."

"But the problem worked in Vetrov's favor," I continued. "He arrives in Russia with four kids, none of whom have a memory of who they are, all ready to accept whatever story he feeds them. He has eight months en-route to build them the identities he wants them to have."

"How did he come up with NASA cryo-tubes?"

"Either a connection to the contractor who built them, or he bought them at a government surplus auction. The feds can work that out. But what I've dug up suggests he's been using them for months to send kids back to Russia. Cryo makes them virtually invisible: no heat signatures for drones to spot, nothing for a dog to sniff out. I figure after he scooped up Leilani Kant, he realized he needed to beat feet."

"Why not just set her free?"

"She'd be a loose end," Barrett said. "One that could identify him."

"The tubes are still at least ten years ahead of the Russian designs. I figure Vetrov swaps one for cash to finance his turnaround in Moscow, starts up again when he's ready."

The cop read through the dictated statement. "He's more well-rounded than the typical human trafficker."

"As Mémé says, 'Milk or cream, both the same when spoiled.'"

The cop's expression suggested he didn't know from Mémé. "What about his injuries?"

"Defensive. He had a .45 and drew. I'm licensed for concealed carry of the baton."

"The knee was a defensive wound?"

"Yeah. He tried to run after the gun."

I got skeptical eyes. "Fair enough. I'll have to pull your permits to verify they're current. Protocol."

"Do what you need."

"Where's his gun?"

I hitched a thumb at the red-hulled boat behind me. "Under the tugboat somewhere."

"Jesus, Robillard. Don't expect flowers from the dive team."

"Someone was going to work all night. The coroner treats me better."

"Is Detective Spencer still your department liaison?"

"Yes. The case file for this is in his registry. #1173."

The cop rotated the screen for my thumbprint. There's a reason kids can't sign their names anymore. The officer verified everything was complete. Balked. "Your name is Cyril?"

"Yes."

"Why does everyone call you Thib?"

"That's my name. Cyril Thibodeaux Robillard. Cyril was my grandfather's name."

"Yeah? Mine's was John."

"How dull."

"He didn't have much say in it. And cloud uplink is complete." The officer touched a couple of controls, folded the flex-screen and keyboard, and slipped them under his vest. "If we need anything else, we'll be in touch." He gave me a nod, tipped his cap to Barrett with a smile, and walked away.

Barrett followed his retreat with her gaze. "He seems nice."

"Back in November, after last time, you asked me to remind you what happens when you date city police officers."

Barrett sighed. "So I did."

We walked to her motorcycle. Barrett had left her hopper, a red sport model, home in favor of her bike—a vintage Indian Chief, crimson over cream paint. She'd restored it herself. The colors matched the 2nd Infantry insignia on her helmet. Barrett was still young, but two combat tours had given her a perspective well beyond her 28 years.

I hadn't planned on another partner after Rojo died, but I'm a better PI with someone batting back the theories I pitch. Rojo had also been better with tech than me. I'd advertised for someone computer and gadget inclined and gotten forty-plus electronic applications. Barrett was the only one who trekked downtown to apply in person. Asked why, she didn't bat her blue eyes or try to win me over. She went blunt: "If I can't do the legwork to get the job, I'm probably not cut out for legwork."

If ambition didn't give her an edge, her Army Recon background did. She'd seen combat, she knew tech, she could take direction and work independently. Her service record and the associated recommendations could have gotten her a position with any law enforcement outfit she wanted, local to federal. She craved a smaller chain of command. As my own army of one, I was happy to bring her aboard. It also didn't hurt she was in better shape for kicking in doors and such.

"Think you let him hit you enough?" she asked as we walked.

"I needed him to volunteer information. He volunteers, he ties his own noose. The minute I take the offensive hit, the District Attorney pulls out the big, red INADMISSIBLE stamp." I didn't tell Barrett there'd also been a police drone circling 500 feet overhead, watching things unfold. I wasn't supposed to know it was there. It had been with me off-and-on for the better part of a month, compliments of Inspector Koi. I suspected it was off-book, warrantless. There was no reason I knew that I needed a shadow. I could have cried foul, but I let him fly his spy anyway. There was plenty of rope to dole out for nooses all around. "The worst part? None of this blood is his."

"You need a medic?"

"No. I need some dinner. Want to come with?"

She looked at her watch. "It's midnight."

"Fête Souvent is open until two."

"My eyes aren't." She pulled on the helmet, tucked in stray strands of chestnut-colored hair. "I'll be crashing through the door around nine. Don't stay out all night. You have work tomorrow."

"Yes, Mother." I was living out of my office. It had been six months since my house burned to the piers, an impolite "hello" from a still-unknown party. You meet all kinds in private investigation. The builders got as far as framing a new structure before the insurance company decided it was my turn over some barrel. Living in the office wasn't ideal, but I had a couch, a coffee maker, and a mini-fridge, plus a gym up the street and a laundromat right around the corner. I was already paying rent. Made sense to squeeze it for all it was worth.

Barrett's bike roared into the night. I walked back to my car. As I passed the police hopper he was stowed in, Vetrov mouthed something at me full of rage and spit. Whatever it was, it didn't need subtitles.

TWO

The chef at Fête Souvent, a skinny guy with two sleeves of tattoos named Dewey Ainsworth, was a Creole-country magician. We'd known each other twenty years give or take, all the way back to mutual trail cut through high and low spots in Louisiana. He'd honed his knives in a half-dozen kitchens along the gulf coast and back to middle school before choosing Houston for his first personal concept. His brick-and-mortar place in the Heights landed on 'best of' lists all the time, made better by its proximity to my house. If I only ate there twice a week, he scanned the obits for my name.

He hovered beside my table, the booth at the end of the bar. He liked to ask after the gory details of cases, as is the wont of friends who see you occasionally on the news streams. The Kant kidnapping was trending and Dewey had seen my ugly mug in the background of someone's live feed, giving my statement. "You're all over the web. They say you were instrumental in catching that deviant."

"It was a collaborative effort."

"His fist and your face?" He studied my bruises. "I hope you got a few licks in."

"He'll never dance the *yablochko* the same."

Dewey wiped his hands on his apron. "I've eighty-sixed the special, but I can preview a soft-shell crab dish I'm planning to lead with tomorrow. I might ask for notes."

"Sneak preview me, Chef."

Dewey flitted back to the kitchen, and I studied the crowd. I liked the booth at the end. It was next to the kitchen; last one the public wants, first one the kitchen sees. It also offered a view of the front door across the bar, under cover of people at the rail and on stools. It was an old instinct, keeping my back to the door, watching the comings and goings.

I was in the middle of the first sip of my beer, a double brown ale Dewey's beverage manager brought in from Florida, when my cell buzzed. Caller ID told me it was Police Inspector Koi. I'd have sooner talked to Vetrov again. I sent him to voicemail, sipped my beer, and watched baseball highlights.

Koi called again ten minutes later. I turned my phone off.

The third time, Koi came calling through Fête Souvent's front door. He didn't make house calls unless someone was dead.

Koi reminded me of the assassins from old Asian action films: compact, chiseled, a little too wide-eyed and tightly wound. The department would pin captain's bars on him one day, in spite of himself. He had fifteen years on the force, seven of them as an Inspector. He'd spent most of his first year with the gold shield trying to railroad me for my wife's murder: in part because I discovered her body, in part because she'd been killed with my gun—stolen from my locked desk—and largely because no one came forward for the first month or so to corroborate my alibi. Throughout the entire process, he was so certain he was right he crossed multiple lines where having a badge was the only thing that kept me from giving him a refresher on assault and battery. In the end, the grand jury refused to indict.

In the years since, Koi had rebuilt from his overzealous black eye, but we were never going to hoist beers together on trivia night, never mind mutual respect or trust. I'm certain the only time I'd be disinclined to piss on him would be if he spontaneously combusted. Even if he was floating drones and hassling me at restaurants, I played nice because I needed to for my livelihood. He still got the barbs for free.

His stride was determined. I wondered if his drone was still somewhere overhead. I hoped it was caught in a tree. My dinner beat him to my table by ten steps. He waited until the server was done setting me up.

"You don't take my calls? You don't like me anymore, Crawdad?"

"That presupposes I've ever liked you, Inspector."

"I need you to come with me."

"Then you'd better dust off your handcuffs."

A thin smile. "I'm saving that for the hard way."

"Koi, I solved the Kant kidnapping tonight. Reunited a city councilman with his daughter, saved her and three other kids from the sex trade, and helped put a bad man in jail. You should try it sometime. Hell, you should have been there. I could have busted your leg too while I was handing them out."

"You could have tried."

I showcased my dinner with my hands. "And Dewey's team just made this gorgeous plate of comfort and victory for me, on account of me being the man of the hour. I intend to appreciate it."

He spoke softly. "Do you know how often the health department gets called here?"

"Exactly never. And if I tell Dewey you're pushing that rumor, you're going to learn how sushi feels." I took a bite. Breaded, fried, seasoned and sauced heaven, set atop a bed of succotash so tender, it might have bruised if mishandled. I made Koi wait while I savored it. "So unless I'm in Miranda-sized trouble, you can watch quietly or go away."

"Let me try this again: I'd like you to come with me. Please."

I'd have choked if I'd had a mouthful. "You actually know that word. Huh. Tell Gildman next time you see him that I owe him a dollar."

"There's a crime scene that involves you."

"Involves me how?"

"That's what I need your help with. And while it would be within my job description to put you in handcuffs, drag you out of here to answer my questions, and spin you loose when you get tired of tough talk, that takes too goddamned long. So I'm asking. *Please*." The last as if it had thrown hooks into his cheeks.

He had a point. It was far too late after a long day to put up with him any longer than I had to. I slugged my beer, then flagged my server to wrap my dinner. I didn't have the heart to tell Dewey I needed it to go. It was never going to be the same reheated.

THREE

We took Koi's unmarked hopper south from the Heights towards Montrose. I didn't own a hopper and had no desire. Personal aerial travel required greater trust in both technology and people, and neither did much to wow me. Most hoppers were driverless control: input the destination, press the button, sit back, and let the on-board computer handle the rest. Manual hopper control required a specific license, a sixteen-week course, and a liability policy that eliminated almost 100% of the morbidly careless. My car, a beat-up Jupiter Jubilee, got me from point A to B, and given a majority of air hoppers used non-petroleum propulsion systems, I appreciated the two-dollar-a-gallon fill-up people swore would never happen again.

At 1 a.m., the clusters of lighted high-rises were like the spikes of the city's pulse, one after another: the classic downtown skyline; the clot of the Greater Galleria; the vibrant color schemes of Asiaton; the hopper-pad topped towers of the Energy Corridor; the fluorescents of the Biomedical Sector. The broad glow in the southern sky announced the whole of the New Space Center, the launch and control hub NASA shared with a dozen commercial space service providers. In between, under meager streetlights, the dirt poor and the filthy rich lived among each other, worked and slept and sweated in the late spring heat. They say DC is cosmopolitan? Of 195 countries on the planet, 144 of them are represented in Houston. You know the score when a guy with Maori roots repairs your bicycle on the same street where you find an Estonian cafe, a Brazilian fashionista, and a fifth-generation Texan serving pit barbecue.

Most of the sky lane traffic at that hour was freight. Chemical and hazardous shipments were prohibited by air, but the goods haulers auto-piloted their way across Texas, clear sailing all the way to El Paso. Koi's hopper was quiet, well-baffled. He was a manual control driver, a requirement for cops. I appreciated how he didn't drive like one. We didn't talk. His radio was tuned to an electronic cacophony posing as music. The occasional interruption by the police band was a balm.

As we descended, I saw the carnival of flashing lights around a charred patch of rubble, half the block reduced to nothing. Fire, ambulance, police, the bright greens of a city haz-mat truck. Multiple columns of thin smoke rose into the darkness from the last remnants of the fire. Koi's hopper touched down outside the secure perimeter.

I couldn't place the smell on the breeze. Sweet, not unlike burnt sugar, and yet somewhat metallic. It permeated everything. There were other scents—a fire makes dozens—but the charred wood, plastics, rubber, even the ozone stink of arcing electric were small whiffs under the cloying and yet somehow industrial stench.

The building had been an apartment house, a horseshoe shape fronted by a half-circle drive and a fountain with a sculpted stallion. The tallest thing still standing was the horse. Fire companies, including an airborne tanker, sprayed debris from three directions to tamp the embers, adding steam to smoke. Charred beams leaned against each other as if grieving.

Koi walked and talked. "7702 Rose Street. The fire call came in about 10:15 p.m.; a driver saw the flames from the sky lane." He nodded at a uniformed cop manning the perimeter. The woman deactivated the light-line and let us pass. "It was already fully involved when fire and rescue got here. Preliminary assessment is arson, originating in the building's resident office. We found accelerant containers in the dumpster."

"You have to love a tidy firebug."

"A master alarm should have signaled the fire department. It was disconnected. Residents say the building alarm never went off either, but someone came through pounding on doors to wake them up. Whoever did it wasn't a resident. We suspect it was the arsonist."

About forty tenants stood in clusters near the rescue squad, dazed stares, mixed anger and shock. Someone had brought the lesser-clad sheets to wrap in, more for modesty than anything, warm as it was. "What kind of arsonist lets everyone know their place is being burned to the ground?"

"Insurance torch job, maybe a guy who gets off by burning things but doesn't want two-dozen murder charges around his neck. Except he overlooked the four deaf college students in a unit on the second floor. They had a visual alarm tied to the building master. Poor bastards never had a prayer. Tick four in the homicide column."

I sniffed the air. "Why does it smell like someone torched Candyland?"

"Ever heard of those smart buildings?"

"This was one of those?"

"Yeah. The organic material they're built from stinks when it burns. I've been past this place a hundred times and never suspected it was one. It's got to be one of the oldest in the city."

One of the bidders on my house rebuild had pitched a compact organic structure for the project. I'd skimmed the literature, but insurance eliminated the cost of organics from the start. The underlying science was supposed to be fascinating. I found it more dense than I cared to dive into. Watching firefighters knocking hunks of what appeared to be slag glass like piñatas from what was left of the frame wasn't a great sales pitch.

"This is all very educational," I said, "and I love a field trip as much now as I did when I was six, but you could have shared all of this over my dinner. Why am I here?"

"The building's digital services provider says three calls originated from the building's office after the fire began. One was to a number that looks like gibberish. One was to 911, but it never connected. The third was to your office number."

"I haven't been back to the office." I dialed the number. When messaging connected, I entered my access code. 10:12 p.m., one new message.

The electronic squeal went through my head, one ear to the other. Random pings and tones followed. I held the phone out to Koi. "Carrier wave. Sounds like an antique modem. Maybe a fax machine."

Koi listened. "A fax? They still make those?"

"How should I know?" I ended the call.

Koi frowned. "Here's my conundrum: why did an arsonist who went to the trouble of disconnecting building alarms and breaking in to set a fire stop to call *you* before fleeing the scene?"

"For that matter, why try calling 911 after disconnecting the master alarm, which would have dialed 911 automatically?"

"I have a forensics team to get me those answers," Koi said. "I'm curious about the connection to *you*. Do you have any active cases involving anyone here?"

"No. Nothing in Montrose for at least a year."

"How about cases involving someone with demonstrated criminal tendencies? Maybe a fascination with fire?"

"No arsons. Unless you count the person who burned my house down six months ago."

"Any progress on that?"

"No. Cold for a month. No thanks to the arson squad."

"Given the call, my concern is this arsonist might be *your* arsonist, and may have been calling to taunt or involve you." Koi enumerated on his fingers. I wished I'd brought my baton along to help. "You have no case ties to the place. I'm presuming you have no friends in the place. But the person who went to the trouble of breaking in to burn the place down stopped long enough to call you. It's not too far a stretch to believe arson—this and yours—is the common denominator."

"Really? That's your theory? Cat and mouse?"

"Sometimes things play out that way."

"Then the message is a great clue. Your arsonist is on the high side of middle age to elderly. Might be trailing a cord, maybe a piece of paper letting you know there was a transmission error. Without an electric outlet, I don't think it will get very far."

"If you want to play this tough—"

"I'd rather play it smart. Maybe if you gave me a little more information and a little less half-assed conspiracy theory, I could be more helpful. Though we all know 'half-assed conspiracy theory' is your milieu."

I saw two uniformed cops trying not to listen. Failing. Koi saw them too. His stare sent them walking elsewhere. His tone went granite-hard. "Information such as?"

"To start, a list of the residents. Someone involved in an old case or someone I'm obliquely connected to could be here without my knowing. If they tried to call 911, they may have been calling me for the same reason: help."

Koi's sideways glance was arctic. "That can be provided."

"I'd also like to see the phone records for the building for the last week or so, to see if there are any patterns or connections there. For example, residents who might be associated with old acquaintances or cases."

"I'll see what I can do."

Cooperation and a 'please'. All the myths are being busted tonight. Are we done here?"

"*We* probably have hours to go before *we* are, but I think *you're* done. Do you want me to give you a lift back?"

"Thanks, but I'd sooner find a large, feral dog to ride."

I used my phone to arrange a ride share, annoyed. I understood why Koi had brought me to the scene instead of talking to me at the restaurant. He wanted to gauge my reaction to the site, to see if questioning me against the visceral backdrop of the fire might wring a visual clue from me— change in expression, body language, inconsistent answers—to tell him if I was holding back. The man was a suspicious tool, but in like circumstances, I might have done the same thing.

Fête Souvent was closed by the time the hired car let me out. Then I remembered my dinner tucked behind the passenger seat of Koi's hopper. I hoped he was parked in the sun for a day before he discovered it.

I grabbed a burger from a drive-thru on the way back to the office, ate it while I drove, and went to bed still annoyed.

FOUR

The strange insect sounds rattling around my dreams resolved into the clicking of Barrett's laptop keys coming through the air vent. Diffused light slipped through the blinds. The clock on the wall said it was a little past nine. I took a glance out my seventh floor window, glad I'd opted for the sunset side.

The building was an old corporate blockhouse tucked among the downtown skyscrapers, a few blocks from Buffalo Bayou. Some wide-eyed developer had bought it empty ten years earlier and chopped it into street-level retail, twenty-eight office suites on the seven floors above, all capped by a restaurant space that took the entire top floor. He'd filled most of the street-side retail, but only seven suites above. The accountant on the second floor was an up-and-comer, some towhead kid fresh out of his CPA program who wanted to try business on his own. I figured in six months, he'd be taking a check from a tax preparer for seasonal work and thankful for things like cheap noodles. Three different medicos formed their own group on the third floor. A graphic designer eked out a living on the fourth. I had no idea what the tenant on six did. He'd been there a year. In his fifties, with a tuft of white hair on his chin, he looked like the bastard son of a billy goat. But I was an investigator, not a busybody. So long as nothing raised a hackle, I wasn't inclined to dig. If I had cause someday, I'd drop by with a belated fruit basket and scan his CV.

With the mattress retracted back into the sofa, I set coffee brewing. I cleaned up in the small bathroom off the side of the office. Then I sifted email. For being offline two days, there was remarkably little of value. I'd planned to run to the gym up the street for a half-hour on the elliptical and a proper shower. Living in my office as I was, the membership paid for itself in hygiene alone. I was also trying to ignore the duffel bag of laundry tucked in the closet. I was on my last clean shirt. I wondered if I could pay Barrett a spot bonus to tackle the pile without losing her respect.

Barrett finally knocked around ten. I imagined she'd already written up her own notes about the Kant abduction, probably so laden with detail my own would seem anemic. I wondered if Holmes ever smacked Watson around for being a better diarist.

She smiled. "You didn't tell me you and Koi were going to have a play date at the restaurant. I'd have tagged along for that."

"It turned into a field trip. And if it makes you feel better, I was last to learn it was happening."

"He emailed a couple of files. Something about a fire on Rose Street?"

"An arson. There should be a list of residents and a data dump from the building's digital comms server. Someone called the office from the arson site last night, about the time the fire was set. I offered to cross-reference the resident and call data against our database and the file on my house."

"You offered to help Koi? How many drinks had you had?"

"One beer, planned for drinking with the dinner I didn't get to eat."

I kept indexes and cross-references of names, addresses, contact numbers, email and other messaging IDs, and more for cases and participants, both employers and everyone I encountered during an investigation. You never knew when someone involved in a case might come back at you like an angry dog. It had been ten years since an irate husband in a divorce case emerged months after things were settled and put two slugs in me. The gun had been small, the wounds non-life-threatening, but it was the first time on a case so innocuous someone had pulled steel. The possibility of death from the past makes one a meticulous tabulator of the facts and players.

"Koi had an arson. I had an arson. I got a call from his crime scene. I figured if I volunteered my help, he wouldn't visit every day this week with a question about whether I was starting some kind of firebug club."

"You think this call is your guy?"

"Did you hear the message?"

I played it for her. She smirked. "You should be honored. The last member of the Analog Phone Mob called you in his hour of need."

"Or he called me because I'm the first detective in the book."

"And you thought changing the listing to 'A C.T. Robillard Investigation' wouldn't pay dividends."

"I'm still only occasionally at the top of the search engines."

She shrugged. "Algorithm's gonna algo."

"Uh huh. I figure at most it was a system glitch at the building. Koi said it was preceded by a call with a jumbled number and a call to 911 that didn't connect."

"I suppose it could have been a misfire."

"Do you think there's anything to translate?"

I could see her making a mental inventory. I'd deeded the closet in the conference room to Barrett for her tech bits and pieces. It was an impressive array. I wasn't sure she hadn't broken through the wall to the adjoining suite by now and created her own Bell Lab. "Good question. There are some digital decoders I can try, emulators to translate a carrier. The tech used in the building shouldn't be much older than the construction, so I'll start with encoders in use when the building was built, and work my way forward. I should also have a vintage box or two in my closet I can try. There's probably not much more to the squeal than a handshake to establish the connection, but that might tell us something. Maybe we get lucky."

"Don't turn too many cycles on it. When you're done, archive the call. If Koi wants a copy, shoot it over to him. If you start cross-referencing the phone data with our files, I'll tackle the name and case data when I get back from lunch with Spence."

She acknowledged me and persisted in the doorway.

"You're hovering."

"A courier came by while you were spinning up." She handed me an envelope, 8x5 yellow clasp.

I turned it in my hands. Saw the return address. I glanced at my watch. "Hells. It's the seventeenth."

"Hells indeed."

It's a minor thing to forget a birthday. It's another when the birthday is your late spouse's. But it's the worst of all worlds when your reminder takes the form of literal hate mail from your dead wife's father.

I grabbed the letter opener, slit the end, and pulled the contents. There was a card. There was always a card. I didn't need to open it, because since Jessica's murder, Colin Maddox has sent me the same card every year on her birthday: on the front, a line drawing of an adult's hand holding a child's and the proclamation FOR MY DAUGHTER; inside, the loving sentiment obscured by a tight row of Xs in black marker, and YOUR FAULT added in block letters beneath. Signed boldly. No anonymous animus on my father-in-law's part.

"He's going to do this every year until one of us is finally dead," I told Barrett as I set the unopened card aside.

"He's got twenty-five years on you. Whoever cleans out the man's house will probably find a case of those cards."

Included in the envelope was a folded sheaf of paper. Unprecedented. He'd included five sheets duplicated from a pad, filled with his narrow, crooked handwriting. There was a terse note stuck to the front page:

I'LL FIND THE EVIDENCE TO BURN YOU

I flipped through the pages. Dates, times, references to reports and interviews, web addresses. Colin Maddox was conducting his own investigation into his daughter's murder from his study in Harrisburg, PA. He'd sent me a master list of the background and information he'd amassed. I saw it for what it was: a taunt. He was going to do what I hadn't, was going to be a smarter investigator than me. He was going to crack the case using his computer, his phone, and the will to see me pay for it, like some armchair cryptographer hammering at a code that once broken would produce buried treasure.

Except he'd started with his desired outcome in mind: that I'd done it. I was married to Jessica. I'd found her body. He hadn't spoken to me since the funeral. That his methodology came with bias was a given.

I tucked it all back into the envelope and held the packet out to Barrett. "Would you put this in the case file?"

"Maybe *you* should file it." She slipped out the door, quiet. Barrett had asked once if she could work Jessica's case warm again. A couple years on, my negative response was still a nettle in her side.

I crossed the room to the safe, scanned my palm, swung the door open. The ROBILLARD, JESSICA S. file was one of a few I kept in the safe. It was three inches thick. It hefted like 30 linear yards. I slipped the materials from my father-in-law in front and closed the safe as if the file might escape with the truth, should I tarry.

I grabbed my gym bag and keys. There was time enough for a workout and shower and to shake off the past before I met with Spence. The laundry would have to wait.

FIVE

If I didn't trust Koi as far as I could throw him, Byron Spencer owned the other end of the spectrum. Every PI operating in the City of Houston required a police liaison officer as part of the licensing process. Then-Commissioner Herrero put the requirement in place twenty years ago, in part to keep those investigators chasing a fast buck from impeding or disrupting department investigations, and in part to leverage private investigators as for-hire manpower for cold cases and the like. All the crime-solving, none of the medical, pension, or union conflicts.

Spence had sixteen years on the job. Both erudite and soft-spoken, he was a no-bullshit detective. If he had a question, he asked. If he had a case to offer, he didn't withhold details. If he thought I was overreaching, he stepped on my neck, as much to correct me as to keep someone else from doing it more roughly. He worked by the book, but appreciated the alternatives a PI brought to the table. People who clam up at a cop might talk to me because they don't like the badge. He saw the perception of competition as an asset.

In my years operating in Houston, Spence had been my only liaison, back to Jessica and I setting up shop. We'd developed a healthy give-and-take in our collaborations. Other PIs had horror stories about interference from their liaisons in things that didn't involve them. Spence encouraged the barriers.

Not to say we don't socialize, though mostly at the 'hang out at the ballgame' level.

We met once a week to compare notes. This morning, Spence had a table at a diner off the 59 when I arrived. He was Houstonian by birth, Senegalese by heritage. He was tall, lower NBA scale. He easily had me by a foot. He looked lankier in a suit than he was. I've always suspected he got them cut larger to mask both his service revolver and his physique. He loved being underestimated. Most cops had bio-enhancements or implanted tech to make them better, stronger, faster. Spence admitted to a single techno-tweak: a quickening on his hands and arms to make him a fast, ambidextrous draw. The absence of tinkering was a plus for me. I'm not a Luddite, but in a world where someone can pluck your identity from your wallet with the right scanner and frequency, the idea of partially mechanized, finely-tuned people makes me uneasy. I like nature. It gives you tics to let you know trouble's brewing. A body-grafted motherboard that some kid in Beijing or Moscow can hack? Not so much.

Spence already had the chair with its back to the wall, so I settled for a view of the rear of the place. He handed me a menu as I sat. "I'll bet you lunch you can't guess how many Federal agencies sent reps to Central this morning to inquire about Vetrov's stolen NASA tech.

I made a quick tally in my head. "Eight."

He blinked. "Lucky guess."

"NASA and the FBI are given. DOD, because if NASA has tech, odds are the military has a version of it made by the same people, and full-bird colonels are safety-first colonels. Space Force, because if you invite NASA, you need to invite her kid sister. NSA, because the words 'National Security' are on this umbrella somewhere. ATF, because Vetrov had a gun and that's their standing invitation if alcohol and tobacco aren't involved."

"Speaking of the gun, Sergeant Trainham would like to thank you for the dive team's 1 a.m. wake up call."

"If I don't sleep, nobody does. Number seven is Sullivan from the CIA field office, the guy in the blue suit who signed up because he wanted to be Jack Ryan, but who's too intimidated by everyone else in the room to say much. He's there because of the Russian connection. And finally, Homeland, because no one is sure where they belong, which lets them go everywhere. And you probably left Interpol out of your count, rightly, because they're not a Federal agency, and their interest is in the sex trafficking thug, not the hardware." I glanced at the menu. "Can lobster be any good at a diner?"

"All this time, I still don't know if you're scary or sad."

"Why not both? I presume the feds are all hot and bothered."

"'We want our suspended animation pods back. You're not cleared to store our suspended animation pods. Your property room better not lose our suspended animation pods. If you talk about suspended animation pods to the press, we'll have to kill you.' The words 'suspended animation pods' have become hate-speak."

"We saved four kids from a living hell and put an international pervert behind bars. I'd say a flock of myna birds are a small price."

"Great. I'll send them your way after lunch."

We ordered from the waitress—name tag Holly—before Spence caught me up on the balance of Vetrov's arrest. "The gun was recovered this morning. The captain of the ship on which Vetrov was to sail claimed no knowledge of Vetrov's plans. He admits he didn't look very far past the balance on the crypto drive Vetrov used to buy his way aboard. Captain Aldred is very happy you didn't beat the stuffing out of Vetrov, and Councilman Kant asked me to extend his utmost thanks to you for your efforts."

"One step closer to the key to the city and C.T. Robillard Day in Houston."

"Meanwhile, beyond general praise the mayor's office remains noncommittal on Vetrov's arrest."

I watched Spence pour a fountain of sugar into his coffee and stir it. Why did the man even order coffee? "Commenting would be too close to admitting the city still has serious problems with human trafficking."

"What's this I hear about Koi ferrying you to an arson site in the wee small hours?" he asked.

"He thought there might be some connection to my arson."

"If he's just dicking around to do it, I'll ask Aldred to stick a boot in his ass. Captain or not, he owes me a couple."

"Thanks, but his question is partly legitimate. I got a call to the office from the arson site just before the building went up. Sounded like a carrier handshake. A phone modem, maybe a fax."

"A fax? They still make those?"

"Don't know. I'm in an old building. Maybe it had a fling with my phone system once. In any case, I told him I'd cross-reference resident info with my files to see if anything makes an X on the map." Plates arrived from the kitchen and I thanked Holly before I finished, "He figures I'm cavorting with arsonists because my house burned down."

"Consensus around Central is Koi's eyes are brown because he's full of shit."

"You came to the wrong table for an argument."

We ate a little before Spence pulled his flexi-folio from the soft-sided case on the chair beside him. "If your docket has room, I've got something for you." He opened it, activated the screen, and turned it towards me. The open document was marked CLEARED FOR LICENSED INVESTIGATOR in red across the top. "Stephen Angelo. Age 48. Engineer by trade. Found dead in his apartment a week ago."

I set my fork aside and began scrolling. "Accident, suicide or murder?"

"The coroner doesn't believe there was foul play. It appears Angelo slipped and fell from a loft in his condominium. The impact broke his neck and lacerated his scalp. His body was found by his cleaning service the next morning. The resident security bolt was active. The landlord needed a lock trip to enter. His keys were on his coffee table. Forensics didn't turn up anything noteworthy."

I skimmed the coroner's report: blunt trauma consistent with a falling impact, fracturing the neck, along with a wrist sprain presumed from a reflexive effort to break the fall. No other wounds, injuries or marks to indicate other possible causes. The responding officers observed the same things. There was a series of images from the condo scene, multiple angles of Stephen Angelo wrecked like an airplane on his living room floor, head at an improbable angle to his body, eyes open and dead empty.

"Appears open and shut," I said, even as I scrolled back to a particular image. I enlarged it, drawn to the back of Angelo's head. It appeared to be resting not on the floor, but in it. A dark stain was visible on his ear. "Is that an indentation?"

"Good eyes. Three centimeters deep in the floor. I thought it was a natural defect in the wood from age or time, but the contour aligned with his head."

"The force necessary to dent a floor should have cracked his skull."

"And yet, there was only the laceration above the line of the floor impression and the broken neck."

"If the coroner doesn't think it was foul play, who does?"

"Angelo's employer. He worked for an outfit called NanoDwell. While they accept it could be an accident, their chief of security was investigating Angelo in relation to possible industrial espionage when he died. Some physical files went missing on his watch. Archived proprietary materials. He was their prime suspect. Now he's dead and the files haven't turned up."

"They think an unknown data buddy may have done this to him."

"Lieutenant Mendoza doesn't really see it in the evidence, and all NanoDwell offered was conjecture about Angelo's extracurriculars, so he told me to farm it. I can put you in touch with their head of security. To be honest, I expect it's a couple days sifting what we collected, going through his belongings, and seeing if NanoDwell offers you something they weren't willing to give us."

Rose Street was nothing but data-mining.; idle time has never paid the rent; and the dimple where Angelo's head met the floor plucked all the necessary strings. "I'll take it."

"Great. I'll log the transfer and send you the file and confirmation. And I'll tell NanoDwell's head of security to give you a call if they're still interested in pursuing it. If you don't hear from her in the next couple of days, let me know and I'll close it out."

"Her? Ex-police?"

"Ex-military. Her name is Dana Sami. Before this, she was a lieutenant in the 1st Special Forces Operational Detachment. You'll like her. Full of two-fisted tales of the Delta Force. Not one of them includes Chuck Norris."

I went back to my plate. "I don't know. I prefer Westerns."

SIX

I was crossing the office threshold when Barrett braced me from behind her desk, now littered with six pieces of gear and her laptop. "Your carrier noise isn't a fax message. It sounds like one because that's the best the machine could do to interpret it."

"What is it, then?"

"An encrypted voice stream."

"How can you tell?"

"Open handshake coding in the lead string to set up the voice translation protocol."

"How encrypted is 'encrypted'?" I sat behind the desk and woke my tablet. She was on my heels into my office and flopped in the chair across from me.

"It's a private encryption. 256-bit AES key."

"I'm assuming that's a lot."

"Let me put it this way: a 56-bit key encryption has approximately 72 quadrillion possible keys. I couldn't break a 256-bit from scratch in my lifetime with a brute force attack running on 50 supercomputers with an AI chaser. Whatever the arsonist had to say, he wanted it kept private."

"Wouldn't that assume I had the key?"

"If the preceding assumption is the message was intended for you. You don't have a key, suggesting the opposite. It may have been a technical glitch after all, but the order of calls makes me wonder."

"A gibberish number, a failed call to 911, and an encrypted call to me?"

"Koi doesn't know anything. The gibberish number? One look, I could tell it was an old-school telephone tie line. Private point-to-point connection via leased hard line."

"Leased by whom?"

"Still undetermined, but I've got a feeler out to a friend at the phone company. It was an important number to someone. It was dialed at least once a day from the apartment office, sometimes multiple times a day, going back the six months of records provided."

"Six months? I asked for the last week."

She shrugged. "What can you say? Koi's a giver."

"Could it have been an employee?"

"They had a concierge service and leasing out front, but the office in question was automated, so probably not. The bottom line is it appears to have been dialed with intent. Whether our number was or not, I can't tell without the right decryption key. Lacking that, it will only ever be noise."

"Whoever's on the other end of the tie-line might be able to sort it out."

"I thought of that, too. When I dial, I get an automated message: 'Unauthorized call, unauthorized number.' Then it disconnects."

I hated when there was more to any case involving Koi. It was like rubbing a lamp expecting a genie and instead getting a flesh-eating virus. "I'll see what I can find out about the owner. Let me know what your phone company contact says. We'll go from there."

"Roger that. I'm also halfway through the cross-reference of phone data. So far, nothing from Rose Street matches up with anything in the case files. How was lunch?"

"Spence passed us a case. Presumed accidental death with industrial espionage undertones. We're giving it a once-over for the employer, if the employer is interested. It's in the Mutual folders. Next on my hit parade, but if you want to give it a read and let me know if anything jumps out at you, feel free. Monday. Not urgent."

Barrett nodded and left me to my devices.

I pumped a Barney Boyette Octet gig from Paris through the sound system. I'd gotten it in trade a week after the BBC streamed it, swapped for a couple of Jazz Fest gigs from a decade ago that a guy in Sarasota was missing. I've been trading concerts with people online since I was thirteen. There are lots of blind download sites out there, but that's just asking for a worm or a ransomware attack. In the beginning, it was about those two or three artists whose every note mattered. My horizons had broadened since then—more quality than quantity—but I still chase jazz and blues the way a stray dog goes nuts at a tennis court. Half a petabyte of live gigs at my fingertips doesn't lie.

Boyette's round saxophone notes flowed from the speakers. Other instruments filled in. Instrumental sets were bread and butter for heavy data lifting. Fewer words to get wrapped around. I pulled on the wireless glove interfaces for my tablet, navigated to the case file database, and dug in.

The closest address in my files to the Rose Street fire was a couple miles away, a home invasion and burglary three years before. The perpetrator in that one was still scratching lines into his cell wall at the Jester III unit.

None of the residents appeared in my name index. Of the two arsonists in my files, one was deceased, the other was living in Mississippi—same thing in my book. My house arson file brought no connections: different accelerant, different methodology, nothing to suggest any connection besides a call from an arsonist to an arsonee. None of the four killed in the blaze tied back to me. I'd never had any deaf clients, direct or indirect. Names get tricky with parents and step-parents, but extended family and associates were also dry wells.

It was bothersome, the methodology. A pyromaniac—with the compulsion to set fires—doesn't worry about disabling alarms or warning residents. Their goal is the flame. Rose Street was calculated, not compulsive. Arsonists burn for a purpose. Insurance money usually, but sometimes it's the same lusts as other crimes: the urge to destroy, to avenge, to make a statement. Fire can be used for murder, but it's sloppy to execute and uncontrollable once underway. Missing your target while killing others is a poor way eliminate someone.

The Rose Street arsonist wasn't focused on general destruction. He went to great pains to run through the building, warning residents, and saved everyone but the deaf students. The disconnection of the master alarm cluster pointed in one of two directions: a personal gripe with one of the deceased, or the desire for a fully-involved building before the fire department could roll a response, with the students unintended collateral damage.

Apart from the call to me, there was no direct connection in any of it. That made it the arson squad's problem. Maybe the owner of Rose Street would have better luck than I did getting answers.

I didn't realize how deep in the weeds I was until Barrett knocked on the door at half-past five to tell me she was leaving for the day. I wasn't far behind her.

I locked up the tablet and drives in my filing cabinet, changed into my cycling gear, and grabbed my helmet from the office closet. I walked to the conference room and hoisted my bike from the wall rack. It was an older Molan. I had no desire for all the high-tech add-ons they'd cooked up for new bicycles. Carbon fiber frame, proper tires, effective brakes, a smart set of gears. Maybe a bell. Everything else was clutter and weight to me.

The tires needed air. No surprise there. I hadn't ridden in several weeks, a combination of work and rain overfilling the bayous. When the first things the flood covers are your trails, you make friends with the gym until the inevitable drying out. I wouldn't bike on Houston streets for cash.

I couldn't remember the last time I'd changed a tube. If it crapped out, there was a spare in the pouch under the seat. I rolled out to the hall and locked the door behind me. It was time to celebrate the birthday I'd almost forgotten.

SEVEN

With a couple of hours until sunset, I picked up the Buffalo Bayou trail on the Allen Parkway side and headed west. Houston maintains one of the most broadly interconnected networks of non-motor mixed-use trails in the country. They spiderweb out from the classic downtown all the way to the far suburbs, following bayous and tributaries, curling under and over highways. You can pedal all day without retracing your path, to the point of exhaustion or loss of interest.

Jessica had introduced me to the trails. At the time, it had been so long since I'd ridden a bike, I was surprised she didn't need to teach me again. Our rides gave us the chance to get together, shut out work, and spend time keeping the marriage half of the relationship on even keel. I didn't bike for three years after her murder. Even with the sounds of the world around me, the silence was too daunting. The exception I made was for her birthday, a kind of rolling memorial that helped me grieve. Even when I picked biking up again regularly, I kept up with her birthday ride, rain or shine.

I'd been so wrapped up with Vetrov, I'd forgotten Jessica. Bad enough to forget. Worse for Maddox to be my reminder. I hadn't opened her case file in years. He'd done more recently to look for his daughter's killer than I had in half a decade.

I crossed a bridge north over Buffalo Bayou, followed the path along low hills until I was beside Memorial Drive. There were more people than I expected. Crazy from being cooped up by rain or heat or work. I considered my route and decided to cut over Memorial, work my way to T.C. Jester, and take the White Oak trail instead. It pointed out of town, north and west towards Cypress. Fewer people. More room to think.

I pedaled hard, trying to outrun the past, but it had a faster ride.

I'd found Jessica's body. That was back in the old office, the one on Shepherd between 23rd and 24th. It was a small place, maybe a little cozy for the two of us and everything the business required, but the rent and location worked. A developer tore the building down a couple years ago. Good riddance to bad real estate.

We'd been working two different numbers at the time. She was doing the scutwork on a cheating spouse case, reviewing and transcribing hours of surveillance audio gathered over three weeks. The wife, Natasha Eberhart, was trying to prove her city attorney husband had someone on the side. Jessica could sit for hours and listen to that crap. My need for background noise when I work is a detriment to transcribing anything but song lyrics.

I was providing eyes at the back door of a neighborhood garage in Pearland. The owner, a Pakistani man named Jitinder, was losing inventory a couple times a month, always at night, usually a few days after restock. He suspected an employee or someone associated, but he couldn't root them out. For three nights running, I'd been watching the back light of Highlife Motors flicker over the door, waiting for someone to let themselves inside. The expected thief never materialized.

The fourth night into my stakeout, Jessica and I ate dinner together up the street from the office at Poquito Puebla #2 before I left. We split up at six-thirty. She went back to the office and the world's dullest podcast. I drove south for cricket chatter and little else. That morning, I arrived back at our townhouse at a quarter to six. Jessica's car was absent. She'd done more than one all-nighter at the office. I freshened up, swung by Ball and Chain for breakfast tacos and coffee, and headed to the office.

She was slumped over her desk. Her cascades of long, dark hair were matted with her own blood. Her blue eyes were fixed open. She'd been shot twice in the back of the head at point-blank range, a traditional mob execution, but we weren't working anything related to gangs or organized crime.

I did non-instinctual things, as much to keep myself together as not contaminate the scene. I called the police. I didn't touch anything. I stepped outside and waited. The police report says it was four minutes from call to the first unit on-scene. Standing on the sidewalk outside, watching the morning commuters go about their business unaware, felt like hours.

Around ten-thirty, Jessica had apparently gotten the munchies and gone to the market up the street for a salad. The receipt was in the trash, the unfinished salad on the desk. The coroner ultimately put Jessica's time of death between eleven and one. She'd known there was trouble brewing: she'd unsnapped the holster under her desktop, where she kept a .357 for emergencies. But she'd left no clues, the whole thing over before she could. Her purse and its contents, including cash and her phone, were there. So were the .357 and all the case materials we hadn't filed. The small safe where we kept emergency cash was untouched. The only thing missing was from my desk: the desk lock had been broken and my Glock .40 removed. I didn't carry on stakeouts. I'd never felt any compulsion to. When the ballistics on the .40 slugs in her head matched the rifling of the pattern on file for my gun, I wished I had.

HPD assigned their freshly-minted rising star detective to the case: Daisuke Koi. The ballistics quickly planted the notion in his head of husband-as-murderer, and he did what a lot of cops do: looked for ways to connect dots to arrive at the picture he wanted to see. He brought me in three times in as many days to answer questions, had me walk him through the office, hit me at home with a search warrant. I suspect he only let me attend Jessica's funeral to observe my reactions. I hadn't reached my car from the graveside when he had me arrested on suspicion of murder, right there in front of God and Colin Maddox.

In the absence of hard evidence, Koi relied on whatever circumstance or opinion he could mine. A waitress from Poquito Puebla said we'd seemed 'at odds' during dinner, though she wasn't sure what about. A utility worker was certain he'd seen my car go past the office three times in five minutes, a little after one, from his flag post two blocks down. The cashier who sold Jessica her salad said she seemed "distracted and unhappy". Koi got Jitinder to admit he'd never actually seen me staking out the store, and how I hadn't seemed able to produce results in his case. None of the traffic surveillance cameras could conclusively support the timeline of my travels.

Koi might have gotten it through a grand jury except for the teen couple parked up the street from Jitinder's garage, who had the only hard evidence of where I'd been. They'd been doing what kids have done in cars for over a century when they noticed me. Most kids would have left, spotting a strange man sitting in the dark at two a.m.; they stayed put because they were undecided whether I was they guy the neighborhood heard had been stealing from the garage, or some psychopath who would follow them home and murder them if I thought they'd seen me. So they remained until I left that morning, texting a couple of friends in case some harm came to them and taking a dozen time-stamped photos on their handhelds of me parked exactly where I'd said.

The rub? They'd gone to HPD after my arrest to tell Koi what they'd seen, and Koi put the report in one of those magical safe places. When no one followed up with them, they came to my attorney, who went with them to the media.

Six weeks of diamond-hard focus on me got Koi nothing but expense and, when the original police report surfaced, a black eye. The media started using words like 'cover up' and 'railroaded'. Detective Lieutenant Mendoza booted Koi from the case and replaced him with a piece of well-worn shoe leather named Ron Webster. Webster performed a fair and detailed investigation that turned up less than zero. The charges against me evaporated, and the rise of Koi's star slowed. He's never said he blames me for his career setback. Then again, he wouldn't say 'vomit' if he had a mouthful.

I poked around the edges for six months on my own, tugging leads, digging into the meat of old cases for possible suspects, seeking connections or clues. Everything was cold. I paid three people to make regular rounds of the pawn and gun shops in the city, on the chance the killer got lazy or stupid and tried to sell my gun. Over three-hundred shops, eleven gun shows, not so much as a partial serial number match. It was probably at the bottom of a bayou.

The whole thing should have made me more determined. Instead, the stress of being the prime suspect coupled with my own frustration at getting nowhere nudged me away from the case. Spence secured a copy of the police file for me after the investigation wrapped. It went into a bundle of failure with my notes and was tucked in the safe. It was easier to ignore there. I didn't want to fail Jessica a second time. Trying and not solving her murder scared the hell out of me.

But now Colin Maddox was shaking the tree, with Koi's intent if not his determination. *I'll find the evidence to burn you.* He'd turned loss into fire. There was a fresh sting of embarrassment that I hadn't.

Damned if I was going to watch Colin Maddox go somewhere I wouldn't go myself. Game on, you old bastard.

It was almost dark by the time I'd pedaled back. I stowed the bike, cleaned up in the small bathroom off my office, grabbed my long-neglected laundry, and locked up again. I made quick use of the Allen Parkway, slipped from the canyons of downtown's skyscrapers, and drove into the Heights. I stopped by my lot to ensure no one had made off with the skeleton of my still-being-rebuilt house. I did two loads at the coin laundry on Main. With a duffel of clean clothes, I grabbed dinner at a cozy Italian place on White Oak, tucked on a stool at the end of their antique zinc bar, and swapped stories with Julie the GM, who I hadn't chatted with in at least a month. It was almost eleven by the time I returned to the office.

I let myself through the front door and dropped my laundry bags. Before I could flip on the light, a hand grabbed my neck and shoved me to the floor. I rolled over to three masked figures and the unblinking eye of a sleek automatic pistol.

EIGHT

"If you don't move," one of them said, "you won't die."

"How gracious."

"If you mouth off, you won't die, but you also won't like the attention."

In the low light through the windows, I could see the outer office had been tossed. I expected the same was true of mine. I wondered if they'd breached the safe. Then I tried to figure out what I had that was so important it took three guys to retrieve.

Head-to-toe in black. Masks and gloves on all. The gun was clean and smelled of oil. Conventional weapon. They weren't high tech bandits. It also ruled out ninjas. One spoke, one held the gun. The third stood there, extra muscle. Only the one appeared armed. He might as well have been holding a rock in his fist. All my weapons were in my office.

"What do you want?" I asked.

"You received a phone call last night."

"I did. Tell your sister I'm still not interested."

The quiet man kicked me in the side. Steel toe. Not hard enough to break me, but enough to refocus my attention.

"From a building on Rose Street."

"Yes."

"Did you listen to it?"

"Yes. It was a whole lot of nothing. Electronic noise."

The mouthpiece glanced over at the silent one. Just a tip of the head, but all I needed to tell me who was driving. Mouthpiece looked back at me. "Did you receive the call, or did it go to voicemail?"

"Voicemail. Office answering system. I erased it. Like I said, it was noise."

He punched the office number into a cell phone. "Code?"

"One-one-three-eight."

He entered the code and listened. In the quiet room, I could hear the system tell him there were neither new nor saved messages. He disconnected.

They wanted me to be intimidated. I played along. "There's a backup system. Burns messages to media when the call comes in."

"Media? You should move to the future. The signal is better." No accent, no unusual inflections, no regional pronunciations. "Where?"

"Locked up in my office. File cabinet."

"Get it." To the gunman. "If he tries anything, kneecap him."

Good. Killing me outright wasn't on the drop-down menu. The gunman waved me to my feet. He kept arm's length and a half between us and followed me into my office.

It was untouched. I'd interrupted them before they got there. I figured my electro was where I'd left it, holstered and slung over the back of my chair. I moved slowly to my desk, held my hand out, and lowered it to the dish with my cabinet key ring. I stepped to the second file cabinet on the near wall and counted to the correct key. I unlocked the cabinet, opened the second drawer, and pulled the optical disc with the safety copy of the call on it. Let them have it. Barrett still had a dub.

I held the disc over my shoulder to the gunman. "Here. Take it. Maybe it says something to you. It's so much noise to me." I used enough motion misdirection in the shadows to palm the pop-knife from its magnetic sling under the drawer. The bastard child of switchblade and stiletto wasn't strictly legal. Neither was mugging me in my own office.

The gunman pressed the muzzle into my back and took the disc. He prodded me out again. He handed the disc past my head to the mouthpiece, a trophy.

"Is that it?" he asked me.

"Yes."

"Dubs on cloud storage? Computers? Phone?"

"No."

A pause. "I don't believe you."

"Why would I make multiple copies of nothing?"

"Private investigators are funny people. You do the most labor-intensive thing to save it, but none of the easy ones? It doesn't track." I caught the nod from the silent one, felt the muzzle leave the small of my back. Death, unconsciousness, or rebellion. I opted for door number three.

I popped the knife's blade and bucked backwards, swinging the knife underhanded into the gunman's leg, twice. I'll never know if he meant to shoot me or pistol whip me. Not knowing is better than finding out by dying.

Unprepared for the backpedal and the knife, the gunman's balance failed. He landed on the floor of my office. I kept my feet, turned and went over him. A kick to the gun sent it sliding into the corner.

I heard the other two coming behind me. I made it to my office chair, drew my electro from its holster, turned and thumbed off the safety.

The mouthpiece came through the doorway, all mouth. "I wasn't going to kill you, but now—" He stopped when he caught the first of the electro's four charge-rounds. The three-prong tip of the cartridge caught him center mass. His body danced to the buzz before he collapsed, twitching.

I tried to put the second one in the gunman, missed to the left. The cartridge thwacked into the door frame as he scrambled past the mouthpiece, crawling and climbing, his cut leg dragging. The third managed quick hands on the mouthpiece's collar and dragged him into cover in the outer office.

I stood from behind the desk chair to follow. Flashes, pops, and two bullets in the wall outside my office gave me pause. Second gun. Glad I hadn't rushed. I expected them to leave through the front door. Instead, I heard a crash from around the corner.

I rounded Barrett's desk in time to see the third of them drop out the conference room window. I heard the whine of rotors as I reached the window, still wary of catching a slug. They were descending to the street, graceless angels. Two of them were strapped into emergency descent packs, the kind the military developed for low altitude bailouts that the hopper industry had glommed onto for safety. Managing the third between them, they were overweight and their landing was harder than it should have been. The gunman folded on the leg I'd stabbed; insult to injury, he rolled onto glass shards from the window. I wasn't going to get to the street in time to pursue, and I'd lose sight of them the moment I tried, so I watched them maneuver up the sidewalk and around the corner. I waited for a vehicle, but only heard a squeal of tires.

I closed the door, bolted it, and turned on the lights. I didn't expect them back. They were heavy lifters. Letting them leave wasn't the most direct path to figuring things out, but they'd return to whoever sent them, believing they got what they needed. It gave me room to maneuver without putting it into Koi's hands before I was ready. I could live with that.

The window was the only casualty in the conference room. The outer office was in need of a complete refile. Some of Barrett's desk contents were strewn about. I left all of it where it was for her to sort out or tell me if anything was missing.

I retrieved the gun from where I'd kicked it. I didn't need to examine it to know it would be untraceable, the serial number a smooth spot anywhere it appeared on the weapon, DNA checkers in the grip or trigger burned out. Between those mods and the trio's gloves, it was useless for figuring out who the men were. Still, I bagged it for forensics. I also bagged the knife I'd used on the gunman.

I reloaded the electro's empty cylinders. I carried a quad-shot Rogers & Scott EV14 electroshock sidearm. It didn't require a permit, which afforded a certain amount of flexibility. Once it was reloaded, I hopped the elevator down to the street to follow in the trio's footsteps.

I found the spent electro charge discarded in the alley around the corner from the building, blood on the prongs. I hoped it tore the mouthpiece a little when he yanked it out. I slipped the charge into another evidence bag. The more genetic samples, the better the odds something might hit in a database. A glass shard with a smear of blood joined the party. There were no other obvious discards. Anything beyond a certain distance down the alley would be impossible to tie to them. There were no security cameras along their path. It had probably informed their choice.

I went back upstairs and thumbed voice control on my mobile to call police dispatch. I explained the basics: break-in, got the gun away from them, cut one in the leg before they took off. They'd get descriptions, best I could give, along with the gun and blood off the various bits I'd bagged. The lab would hold them as evidence if the case broke open. I omitted the Rose Street questions and call. It kept space between Koi and my affairs until I wanted him there.

It had been less than 24 hours. Wherever they'd come from, they were already privy to my connection to Rose Street. An arsonist with friends was certainly possible. Organized crime enjoyed the occasional group outing, same as anyone. But their concerns struck me: if I'd listened to the message, and if I'd made a copy. Both suggested it could be deciphered, even with the encryption, and someone was worried enough about what it said to want to contain it.

NINE

I was re-settling files in the lateral cabinet in the outer office when Barrett walked in. She occasionally worked a half-day on Saturday to keep in front of things when it got busy, but I wasn't expecting her. I hadn't called to tell her what had happened.

She sniffed the air. "Smells like crime scene in here."

"Uh-huh. Tell me, Kreskin: how many cops responded?"

"Three cars worth?"

"Did unit call signs go a little fast for you on the public live-stream when they responded?"

"In fairness, I counted three, but they all mumble. I don't know how the dispatcher keeps them straight."

"I'm touched you rushed right over."

"No one called for the coroner or the flying fridge. I figured you'd be here to tell me what happened." She studied the mess around her desk. "And you didn't disturb anything. That'll help with inventory. Thank you."

"It helps to know your audience, but I don't believe they had any interest in your bits and bobs."

"How insulting. I have some primo bits and bobs." She removed her holster and locked her Colt inside the gun box bolted under her desktop. Private firearms get locked up on entry. Barrett understood my history and rationale. She was responsible with her .45 at all times, but it still came down to whose name was on the door. She endured the requirements with grumbling reluctance.

"They were all about the Rose Street call."

I gave her the short version of events. The mention of emergency descent packs piqued her curiosity. "Could be ex-military. Team training, offbeat gear, preplanned route."

"It's possible. I'm more concerned with how quickly word got around that I even received a call."

"It's a question? HPD is equal parts former soldiers and loose lips. And if Internal Affairs can't ferret them out, your odds are slim."

I was about to retort when my mobile rang. Spence. I stepped into my office. "Word travels fast," I said.

"Word?"

"I got burgled last night. Figured that's why you'd called."

It wasn't. He hadn't heard yet. "I was calling because when I reached out to NanoDwell, Dana Sami was happy to accept your help. She's going to contact you directly if you don't reach out. In the meantime, I've set you up at Angelo's building." I grabbed a pen and jotted down the couple of contact names he provided. "They'll be expecting you. You're good to look over his unit and examine his belongings."

"What about next of kin?"

"None identified. He appears to be the end of the line."

I thanked him and disconnected. I always found that depressing, the idea of dying alone with no one to take care of the details.

Barrett already had her scattered things sorted into piles on her desk when I emerged. "When you're done straightening up your collateral damage, lock up behind you."

"Heading out?"

"Yeah. Spence made the arrangements for me to call on Stephen Angelo's building and go through his things."

"Give me two minutes. I'll grab my kit."

"It's your weekend. Go home."

"Please. You can't offer me a puzzle and then send me outside to play. And are you going to know what to look for if he was actively swapping secrets with another computer?"

I stashed my baton in my back pocket. "You read the file on your night off?"

"Eh. Nothing better on the streamers."

"It's your weekend," I repeated, more slowly.

She blinked at me.

I sighed. Her name should have been City Hall. "Who am I to argue with work ethic? Gather your gear."

Angelo's building was compact, well-designed for its constricted lot. It towered twelve stories, a bully looming over its neighbors. Despite its height, the builders had tried to style it to the buildings to either side. It didn't help. It's a problem born of a lack of zoning and sensible building codes. No hope of resolution unless Mexico decides to come back for Texas. I'm not holding my breath.

I parked in a visitor space and we walked through the front door. I presented my credentials to the dark-suited concierge, dropped the first name Spence had given me, and explained my connection to the investigation of Angelo's death.

"Yeah, that was a shame," the man said. "He was a quiet guy. Didn't entertain. Worked a lot."

"Were you on duty the night of his accident?"

"I was."

"Did you notice anyone about the place who didn't belong? Visitors who weren't logged, strangers skulking around the lobby?"

"No sir. We had an issue once with someone trying to sublet their unit as a hotel room on the Internet. Found him out the first time he had 'guests' appear unannounced. Ended it in a blink. I don't mess around. I take my job seriously."

I nodded. I wouldn't have tried to slip past him.

He rang for one of the other building office staff to show Barrett to their storage room to begin her review of Angelo's belongings. Then he called someone to cover his post while he led me to the elevator up to the unit. "Or what's left of it. They've already started preparing it to show potential tenants."

He'd been dead a week. Everything on the planet was in a big damned hurry.

The concierge escorted me to the tenth floor. The building was a monument to swank. Reproduction marble sculptures, tile hallways, chrome accents. My wallet ached looking at it. Outside Unit 1006, the concierge hovered his watch over the lock. With a low *ding* the door slid open.

"That's handy," I said.

"The unit's in Realtor mode. Makes it easier to tour. Otherwise, I'd have to sift through a bunch of keycards every time they showed a unit. Big PITA, going through them several times a day."

"Is it easy to put a unit into a different mode?"

"No. It takes an act of God by the home office. Unless there's an emergency. Emergency overrides, we can do from downstairs."

"Including the security deadbolts?"

"We can only trip those with a management activation key."

"Do you have many emergencies?"

"Besides Mister Angelo? Only one in the last couple of years. One of our lifers. She passed away in her sleep. A nice Mexican lady. Never a bad thing to say about anyone."

The concierge led me inside. I passed through the foyer into a main room, intent on the spot Angelo had landed. But the layout in my head from the crime scene photographs was useless. The large, dual-level main room was smaller, with a metal spiral staircase in the corner. Square-arched doorways led off in different directions. The floors were no longer hardwood, but ceramic tile.

"Are you sure this is the right place?"

"He only had the one."

"This looks nothing like the pictures I've seen."

"The layout is new. They just did this today." He returned to the foyer and touched a button set in the wall. A panel slid open to expose a touch screen that faded up to a glow. "You probably remember it more like this." He touched a couple of controls.

The walls of the room desaturated from green to deep gray. The tile lost its features. A series of laser-lights glowed through the apartment. The layout I knew from crime scene photos emerged in skeletal blue lines: the loft, the wooden floors, the old walls and doorways.

"That's fascinating."

"State of the art. Only six months old. Ever seen one of these?"

"No."

"The entire condo can be redesigned on the fly. This database stores the previous layouts. You can use them as overlays. It helps prospective tenants see how other people used the space."

I moved to the spot Angelo had landed. It was easy to find. A flicker in the image marked it, a scoop of blue fire where the indentation and the flat surface of the floor fought for dominance in the presentation. "What's this? A glitch?"

The concierge walked over and looked. "I've never seen it shimmy before. Strange." He returned to the controls. "Let me step it to the next configuration back." There was a surge in the blue outline of the room, then it stabilized again. "How about now?"

The flicker in the floor stopped, but something else caught my eye, above me. "Can you step forward again?"

The concierge complied. I studied the outline. "Now back again?"

I watched the edge of the loft retreat four feet.

"Go back one more?"

The concierge huffed. "I'm not an interior designer."

"Please. Humor me." I took out my cell and started recording video. "Now, step forward from there, at five-second intervals."

The concierge sighed, but complied. I recorded the final three states of Stephen Angelo's apartment: as Angelo knew it; then with a four-foot width of the loft edge and supports removed; and finally with the loft edge restored, and the blue indentation marking where Angelo's head impacted the floor.

I thought about the file on Angelo's death. "Do me a favor? Try the front door."

The concierge turned the knob and pulled. The door refused to open. "I don't understand."

"Unlock the security deadbolt."

"I didn't lock the—" He stopped as it snapped open with a twist of his hand.

"I know," I said. "Neither did Stephen Angelo."

"You're saying someone literally pulled the loft out from under him?" Barrett watched the video a third time.

"So it appears. And locked the security deadbolt behind them when the room reconfigured."

"Handy detail to command."

"Yes and no. As locked room mysteries go, it's a hell of a cheat." The storage room of Angelo's building was in the building's first basement. It had nothing on a basic police property room. A locking door led to a small anteroom with a large caged-off section, within which were racks of smaller locking compartments holding combinations of bins, boxes, and miscellaneous receptacles. Barrett had set up at one of several tables on which residents could go through their things. She'd daisy-chained her laptop to Angelo's through an intermediary device, wires snaking to a power bar plugged into an outlet on the other side of the aisle. Three totes were set around her, lids ajar. A cascade of clothing laid over the side of one. "Seems like you're having fun."

She didn't look up from the screen. "Angelo didn't have a lot by way of electronics. There's a small digital camera with about forty photos, most of them from Galveston, nothing suggesting industrial espionage. There's a standalone audio player with a few hundred files. I'll dub that drive to make sure they're all music."

"Email?"

"Tidy, and he was a password saver, so also easy. Bills, spam, a couple of industry newsletters, family and friends. No sore thumbs."

"Mobile?"

"No sign of one. Work or personal. I found bills in his email, so there is one, but it's not with his stuff."

"Police inventory of his belongings didn't list one on his person. Location trace?"

"Already tried. No response. The location function was never set up, turned off after it disappeared, or the phone was tossed and is out of juice. And there's just the one personal laptop. I expect his work device stays in the office, so their security can sweat that."

She had about eleven windows open on the screen before her, some of them mirroring Angelo's device, others running processes I could only guess poorly about. "Anything else interesting?"

"Full disclosure? Thib, if the man wasn't already dead, I'd drone-deliver a *coup de grace* to him." She took a long drink from a thermal mug I hadn't seen her bring in. "I'm not a medical professional, but this guy was full-metal paranoid. He safeguarded his laptop like he expected to be found with red hands. Up top? Multiple levels of basic security—easy enough to overcome—but he password protected some really random stuff at the surface, which took time to crack. For my efforts, I got his mom's peanut butter cookie recipe, the maintenance records for his hopper, and his pirated copy of *The Complete Stephen King*."

"A non-lethal data minefield."

"Hassle most people enough, they'll give up looking. I'm not most people, so I pressed ahead. That's when I found the nested folders. Some of them up to forty levels deep. About a hundred of them. Know what was down those wells?"

"Jessica McClure?"

"No. His secret life writing online fan fiction. Volumes of it. Mostly *Shawn of the Spaceways* stuff, focused on 'relations' between Henri and the Yangabot—"

"He doesn't understand the show at *all*."

"—with a smattering of other pursuits, some of pretzel-twisty. While not wholly committed to tentacle porn, I'd call him cephalopod-curious. But each of his stories had its own folder, buried at the bottom of a forty-tier directory tree. What he didn't have were hidden or encrypted files, or any NanoDwell materials, or any local mail storage. So I went to his cloud storage. It was the same thing: a slew of little, meaningless speed-bumps, needlessly buried files and further evidence suction cups were a thing for him."

"So lots of rabbit holes, no rabbits."

She laughed. "Oh no. It's *Harvey* knocks up *Watership Down* in here. Even someone concerned about kink-shaming doesn't nest folders that way. It was purposeful. So I started looking through what he might have gotten rid of."

"I'm guessing this wasn't as easy as 'I undeleted his trash.'"

"Much harder. The vids lie. Angelo was paranoid, but in a hurry to cover tracks to somewhere, and even people who know what they're doing make mistakes in a rush. The most common is not performing a true uninstall of software. Drag and delete a program file, you still leave all kinds of pieces behind."

"Sure. Preferences, control files—"

"—interface bits with other programs, logs, crash reports. Deleting the program file still leaves crumbs. So I went looking for traces of old programs and stumbled on this." She maximized one screen, a list of file names with extraneous data I couldn't parse.

"And this is?"

"A log file from a piece of software for the distributed generation of encrypted data. Think striping across an array, but instead of your supercomputer, the redundant array of independent disks is the Internet itself."

"In English, Persephone?"

She sighed. "I presume with all the music you trade online, you know what a torrent is."

"Sure. I have a concert. I create a torrent file with the data specifics—number of files, sizes, and so on. I load it to a tracker that announces to anyone who cares, "Hey, this concert is available." A second user fetches the torrent and begins downloading the files from me. Then someone else comes along, but they download from me plus the other user, and so on. As more people join in, you get hundreds of people seeding the same files, with each new person grabbing bits from all the available hosts. A hash check file verifies all the bits from all the hosts are complete and assembled correctly, ensuring the copy is true."

"Thank God. I hate teaching the hundred level class." She indicated the screen. "This is a list of torrent files. Thirty-one of them."

"You think Angelo slapped the data he stole onto a bunch of file sharing sites?"

"That's exactly what he did. Around the globe. It's the 'how' that's pretty far out-of-the-box. This log file belongs to an encryption program. It's an older one, a little convoluted, but effective. Ever had a decoder ring?"

"It was a necessity. Mémé spoke Cajun."

"Same principle, massive scale. I want to send you a secret message. I use a program to encode it, then divide it into pieces, but I need to put those pieces into other things to smuggle them out. Sticking with the music example: I have a ten song concert. I give the program the list of the ten song files. To the program, they're ten data buckets. With me so far?"

"So far."

"The program takes the pieces of the encoded message and sticks those pieces randomly in the data buckets. It creates a key so they can be found and reassembled later. The concert is treated like any other torrent file: it gets announced and users start propagating it. Meanwhile, I provide the file name list and the decoding key to you directly, so you can retrieve the message after you download the data buckets."

"I'd think spreading your secret message to Kathmandu and back would be insanely risky."

"On the contrary. You, as recipient, have dozens of pickup points for slivers of the message if my source goes away. And without the software *and* the key, all anyone else who downloads the same files gets are the media they expect. Unless they dig into the coding, and no one does if they get what they expect, they'll never know the bucket has a snippet of code belonging to something else. And even if they like to pry open the hood and tinker—"

"Without all the bucket files, the key, and the software it's impossible to reassemble Humpty Dumpty 2.0."

"Go to the head of the class." She indicated the list again. "The key is gone, but he used his fan fiction for the data buckets. He hid his message in them and scattered it to all the spacers and tentacle fans and lord knows who else."

"Meaning it's still out there, on drives around the world."

"For what it's worth. It might as well be one of those tubes of confetti money from the federal reserve. But we have one pointer: where he sent the key." She indicated an IP address buried in the bottom of the log. "The program sent the list to this address. If it wasn't spoofed in some fashion by the program, finding where it went becomes a lot easier."

"It doesn't mean the message pertained to stolen data from his job."

She gave me a look suggesting what she thought of my devil's advocacy. "No one goes to this much effort for things they shouldn't be sharing. I'd bet a month's pay it does."

"That presumes you'd find someone to bet against you."

She was cloning the drive and had about forty minutes to go. I took advantage of the lull to call Spence and fill him in on Angelo's disappearing loft. "The indentation in the floor appears to have happened while the room was changing."

"It could explain the dent without the associated damage. He lands on his head but doesn't crack his skull. It's like falling into mud." I could almost hear Spence's wheels turning. "If he didn't get the scalp laceration in the fall, someone split it for him before-hand."

"The concierge believes the unit timestamps every change made. If so, a timeline can be derived from them. I'd do it, but he wouldn't give me the data."

"Despite the PD authorization?"

"He was worried about oversharing. Said a warrant would make him happier."

He chuckled. "You must be losing your touch."

"Easy. That's how rumors get started."

"I'll get a warrant and send someone to collect the unit's data. We'll go from there. Anything else?"

"Some theories. Still too young to bring home." I kept the transfer thread to myself. No use getting anyone excited until I knew if it was worth the confetti.

I dialed Dana Sami next, expecting to get voicemail on a Saturday afternoon. Instead, a man answered, announced himself as her personal assistant, and asked what he could help me with. I introduced myself and gave him the thumbnail version. He very helpfully scheduled a meeting at the office for Monday morning and preemptively asked about my rate, so I gave it. The case was curious enough for me to continue pulling threads whether the company or the cops wanted to pursue it or not, but it wouldn't hurt to accept a corporate deposit or two for the effort. As Mémé says, working for free doesn't fill the fridge.

TEN

Barrett's phone made some unholy noise for a message tone twice on the way back to the office. She read and replied before telling me, "My friend on the PD forensics team confirms on the hush that the building's comms box, located at the back of the complex and thus not reduced to slag, contained an encryption/decryption module. He's going to see what he can do to provide the decryption key, or at least let me access the unit to run the Rose Street call through it. What do you think: worth dinner?"

"With drinks if there's anything worth decoding."

Barrett stopped in the office long enough to drop her gear. Once she was underway, I replaced the makeshift tarp on the broken conference room window with a piece of nailed-in plywood—infinitely better against birds and bugs—and researched companies to replace the window. Then I caught up on email and ordered a pizza from Renaissance, the better of two pizzerias up the street. I locked up after settling with the delivery driver, opened the safe, and extracted Jessica's file. It felt heavy in my hand. I loaded Kiki Sharp live at the Schloss Salzau and ate while I organized: cleared my desk, laid out my investigation notes, loaded the digital copy of the police file onto the tablet, and scanned Colin Maddox's sheaf of paper.

The first thing in the file was a picture of Jessica and me. She's still as clear in my head as she was in the photo, taken in judge's chambers at the Harris County Court House the afternoon we got married. I'd had it framed for a while on my desk before dropping it into the case file when I realized all the folder held were crime scene images. It was counterintuitive, but the picture anchored me against the riptide of images of Jessica in death's hands.

I began my three-way comparison of the case resources. Maddox's list was by no means comprehensive compared to the other two files; there were things he'd never be privy to without copies of the police department's jacket. But his list offered a decent index for easing into the past. An old case doesn't freeze in place. Players and elements keep moving. Diving in after several years means starting from scratch.

As I developed a rhythm, it got easier building a new composite timeline from the three sources. Details pulled loose from the mortar of time. They say the less your brain touches memory, the sharper it stays. Some of the names resurrected long-forgotten faces and details about the office on Shepard, the routines Jessica and I had, the people who hired us and the others we interacted with. Spence had been our liaison from the beginning, but there were other players on the field in the pre-Koi days: ambitious city employees like Assistant DA Montez Clayton, bad egg cops who met bad ends like Rory Tinker, or simply disappeared like Adriana Cross; shifty characters who hired us for sketchy work thinking a PI takes everything they're told as gospel or will overlook sins for the right price. Some of them became fresh notes in margins for additional research.

It was easy enough to cross-reference Maddox's list with the other files. He'd noted names and dates of official reports and interview transcripts where he had them, which made reconnecting them a breeze. It was two hours before I whittled down to the only original information Maddox had, a single-line entry with no additional notations:

LEON DUSHANE? (23)

I didn't remember a Leon Dushane.

Sometimes memories disconnect and go their own way. You lose bits. You can even gain things. I had a friend whose imagination was so formidable, he'd swear he remembered scenes in vids that never existed. He picked them up from the novel or screenplay or his own imagination, and his mind integrated them where it felt they belonged.

It had been seven years, and it was one name out of dozens, but it made no ripples. I sifted the electronic index of the police file. No hits. I scoured my own notes. Also nothing.

From where had Maddox conjured it?

I picked up the phone. I didn't put it past him to give me something to run me in circles, a placebo to replace flying to Houston and simply killing me on his personal suspicion. Calling him on it made the most sense, though it would be like crawling naked over broken glass.

Harrisburg was an hour ahead. After nine there. I dialed his cell. His voicemail picked up on the fifth ring. I didn't leave a message. He preferred overnight dispatch shifts at the rail yard, and didn't answer his cell at work. The FTA had rules. If anyone was a stickler for the rules, it was Colin Maddox.

I hunted down a number in the archived file of Jessica's emergency contacts and dialed the yard control room. Corporate entities are slowest to change infrastructure. There was a single ring before I connected. "Yard watch. Kosinski."

"Is Maddox there?"

"Who's calling?"

"His alleged daughter-murdering son-in-law."

"Oh." The shift in tone said Kosinski imagined me with a knife in one hand and a carton with a severed head in the other. "Just a sec."

I heard the sounds of the control room in the background, a half-dozen men managing track assignments, reviewing Positive Train Control systems, adjusting hookup schedules on the fly. No one yet had figured a way to replace rail. Improve it, maybe—add long stretches of magnetic bed, or convertible stock that was hot-swappable between mag-bed and old steel rail. The movement of goods was never going all the way to trucks, no matter how many you could cram into the sky lanes.

With a cough, Maddox was there. I didn't recognize his voice at first. We hadn't spoken since before the funeral. He wouldn't even see me after my arrest. He'd appeared on the local news once, a sputtering affair where he swore he'd see whoever killed her—hedging his bet against me—hang for the crime. His voice was seven years more haggard. Probably still smoking. Certainly still drinking.

I thought he might be discreet, even polite on the job, but the control room was apparently one big, happy family. "You've got some goddamned nerve calling me at work."

"I got your list. Smart investigators never lay it all out for the person they're investigating. That's PI 101."

"Blow me."

"Who the hell is Leon Dushane?"

"Why? So you can murder him too?"

"I think you put some random non sequitur bullshit on your list. Tossed in a name from your back pocket, made it cryptic with a question mark to see how many cycles I'd turn chasing my tail."

"Oh, he's real. You didn't know about him? That's your shoddy work." He chuffed at what felt like an upper hand. "Or you already know him. Maybe he was your accomplice. Did it for you. It sounds like you might be worried I found out about him."

"You should exercise your health plan and consult with a psychologist about your paranoia."

"Yeah? Sounds like he's a bee up your ass. Maybe I'm a step ahead of you, mister big-shot private eye."

Not if you have a question mark after his name, I thought. "Don't fret, *Dad*. I'm like Paper Crane on Derby Day: slow out of the gate, lightning down the stretch."

He started to shout about me calling him 'Dad'. When Jessica was alive, it grated him; now, it was a profanity. I hung up. I'd learned what I needed. Maddox wasn't bluffing. Leon Dushane was an actual name he'd come across in some fashion.

But who the hell *was* he?

ELEVEN

I started Sunday by running online searches for Dushane. It was little more than pushing pins in the board. Most of the online people-finding services copped data from each other, amplifying facts and errors alike in a hellish game of Identity Telephone. Some were steeped in information so old and distorted, it had passed into legend. I'd winnowed the providers over time to a couple I could trust, based on the accuracy of my own history in their databases.

Three Leon Dushanes turned up in Houston, ranging in age from 24 to 83, all in different parts of the city. Leon 24 came closest to the age on Maddox's sheet. He'd only resided in Houston for three years, Pittsburgh before that, officially arriving well after possible involvement. Leon 44's Houston address and number appeared in one of three databases, and didn't cross-check. I couldn't confirm Leon 83 was still alive. With the volume of public records floating around, I'm always boggled by how few capture a date of death. Algorithms compute current age based on what they'd been fed, and some never stop eating. Pépé had been dead forty years. He still occasionally turned up as a 112-year-old phantom.

Spence called in the middle of my process. "We got the results back from the system for changing layouts in Stephen Angelo's apartment. Based on timestamps on events, there were two changes in his residence the day he died, about 90 minutes apart: one to remove the loft, one to restore it. Both times fall within the coroner's time of death estimate."

"How are changes authorized?"

"They require a four-digit pin, but it doesn't record the pin in the record. Could have been Angelo, could have been an override, could have been a short in the system."

"An override?"

"According to the maintenance super, the only override he's aware of is the pin he received when he took the job. It sits in a locked file."

"But the changes were made via the unit in the apartment?"

"Yes."

"So Angelo may have opened the door for a killer. No doorbell cam?"

"No. But if the concierge is right and no one came in who shouldn't have, you've narrowed the suspect list to about 275 residents."

"Thanks." I wasn't convinced the concierge was right. My gaze settled on my people-searching notes. "On an unrelated matter, when you have a minute could you submit a records search request? Nothing urgent. Closing some loops on an old case. Any police jackets you turn up."

"Fire away."

"Last name Dushane. First name Leonard or Leon, may also be shortened to Leo. I'm not certain which form he used. I suspect Leon."

"Date of birth?"

"Unknown. Approximate age is 23."

"Most recent address?"

"Also unknown."

"I'm going to guess you don't have height, weight, or physical description."

"You're lucky I know he's a him.

"But do you?"

"Fair point."

Behind him, police central buzzed. "That's a big ocean for my little fishing net."

"I believe he's local. My search has three possibles, ranging in age from 24 to 83, but I've pushed over all my rocks."

"How far back do you want?"

"Call it ten years."

He was quiet. Weighing it. I didn't usually come to him with so little on which to hang a search. "Is this a case I need to be concerned with?"

"Not at this juncture, no."

"Will it become a case I need to be concerned with?"

"The Mystic Seer says 'ask again later.' Besides, it's your file system. You'll know before I do if it's radioactive."

He let the non-answer slide. Proven reliability has its privileges. "I'll submit it, with the usual caveat about Records moving like they're running in mud unless it's an urgent case. Two weeks would be an optimistic guess."

I thanked him and clicked off. With police wheels in motion, I set out to see if any remnants of Leon Dushane blew in the gulf breeze.

Maddox & Robillard had operated out of a four-room building near Shepherd and 24th. We'd tapped a number of people for local information back then. Every investigator does. You can't be everywhere at once, and there are places you don't fit if you turn up looking for clues—a lot of them in a city of five and a half million people as diverse as Houston is. A database can tell you things, and people may or may not share what they know if they don't feel like you 'belong', but they'll be themselves in front of their neighbors or other known quantities. A search for a potential troublemaker who kicked around the old neighborhood seven years earlier needed to begin with Lottie.

Lottie Sandovar had been driving a cab for Wing Tip Taxi for a dozen years across the Heights and downtown. Her life prior was two verses from a country song: husband did her wrong and ran off with a debutante, dog died on her birthday, kid stole her car. Even after she bought controlling interest in Wing Tip a couple years before, she wasn't one to sit behind a desk and manage. The news made big-type headlines of her hands-on approach. Lottie didn't care. "You lose touch with what your drivers go through if you're not out there, in the same conditions they are," she'd said at the time. It helped that no one in their right mind messed with Lottie. She was full-bodied and, when crossed, mean-spirited about making sure you knew where you'd turned left on red—the kind of person who'd just as soon shoot you with your own gun as file a police report if you tried to rob her.

Wing Tip's dispatchers sent me to the queue at U of H's downtown campus. Lottie was waiting for fares. Groups of parents and students milled around the main walk, small clusters passing the stand at irregular intervals. "Campus recruiting tours," Lottie explained. "Three, four trips to the airport and I can knock off early today. How about you? Heard you were involved in some grand high muckity-muck arrest. The degenerate Russian sex-merchant."

"Yeah. For the record, you put it way better than the late local news stream."

She shook her head, her expression grim. "I don't condone the forced sex trade. Prison's too forgiving. I say mash his bits up. Guarantees he doesn't forget right and wrong again, and doesn't reproduce."

"I'm mystified how you haven't been elected mayor."

"Gotta be in it to win it, Thibodeaux. To what do I owe the pleasure?"

I explained who I was searching for. She repeated the name a couple of times, shook her head. "Doesn't knock anything loose, but I'll admit my memory isn't so good anymore. And the only sixteen year olds I ever saw were troublemakers. If he was trouble, he wasn't the 'stick a gun in your ear and demand your wallet' variety. Them, I remember."

My next stop was Rudy Wilkie. Rudy was one of the guys who'd run down guns in pawn shops for six months after Jessica's murder, searching for my missing Glock. He was a walking stick with eyes. It was hard to not offer to buy him a sandwich when you saw him. He took care of his city every way he could: volunteer firefighter, head of his neighborhood association, constable patrol volunteer, and occasional crossing guard. I suspect he picked up trash along the 610 on his weekends because he could.

The name stumped him as well. "Closest I recall is a guy I went to school with. Total blue screen named Dukane. Couldn't get out of his own way. Heard he got shot-up in California. Salinas, I think."

"The riot or the city?"

"Shit, Thib. It was the same thing back in '37."

I couldn't disagree.

After a couple other negatives from other familiar faces, I drove past the location on Judiway provided by the background check website. The most recent address for 44-year-old Leon Dushane was in clear disrepair, blue paint peeling in long strips, the yard a bed of weeds. Even the For Sale sign out front was sun-faded. The name on the mailbox, which was missing its door, was MARM. No help there. I made a note to check tax records for the lot.

I circled south again, headed back into the Heights, and decided to stop at Mintz Brothers BBQ on my way back. It crouched at the end of 18th Street, a troll of a restaurant where the local road passed under the looming bridges of the 610 and 10. It also had some of the best ribs in this part of the city.

I was headed inside when I spotted Ramon González sitting on the restaurant's patio. He'd owned a store on 19th Street in the classic Heights—antiques, bric-a-brac, junk, whatever else they call it. He was the only nearby buyer/seller at the time who still dealt in old audio formats, which was how we'd met. I haunted his store for rare live recordings until he simply started calling me when he got jazz and blues sets in the door. He was a delight to talk music with, a big fan of the old Cubano sound and the Caribbean bands. Best organic knowledge of sidemen and venues this side of a search engine. He was never a contact for cases; some people are simply satisfying conversation.

If Lottie's history was a country song, Ramon's was Shakespearean tragedy. He'd run his store for over twenty years before the night two guys rolled in to rob the place. Shot and paralyzed from the waist down, the cost of saving Ramon's life was even more debilitating. He'd never married. He'd only had minimal insurance. Even though the community rallied behind him, in the end he had to choose between keeping his home or risking it on biomech prosthetics offering a scant 7% chance of walking again. He kept his home. He dealt the shop and most of the contents. Some of the joy in his eyes went in the sale.

My old friend broke open a smile when he saw me. He was parked in the shade of Mintz's patio in his wheelchair, sheen of sweat on his face, sipping what could have been tea or bourbon from a plastic cup. It could go either way with Ramon. He called to me, shook my hand with both of his when I walked over. "C.T. Robillard! Think of the devil."

"What'd I do?"

"Popped in my head, then into view. Got a guy who called me the other day, asking if I had any weird Coltrane sides laying around. I immediately thought of you."

"Nothing says 'Robillard' like weird Coltrane sides. Do you have any?"

"Who knows? Everything I have left is in my sister's garage in Katy, full of silverfish and regret."

I sat on a bench next to him in the shade of an umbrella. Intermittent clouds did nothing to cool the day. "How've you been?"

"I'd say my toes tingle when it rains, but they're quiet rain or shine. Otherwise, life is what it is. I eat a little too light, drink a little too strong, find ways to amuse myself. What brings you this far from downtown? Hell, you're almost out of the loop. Need a map of the western wilderness?"

"Talking to a few old faces about business before I slink back to the office. Figured I'd grab some lunch along the way."

He squinted at me. "House building business, or snoop stuff?"

"Snoop. Someone named Leon Dushane. Needles and haystacks. I'm beginning to think he might be a ghost my father-in-law cooked up after all."

"Leon Dushane? Lived over on Judiway. Big guy. Flew jets for the Air Force until he went blind."

"Blind?"

"Yeah. Some kind of infection of the optic nerves. Damn shame. He was only thirty at the time. Shipped himself off to Montana. There was a doctor there he knew from the service who thought she could help him. She couldn't, but I hear they got married. I guess there are all kinds of ways of helping."

"He was thirty? So fourteen years ago?"

"Sounds right."

"Then he's not the Leon Dushane I'm looking for. Too old."

"Hmm." He rubbed his chin with the knuckle of his index finger, glanced at me. "Could you be thinking about little Lenny Dushane?"

"I don't know. Who's little Lenny?"

"He was a kid. Well, a kid back then. Lived on the edge of the Heights, in Timbergrove. His mama was a funny lady. Her husband was in the wind, and she was making due. She used to come into the store a couple times a month. Her big thing was little ceramic ducks."

"Pretty specific."

"It takes all kinds. But you remember my place. I had a few of everything come through now and then, Anyway, she always had her two kids in tow with her. Lenny was the baby. Bright boy. Quiet. Always looked bored when he came in, like the old stuff really didn't matter to him. His brother Barry was a few years older. He was nothing but trouble, that one."

"How so?"

"Barry ran with some real *gallos* in high school. You'd see them all over the place, raising hell. Not really a gang so much as a pack. He'd gone in and out of jail a couple of times, here, Oakland. Finally shot a boy out in California a few years ago. Drew some hard time in San Quentin. I wager he's still inside." He frowned. "Barry was dim, a sheep. Lenny was smarter, more ambitious. And one afternoon, I caught Lenny trying to lift something from the store. He was twelve, and it was dumb. It wasn't even valuable. Junk stuff from the dollar box, not even worth calling the cops. I closed the shop, drove him home to his mama. Dolores shouted up one side of him and rappelled down the other. He never came in the shop again, probably because he thought I was a rat. And she never came in again, either. I think she was ashamed of what he did. I should have let the cops scare him straight."

"You tried to give a kid a break. It was a good thing to do."

"Except instead of thinking about not stealing, he started thinking harder about how not to get caught. He kept—what do the vids call it? 'Refining his technique'? Other shops, bigger grabs. Like I said, he was smart. Cops picked him up a few times, but always when it was petty enough for them to cut him loose with a fine or a warning. Jails were chocked full, Dolores kept making restitution. I kept thinking, 'maybe this time, he'll figure it out.'"

"Know what became of him?"

He swirled the liquid in his cup. "No. When he was seventeen, he disappeared. Like he slipped off the planet, to hear Dolores tell it. Went out one Friday night and never came home. You never know how hard the cops looked, though. I always figured he either stole from the wrong person and wound up fish food, or he went somewhere he could fill his pockets faster. Either way, it broke his mama's heart."

"How long ago was that?"

"Lessee. I got shot five years ago. Seven? Eight? I'll be honest, I was on painkillers for so long, the time is muddy in my head."

"Is Dolores still around?"

"No. After Lenny never came home, she decided there was nothing here for her. Packed up the house on Beall Street and left. I don't know where she went. Probably closer to Barry."

"Where on Beall?"

"Between 20th and 21st."

A few blocks from the old office. "That helps, thanks. Have you had lunch?"

Ramon shook his head. "Nah. I'm not a 'cue guy."

"And the mayor lets you live here?"

"I stop here for the sweet tea. I'll probably roll over to the truck parked up the street. Barbacoa. Lengua. Al Pastor. Lady that runs it has been doing it for 15 years."

I gaped. "How have I never known about this truck?"

Ramon chuckled. "A snoop like you. That has to be hard to admit."

I bought him lunch for the opportunity to talk about Urban Junco's set at Jazz Fest, a trove of old soundboard recordings discovered behind a wall in a club being demolished in Chicago, general musings on the state of the Houston music scene. When we split, I tried to give him a twenty for his insight into little Lenny Dushane. He refused. Laughed. "If someone thinks I'm a snitch, I'll never outrun them in this piece of trash chair."

"It's Sunday," I told Barrett when she rang.

"Are *you* breaking the Sabbath too? Small world." If there's a problem with Barrett, I worry she's going to burn herself out because she's unable to use or appreciate downtime. At least she called the office that afternoon instead of coming in. "I'm about to send you the highlights of my deeper dive into Stephen Angelo's computer."

"You know my mobile tells me when you send things, right? You don't need to announce them."

"I didn't want to bury the lede. While I can't prove my theory regarding whatever secret message Angelo sent into the world, I did find two additional instances on Angelo's computer of the IP address the decoding key was sent to, both of them in emails recovered from his trash."

I got on my computer. "So we have an email address?"

"Even better: a name. Herb Young. Not sure of how they connect yet. I thought I'd leave you something."

"How generous considering it was your day off." I began an online search. "What were the messages?"

"One was a 'Thank you' with no context. The other was a cryptic single line from Young with no additional thread, subject SVMS v CoCat: 'If you look after my kids, I'll see to yours.'"

In spite of a forthcoming email, I jotted notes. Leave nothing digital to chance. "Angelo being unmarried makes that curious."

"More than a little."

"Anything else unusual?"

"No threats, no concern he was in danger in anything he'd sent recently, no cryptic codes. If this was industrial espionage, he didn't talk about it where he actually performed it."

"Thanks. Nice work," I said. "Now, go enjoy the rest of your day."

"Okay."

"And if you call, write, or otherwise reach out again before nine a.m. tomorrow without it being a threat to your life or limbs, you're fired."

She begrudgingly hung up. Sometimes tough love is the only way.

Herb Young turned out to be an easier find than Leon Dushane. The email subject letter-jumble was more ignorance than mystery: both were abbreviations for youth basketball teams, Saint Vitus Middle School and Braeburn Catholic, also a middle school. The two teams had played each other four times the preceding season. Young served as Braeburn's coach. He was also a shop teacher. Braeburn called one of the city's Reformed Catholic enclaves home, and a quick background check bore out my hunch Young lived there. Pieces fell into place quickly then: no spouse or children, no criminal record, not even a parking ticket to speak of. Also no apparent reason he'd be receiving encrypted information from Angelo.

I added Young's address to my mobile, plus a contact number for the residence offices. Then I set it aside and began sorting through what I wanted to share with NanoDwell's chief of security in the morning.

TWELVE

For a woman in her early thirties who'd been elite military before becoming NanoDwell's head of security, Dana Sami didn't look like she'd had a single long march in the service. I'd have believed her younger had I not done some research. She was tall, lean. Her raven-black hair was trimmed in a tight, neat bob. Her suit, indigo over a white blouse, had been tailored by a professional. It hid the lines of the firearm and shoulder holster with near-perfection. The suit complemented her eyes. She carried a compact black briefcase. She gave me the same python grip she used on its handle. "Thank you for seeing me, Mister Robillard."

I ushered her to the conference room and closed the door behind us. "The pleasure's mine."

She took a seat. "Detective Spencer speaks highly of you."

"We've known each other a day or two. I do alright by him, and he helps me keep the lights on."

She opened her briefcase on the conference table, her movements graceful, composed. There was something attractive in the way she carried herself. She knew it, too. "I wasn't aware private investigators worked so closely with the police."

"The smart ones do. It's steady work. And if you have a good liaison officer, it's rarely wasted time."

"I understand you've read his file on the death of Stephen Angelo."

"Cover to cover. Report from the scene, coroner's report, witness statements, your interview. I've visited the apartment, though there wasn't much to see."

As natural as her movements seemed, her smile was a practiced thing, and still imperfect. "Thorough. I like that. So you understand the company's position on this."

"Only in that you suspect he was murdered, and industrial espionage may be at the heart of it. The details were thin."

"I know."

"A little more information about the case you were building against him might be helpful."

Some of the gloss came off her smile. "Before I can discuss things in greater detail, I need to be clear. Some of the information I'm going to share is of a confidential corporate nature. To give me the latitude to speak candidly with you, I've pre-cleared my discussion points with our attorneys. But I need reassurance you'll embargo anything I request until we clear it for release to the media."

"No worries. I'm not a press conference guy."

She slipped a tablet from her briefcase and across the table to me. "Still."

I skimmed the file opened on it. Standard confidentiality agreement with protections for both of us. I saw no red flags. They'd already been digitally signed by someone in NanoDwell's legal office. I added my autograph to the correct line, and a thumbprint for good measure. Sami initialed as witness and asked for a mail account for sending. I gave her the office address.

"Thank you." She tucked the pad away. "What do you know about NanoDwell?"

"Only what I gleaned from the file. You're in biotech and construction."

"We develop and manufacture buildings. Alteration-friendly structures. You may have heard of the Smart Shuffle line of residential buildings? Maybe the Exec Smart mid-rise modular offices?"

"Only in passing. I gather Angelo lived in one of your buildings."

"Yes, but that's not uncommon. We incentivize employees to live in them. Helps us troubleshoot on an ongoing basis. No one likes to say 'free labor' but..."

"How long have you been building them?"

"We're the oldest and foremost company in the field, founded right here in Houston, sixteen years ago. I'm the Chief Security Officer for Intellectual Property. I'm responsible for protecting every byte of data we generate. We make money through our own construction projects, as well as by licensing intellectual property. How we do what we do is worth billions in annual revenue."

"What was Angelo's role with the company?"

"He was an engineer in our control center and nano-integration department."

"I'll admit, I'm willfully ignorant of tech-speak."

"Our structures, no matter what size, are comprised of three proprietary components: the building material, which is a nano-sand of our own design; the builders, a collective group of programmable nanobots that shape and process the nano-sand into structural elements; and a control center that acts as an interface between the human element and the builders. Through this trinity, we can provide structures that grow and change as the owner's needs do, offering unprecedented freedom of design and a deep portfolio of features to our customers."

"And he worked on the interface for control of the builders."

She nodded. "He developed and coded programming language used by the control center to communicate with the nanobots."

"How long did he work for you?"

"Eight years. He came over in a buyout of another firm."

"A competitor?"

"No. A company we sometimes outsourced work to. They became available cheap, so we acquired them. He passed his background check, never failed a workstation audit, never so much as a memorandum of warning in his jacket." She consulted her tablet. "But a couple of months ago, he requested some materials from records retention related to the development of our initial building computer control centers, very old R&D design documents."

"How normal is that sort of request?"

"Fairly common. Engineers often review background to understand progression of designs. But he wasn't authorized to access the materials he requested. It happens. We compartmentalize to reduce the possibility someone could walk out the door with a chunk of intellectual property if a competitor poaches them from under us."

"What happens when someone makes an improper request?"

She blinked. "Their request gets denied."

"But there's no reprimand, no black mark in the file, no one goes to his office and gives him a mighty shake?"

"Oh, no. We don't expect everyone to know everything they can and can't ask for. Usually, the request is denied and life goes on. You can appeal and explain your need. Make your case, and you're allowed supervised access with the material. But Angelo never filed an appeal. Instead, he used a skillfully forged order and duped a relatively new clerk into giving him access."

"And that's how he got on your radar."

She poured herself a glass of water. "Yes. The clerk's supervisor saw the notation on the woman's weekly report of filled requests. It rang a bell with him. He called me."

I considered Angelo's options. "I'm assuming these files are accessed in a controlled environment, like a SCIF."

"Exactly. And supervised via vid feed. Notes can be taken. He did and they were reviewed. Some computations, according to the clerk's review. There's no digital or physical imaging. Tablets and phones aren't permitted, and even if they were, there are electronic counter-measures designed to specifically disrupt picture-taking by such devices—infrared pulses, light-scatterers, that sort of thing."

"Like backflash drones at a crime scene. The paparazzi stoppers."

"Exactly. When I was notified, I performed a physical inspection of the files he requested. On review, I discovered he'd managed to swap filler into the files for specific pages of data. I presume he smuggled the originals out on his person. We inspected his work area, found nothing, and were preparing to pull him in for an official inquiry when he had his alleged 'accident'."

"Who do you think killed him?"

"That would be your bailiwick, no?" It came with an edge I wasn't expecting, a touch of sarcasm, maybe annoyance.

"You wouldn't be wasting your time with it if you didn't have thoughts."

It seemed to put me over whatever unseen bar she'd set, and the tone was as quickly gone. "My suspicion is he was fishing for some first-level engineering notes to help a competitor catch up. He stole it thinking it was so old, no one would give much thought to it being accessed. I believe he tried to sell it and the deal went sour, and his interested party killed him to steal the information from him, or to cover up their dealings, or both."

I nodded. I kept Herb Young in my pocket, wanting something more tangible than IP addresses. "I can search competitors, find industry personnel with overlaps—professional associations, conventions he might have attended, that sort of thing. It's a bit of a long shot, but sometimes people get careless. Can I get a copy of his employment file?"

"That shouldn't be a problem. I'll speak to HR."

"Why do you think he'd do this now, a straight arrow like him?"

"Opportunity. Our initial public offering is coming up. Analyst projections suggest we could generate $50 billion in revenue on day one." She paused. "We have five competitors snapping at our heels. A leak of intellectual property, even as old as this, could bring any of them even with us and damage our value right at lift-off."

I tapped the table with my thumb, a slow rhythm. "But you don't have evidence of anything except missing technical data. No specific competitor ties, no bank records showing large deposits, no intercepted communications, no suspected accomplices. Correct?"

It sucked the wind from her sails. "That's right."

"What about the clerk?"

"She was a dupe. But her employment was terminated." There was an air of satisfaction. "I'd have pressed criminal charges if you could for not being discerning enough."

"And everyone else in his department came out clean?"

"As if bleached."

"No trace of documents in his apartment after his death?"

"Nothing was found by police when they searched."

"I understand the possible motives for theft. It's a solid assumption. But murder is a poor play. It just draws attention to the crime. Why kill him?"

There was a flicker in her glance, an unguarded moment confirming she was studying me as much as I was her. "I expect we've both seen the same photos from the scene of his death, Mister Robillard. Tell me there's not something wrong with how he died."

"Indeed." I tapped my stylus on my tablet. Fifty billion dollars of valuation was a tempting reason to pull the floor from under anyone. Still, I noticed she'd dodged the question.

"The police seemed uninterested. On the other hand, you at least appear willing to take a deeper look. I can send over our internal investigation file, such as it is, and answer questions as they arise. What kind of latitude do you have from law enforcement?"

"Autonomy to investigate. Certain requests need to go through them, but there are a number of avenues I can examine on my own: building visitor logs and security tapes, GPS data for his vehicle, data on his phone. Some of that is already underway."

That got her attention. "I'd be curious to hear what you find. We were denied access to his cloud accounts and computer."

"If there's anything, I'll let you know."

"To be honest, I just want to close the book on the whole thing. Everyone's on eggshells between his death and the initial public offering. It doesn't help the company suffered a devastating loss this week."

"Oh?"

"One of our earliest prototype buildings was burned down three nights ago, over on Rose Street. House Doris."

You never think about your hackles until they go up. "I wasn't aware you named houses."

"House Doris was a milestone. To Victor Phalen, our CEO, it's as the James Charnley House was to Frank Lloyd Wright. It was the first multi-unit dwelling to successfully deploy the first version of the Shuffle Smart technology."

"Why 'House Doris'?"

"Mister Phalen felt his initial constructions were like having children, so he named them. House Alan was a single-family model. It failed several hours after going on-line. House Barbara was his first success in the same design. House Charlie was his office building prototype. It still serves as our corporate headquarters today."

"A testament to its versatility. And House Doris?"

"First apartment building. A logistics miracle for the control center. It paved the way for today's designs. You could say Angelo's apartment building is a descendant of House Doris." Her eyes widened at a notion. "Do you think it's possible the fire and Angelo's death could be related in some way?"

The thought had crossed my mind, but I wasn't sure it hadn't been led there. "I'll certainly examine that angle."

"I spent most of today with HPD, reading their report about the fire, sifting evidence with the inspector handling the investigation." She paused, deliberating. "I understand you received a phone call from Rose Street at the time of the fire."

"Inspector Koi is nothing if not thorough."

She picked up a note in my tone. "Does he waste your time?"

"Mémé says if you can't say something nice, there's probably a reason."

Sami got my gist. "He said it was electronic noise."

I nodded. "It was as far as I could tell. Any idea what it was supposed to be?"

"In our earliest models, we integrated security features for common areas—A/V digital monitoring and recording. It was an attractive selling point for potential rental companies. In an emergency, they were designed to dump the most recent half hour of security footage to a compressed file and send it via digital line to a data holding server at our headquarters. It could assist owners and insurers in determining culpability by seeing how an emergency unfolded."

"I'm sorry I deleted it. Odd glitch to send it to me in the first place."

"The digital number to connect with the server isn't far off your office number. It's possible the heat of the fire fried the circuits and caused this A/V stream to be misdirected to you."

It was feasible enough, so I let it go. "Yours sounds like a fascinating field."

"You should visit our headquarters. We've beefed up the public tour ahead of the IPO. I can even conduct it personally. It might help you better understand the nature of Angelo's work."

I considered my follow up on Young and whatever Barrett could tell me about the Rose Street comms. "What's you schedule look like tomorrow?"

She checked her tablet and made a notation. "Actually, it's pretty clear. I'll send a car. Pick you up at noon?"

THIRTEEN

When I emerged from the conference room with Sami, Barrett was at her desk, working her laptop over. I made brief introductions before Barrett watched us out the door.

When I returned from the elevator, Barrett looked up from her screens. "Is she former Delta Force?"

"How could you tell?"

A half-shrug. "They pick up a certain swagger." I couldn't tell if Barrett was put-off or amused.

"I'm visiting their facility tomorrow."

"You never take me on field trips. Are you ashamed of me?"

"You were just at a death scene and elbows-deep in the dead guy's stuff."

A shrug. "That was work."

"She didn't say you couldn't come. They're sending a car."

Barrett scrunched her nose. "Pass. Too fancy. Besides, I have too many jets burning to leave them unattended. That's when things burn down."

I wasn't going to argue for an additional fire in my week. "Jets. Enlighten me."

"Item One: I talked to my contact at the phone company. The tie-line used at Rose Street is leased to NanoDwell. Direct pipe to their headquarters. It's been in place since Rose Street was first put up, without change." She waited for some reaction and was puzzled by the lack of one. "She told you about the Rose Street connection already."

"She read Koi's report."

There was a rare Barrett huff. "I hate those Delta Fraus."

"Any idea what it's for? Diagnostics monitoring, something like that?"

"Doubtful. A diagnostic line would have been fiber for speed and load from day one, unless the computer was intended to read aloud to the technician. It's a standard telephonic hard line. Still live for arcane reasons. It could have become co-opted."

I started a fresh pot of coffee. "By?"

"Show me a hacker thug who wouldn't crack a hot, easily overlooked communications path they could exploit."

"Fair. You said the call was encrypted voice."

"Yes."

"Sami said it was transferring security A/V."

"No way what you got was a video file, fragment or otherwise. She's mistaken. Though given her line of work, she'd know that, and it's more likely she lied to you."

"Well, I lied to her and told her we no longer had a copy."

She smiled. "Deceit and omission on both sides. When's the wedding?"

"Nice. Anything else I need to know?"

"My digital forensics guy couldn't get me access to play with the Rose Street encryption box."

"I hope he goes thirsty."

"He did give me the next best thing: slipped me the operating system. Passworded, but I've got a cracker working on it. Once I'm inside, I have a subroutine that will exploit a few things and sniff out the encryption key. I plug that into a translation program, I should be able to turn your digital noise into an actual voice."

I sighed. "If it gives me weather and time, I'm going to be very disappointed."

"Yeah, yeah. Everyone wants the piñata with candy. Hate the message, not the messenger." She watched me fill my travel mug. "Headed out?"

"To the Reformed Catholic Community Enclave in Braeburn in search of Herb Young. Interested?"

Her bemused head shake suggested I was lost. "You don't get my field trip needs at all."

I left Barrett to her devices. I slipped out of downtown and over to Washington Avenue, then cut north on Sawyer through the Warehouse District to pick up the freeway. There weren't any warehouses anymore. What hadn't been torn down for apartments had been carved up for art studios, strip malls and the like. The only ghost of industry in the ongoing sprawl were the old storage silos of a rice company. Nestled beside the railroad tracks, the company's turbaned-genie logo had long since been painted over with rockets, themselves riding on jagged plumes of more recent graffiti. They were the only trace of a thriving rail system that used to dominate the corridor north of downtown. Three lights later, I picked up the freeway and headed west on the 10, bound for the Braeburn enclave.

It stood to reason Young would be working. Dropping in on him in front of students wasn't my style, but I needed to decide where to wait, so I called the office of Braeburn Catholic Middle School and asked if Young was on site.

The secretary was polite, direct. "Mister Young's currently on leave," she informed me.

"Really? For how long?"

"Indefinite. He hasn't been in for close to two months. Would you like to speak to his substitute, Miss Wallace?"

I declined and thanked her. His residence, then.

The Reformed Roman Catholics were born from schism. Like Martin Luther before them, they'd taken a critical look at the state of the church and assessed where it was weak, where it failed, where it sinned. Their de facto founders—a clutch of believers from northern Virginia—decided after one scandal too many to take their grievances to the Vatican. The Pope was neither hearing confession nor suggestion and decided the old ways of jettisoning rabble via excommunication might still work. It went over about as well as it had with Luther, except the group was far better connected and had both too much time and money on their hands.

Thirty years later, their more modern branch—which had dubbed themselves the Reformed Catholic Church—had severely chipped away at Rome's head start through a deft combination of spirituality, modernity, and inclusiveness, while pitching down the memory hole things like restricting clergy by gender and hiding pedophiles in new neighborhoods.

It was a protracted fight that split not just the faith, but parishes and families. Both still considered themselves the "true" Catholic church, one hunkered in Vatican City—presumably because it was paid for—while the other had started in the U.S. and ultimately relocated to Rio de Janeiro once they got global traction. I didn't have a dog in the hunt, but I figure the RRC's claim to the throne is as good as any of the hundreds of earlier chips off the rock, especially if they're honestly practicing what they preach. Part of their design to build community was by establishing enclaves: church-owned neighborhoods where its members could live, buffered from the negative influences of the greater population, supported by their fellow parishioners.

Braeburn was the largest of the RRC enclaves in the Houston area, and with good reason: the bishop of the diocese resided there. Another RRC flourish: the big-time shepherd who lived among his flock. His residence was larger, but not especially opulent or out of place, aside from the shingle hanging out front to identify its resident. I passed it on my way to Young's address, which was a comparative outlier on the far south side of the community, almost out the end into Brays Oaks.

Young's address was an apartment building, a six-story job that was well-kept and, based on the brightness of the finish, recently painted against the Texas sun. It was denoted by both the street number and a numeral 2 on the side. I didn't have to guess what the latter meant; there was a map adjacent to the parking lot. Young's building was one of three specified for adult singles at that end of the enclave. I parked, got my bearings and found the stairs up.

Eight apartments to a floor, and Young's was on the back left side of the third floor breezeway. I wondered as I climbed stairs about his leave from work, whether it had bearing on Angelo's fatal fall.

Doorbell with camera. I rang and waited. Absent a response, I rang again. Listened. There were no sounds from within. In spite of the camera, I tried the door. Solidly locked.

The map identifying Young's building was equally helpful in pointing out where the resident office was.

Adjacent to the church—a classically styled brick affair with twin spires and SAINT ANDREWS carved in the stone beside the doors—were the enclave's offices. They'd been re-purposed from the church's original rectory. If the bishop lived an austere life, he worked in relative splendor. Four broad steps led to the front entry. The outer door was open, an invitation. I showed myself into the foyer. It was dark wood, bare except for a cross and a picture of the RRC's Holy Father inside the door. A long staircase on the right lead upstairs, presumably to additional offices. Down the left side, three arched doorways at regular intervals led elsewhere. The two farther sets were closed, so I stepped through the nearest arch, into a small office.

The clerk looked up from a stack of folders, harried. His brown suit might have been crisp when he started the day, but it had become a casualty of activity. His goatee was neat, his eyes weary. "Can I help you?"

"Possibly. I'd like to speak to you about one of your residents."

Weary eyes widened like he expected me to whip out a subpoena and serve it. "And you are?"

"C.T. Robillard." I handed him my card. "I'm a private investigator. I'm trying to reach Herb Young, resident over in the Mayfair neighborhood, single resident building 2."

He read the card, eased. Not the bullet he was expecting. I wondered what he needed to dodge. "Miles Egan. Bishop's clerk. Have you tried knocking on Mr. Young's door?"

"I did. The office at the school said he was on leave. I thought you might be able to tell me if you knew whether he was in town, had gone away, was—"

"We have thousands of enclave residents. I don't see everyone every day." And back to his stack of files, as if they might multiply while he wasn't paying attention.

"Do you remember the last time you *did* see him?"

He sighed. "I couldn't say. For certain not lately, but that doesn't mean anything." He studied me as if trying to decide what I was selling. "If he took an extended trip or something similar, there might be a note in his resident file. Let me see."

He leaned over his computer. I'd have taken a seat, but there were also stacks of aged folders crammed with paper in both guest chairs. "You appear to be very busy."

"We're digitizing old church records from parishes around Texas. We're building a genealogical resource not unlike the one maintained by the Latter-day Saints. Old files, document lists, genetics databases. It piles up quickly, especially when you're understaffed." He touched the screen, swiped, touched again. His energy was nervous. I attributed it to a general dislike of strangers wielding questions. "Here. He notified us he would be unavailable for coaching in the Saturday youth sports program until further notice."

"Did he say why?"

"'Personal reasons' is all he wrote."

"When is the note dated?"

"A month and a half ago. The eighteenth."

I jotted it down. I felt him staring at me.

"What is this about?" he asked.

"An acquaintance of Mister Young's was killed last week. I'm following up to see what, if anything, he can tell me about certain aspects of it."

"Unsavory aspects, no doubt."

"Not for me to judge. Just inquire about. Does he have an emergency contact, someone who might know where he is or how to check on him?"

You'd think I'd thrown an equation at him. "What?"

"A man suddenly changes his routine, abandons his job and responsibilities, doesn't answer his door, loses a friend. I'm curious if anyone has heard from him or checked on his mental well-being."

Something in my words flipped a switch in Egan's head. He chortled. I'd crossed an invisible laser-line into his domain. "I suppose you want to be let into his apartment. That's where this is ultimately going, right?"

"No. And if I did, it would only to be sure he was alright."

"I'm sorry, I can't authorize that without some kind of warrant."

"I'm not a police officer."

"Perhaps you should go get one. One with a warrant." He wore the expression all men of little power and less sense wear, the look of a man who now was going to play with me because he could.

"Could your boss authorize it?"

"My 'boss' is the bishop."

"So you said."

"I suppose he could. But he won't."

"I'd like to speak to him anyway."

Smug. "Do you have an appointment?"

"Don't you think I'd have mentioned already if I did?"

"Mister Robillard, I don't like your tone. I suspect you're less a private investigator and more a con, trying to exploit some circumstance of Mister Young's of which you became aware to gain access to his apartment for some illicit purpose. How do I even know you're a real investigator?"

"Would you like to see my credentials?"

"I could make something resembling your so-called credentials right here in this office."

A voice like an approaching dump truck rolled in between us from behind me. "You'll have to excuse my clerk. Miles sometimes lets human weakness, such as gate-keeping, cloud his decision-making process."

I watched Egan wilt. I turned, face-to-face with Bishop Hudson. He was a short man, linebacker broad. A deep, hook-shaped scar curled catlike at the corner of his left eye. His hair was gray at the temples. He wore the crimson garb of the RCC clergy, square of white at his throat like a raft in a red sea. He carried himself with the authority of his position, and still managed to exude a friendliness. I wasn't sure how long he'd been standing within earshot.

"C.T. Robillard," I said, hand extended. "I'm a private investigator."

The bishop's grip said all I needed to know about his confidence. "Emmanuel Hudson. Bishop of the Texas Gulf RRC diocese."

Egan went mouse-timid behind his desk, "Sir, I was just explaining to Mister Robillard—"

"I heard what you were explaining. Do you know what else I heard, Miles?" He waited a moment to see if Miles would jump in. "I heard that a man has died, that Mister Robillard is looking into it, that Herb Young might be able to help, that no one is certain so far where Herb is, and that he stepped away from his job and other interests suddenly in the past several weeks. Did you by chance miss any of that?"

Miles remained still. "No sir."

"Does he have an emergency contact?"

Miles looked like he wanted to spit a nail. "Donna Pascal." I noted how he'd conjured her name without looking at his screen. I wondered if he'd noted it when he'd reviewed Young's file. If not, it was a curious bit of information to pull at random from memory considering thousands of residents.

"See if you can reach Miss Pascal, and inquire if she's heard from Herb. And hold my calls." To me, he indicated a direction down the hall towards one of the arched doorways.

The bishop's office was as modest as I expected his home in the enclave was. The floors were hard wood, varnished blonde and worn. The walls were pale yellow and undecorated. Two windows opened into a courtyard not visible from the road, a square space with a birdbath in the center. One wall of the room held floor-to-ceiling shelves, crammed with books, some centuries old, many in other languages. A rolling ladder offered access. The bishop's desk was oak, plain sides and top. Shaker in design, if not age.

Instead of sitting behind the desk, the bishop motioned me to one of two green upholstered chairs facing the windows, and sat in the one beside it. "I have to apologize for Miles. He's been under a lot of stress. We've come up short getting him some clerical help."

"It's not every day a private investigator walks through the door. But if you don't mind an observation, he seems to have an issue with Miss Pascal."

I could see the bishop carefully selecting his words. "We work hard as a progressive congregation to honor Jesus' words and spirit. He kept company with sinners to help them closer to the Father. Miles sometimes forgets forgiveness of sin is a cornerstone of the faith. And Donna Pascal came to us through some rocky personal straits, going back to her childhood. Miles disapproves of who she used to be, rather than accepting who she's become."

"That's not a very Catholic attitude."

"No, but it's too typically a human one. And to be fair, Miles works on it. He's as imperfect as the rest of us."

"I understand Young is a teacher."

"Middle school, right here in the neighborhood. Also coaches the school basketball team and in our Saturday youth league. I was sorry when I heard he was taking a leave of absence. He's adept at instilling fundamentals and inclusive of every child. Everyone got playing time. The kids adore him."

"He didn't give a reason for withdrawing?" I watched a bird land on the lip of the bath. It tipped forward and flapped, sending water everywhere.

"Only that it was personal." Hudson picked at the cuticle of his middle finger with the edge of his thumbnail. "So what is this all about, Mr. Robillard?"

I laid out Stephen Angelo's death, the question around it, and the possible connection between Angelo and Young. I gave him my credentials and the cooperative agreement for the case with HPD. I didn't air any suspicions about Young's connection to it all short of knowing he and Angelo were familiar. If I committed a sin, it was in playing up concern that Young might have been in a state of mind suggesting someone should peek in his apartment to check if he was inside and alright.

In the end, Bishop Hudson admitted what I'd laid out was concerning, and he respected my station adjacent to the police enough to let me look behind door number one.

FOURTEEN

Bishop Hudson paired me with the apartment complex's superintendent, an older man named Jaworski. He was built like a fuel drum. His ruddy complexion suggested he could hold as much liquor as one. I followed him through the complex back to Young's building.

"Have you worked here long?" I asked.

"Ten years, give or take."

"Do you like it?"

"It beats a swift kick in the crotch. Most days, anyway."

"Anyone give you trouble?"

Jaworski grunted. "I'm a superintendent. Everyone here gives me trouble."

We climbed the stairs back to Young's door in building 2 and stopped outside unit 304. I studied the bristly red hair on the back of the man's hands as Jaworski flipped through two hundred keys on a wide ring, a living dungeon master.

"To be honest," he said, "most of the time I daydream about being somewhere else, doing anything else."

"Why stay?"

Jaworski froze, key in hand. Eyes yellowed at the corners stared past me. "You know how lapsed Catholics still go to church on the high holy days?"

"I suppose."

"There you go."

I had no idea what it meant, and even less desire to ask. Jaworski shuffled several more keys. Held one aloft. It looked like all the rest to me. "If the security deadbolt inside is locked, we're gonna need to bust the door down. Building's older than Christ. These things don't have those fancy override do-dads you find in new apartments."

"If it's security-locked," I said, "he could be dead inside."

Jaworski sniffed the air and shook his head. It was weirdly reassuring.

He slipped the key into the lock. "Before I do this, we need some ground rules. The bishop explained you're licensed and bonded and on police retainer, so you can do your thing. I'm going to keep out of your way. But I'm not going to let you take anything. I'd appreciate it if you even kept touching to a minimum. These are someone else's things, and while we have some landlord powers under the law to enter without permission, I take my job seriously regarding personal possessions. Cool?"

"Set, settled and shiny."

He unlocked the door, twisted the doorknob, and pushed. The door swung inward. The room beyond was a shambles, lighted by a single lamp on a table by the window.

Jaworski gaped. "This isn't a good sign."

"No. Not usually."

The view spooked him. "You mind if I stay outside?"

"You're comfortable letting me roam without you?"

"No, but I have some priors. Old stuff, but if anything's missing or he turns up dead, I'd rather not leave DNA or fingerprints in his place. I don't need the hassle."

I gave him a Boy Scout salute. "I'll keep my hands inside the ride."

"Smart lifestyle choice. Mind if I prop the door?"

"If it makes you feel better."

He pulled a door stop from his belt and set it, careful to not touch the door. "I'll be out here if you need me."

The door settled closed to a couple of inches.

I thanked him, fished a pair of gloves from my back pocket, and went to work.

The place had received a thorough going-over: every drawer from the living room furniture, including a corner desk and the entertainment center, had been opened, contents strewn on the floor. The pattern was repeated in the single bedroom, dresser drawers emptied, mattress flipped. Whoever came calling had refrained from filling the laminate kitchen floor with silverware. There was no sign of Young, alive or otherwise.

A living room window fronting a fire escape was unlocked and ajar. Probable point of entry for the break-in. I photographed it, then closed and locked the window and made a note to tell Spence when I called it in.

The goal wasn't valuables. Young's A/V components were still extant. Something else, then.

I took pictures as I went. HPD would too, but there was no guarantee things wouldn't change between now and their sweep. I started with the bedroom and bathroom. There were indications of trip preparations: the absence of a toothbrush, an empty box for a travel-sized tube of paste in the bathroom trash, but no tube. The bedroom wastebasket held a receipt for several travel sizes from a nearby drug store, another for a suitcase from a store a few blocks over. Nothing else stood out.

There were no car keys. I didn't know if Young had a car, walked to work, took a bus. More search-engine-fu required there.

"Is he inside?" Jaworski called when he heard me back in the living room.

"No sign."

"Well, that's something."

In the living room, I stepped with care over the debris, taking pains to avoid shifting anything. I studied the visible paperwork scattered on the floor: old utility bills, financial and health insurance paperwork, the mundane business of life and little else.

The desk was a built-in. The power cord testified to a device. The router blinked at me from the corner. No telling if the device was with Young or whoever ransacked the place. The desk drawers had been rifled, but hadn't been removed.

First rule of information: if it's worth stealing, sometimes it's not *in* the drawer.

I pulled the first drawer all the way out, checked underneath. Nothing. I repeated the action with each of the other three.

I found the tan document envelope secured to the back end of the file drawer. I removed it, uncrimped the clasp, and opened the flap. Inside was a stack of paper stapled together at the corner. Printouts.

I laid the stack in a clear spot on the desktop and photographed each page, eleven in all. The first four comprised a medical report: typical blood work, comparative charts, some additional tests with which I was unfamiliar. The report was fifteen years old. All four pages had the same control number.

The next four summarized multiple test results. The font, layout and date were different, the product of another place and time. Multiple diagrams highlighted specific values, percentages, levels. I had no idea what any of them meant. The control number from the first report appeared again, circled on each of these pages. A stamp on the original pages identified the document as CERTIFIED. For what went unstated.

Three more pages of unfathomable table data followed: columns including a date, a long alphanumeric string, several columns of numbers that could have been computer-related, and one titled "Contract Number." The entire thing was headed LALO MATRIX.

I finished imaging the pages, verified the pictures were usable, and slipped the sheets back into the envelope. As I did, I noted the logo in the right-hand corner of the first page: Medical Explorations Corporation.

I set the envelope on the desk. There was no point in having the police department play treasure hunt.

The kitchen offered minor clues. The milk in the refrigerator was two weeks past its Use By date. The remains of a head of lettuce had gone black and slick. The kitchen garbage can was empty, an unused bag hung inside. All suggested Young planned to return.

I was wrapping up when I heard voices outside the door. Jaworski and a woman. The voices grew in intensity before the door swung open. The woman crossed the threshold but jerked to a halt when she saw me, expecting Herb. She took in the disarray. I couldn't tell if she was hurt or angry. "He's missing, isn't he?"

"If he isn't, his housekeeper is ripping him off."

"You must be the detective Egan mentioned."

"Private investigator. Is there somewhere we can talk, Miss Pascal?"

She suggested the community room in the clubhouse building up the street. I asked her to lead the way. As we crossed the foyer, Jaworski locked the door. "You didn't take anything, right?"

I crossed my heart. "It's like they say when you pack into a national forest, Jaworski: take only pictures, leave only memories." I advised him to keep the key handy. He was going to need to let the police department in after I called them.

FIFTEEN

"Did he make that mess, or did somebody break in?" Pascal stirred a vended latte. She was every young woman Norman Rockwell ever painted, fresh-faced and smooth-skinned. I guessed she wasn't yet thirty. Her pale blue blouse was buttoned to the neck, complimented by a long, black skirt. Her brunette hair was held back by two clips, one over each ear. She wore no make-up. The plainness made her brown eyes pop. It did little to mitigate her frown.

"It appears to be a break-in, though I'm not sure what the goal was."

"Goal?"

"Thieves steal valuables and leave through the front door. Everything worth a quick pawn was still there. Vandals tag walls or bust breakables. There was just disarray and an unlocked window."

"Like whoever came in was looking for something."

A couple of teenagers were across the broad room, watching a basketball game on a large screen and paying us no attention. Otherwise, the place was quiet. Spence was still a half-hour out, owing to organizing a squad to join him. Talking to Pascal was good use of the time. "How do you know Herb?"

"We date. Casually. A few months now. I suppose that makes him my boyfriend. He hasn't introduced me to any of his colleagues, so how serious could things be?"

"Serious enough that you're his emergency contact. That counts for something."

"I'm still not sure how much help I can be." I'd explained the broad strokes of why I'd been there on the walk over. She'd offered no objection to my recording the interview, but now she stared at my mobile, its display counting time and showing the waveform of her voice, and seemed uneasy. "But ask your questions. Maybe something will occur to me."

"When you came in you asked me if he was missing. When was the last time you saw him?"

"About six weeks ago. We were going to have dinner that night, and before we got together, I got a call from that little weasel Egan, pressing me for details about Herb notifying them of he was taking leave from coaching. That was how I found out he'd stepped away from everything. I expected he was leaving, going somewhere, and didn't have the nerve to tell me."

"And then he told you at dinner."

"He did, but it was odd, even for Herb's sense of humor. He told me he needed to take care of some business. I didn't know what business. He's a school teacher. Short of conferences, his business is all right here. So I called him out. And he gave me a bit of run-around, before he told me—" She stopped. "It's going to sound insane."

"Try me."

"He said someone had stolen his soul."

From her expression, I might have done a double-take after all. "Stolen his soul? As in the prince of darkness?"

"Satan buys or barters or gets it at your immoral end. I'd be surprised if he had to steal one in this world. But that was Herb's story, and he said he was going away for a while to make it right."

"And you said?"

"I told him he didn't need to lie to me if he wanted to break up. He insisted he was being honest." She frowned. "And I said he needed professional help. He didn't appreciate that. We got past it, but we were both stung. He messaged the next morning. Said he was sorry and that he'd message again soon. That was the last I've heard."

"And he didn't elaborate at all?"

"I wish he had. Not knowing where he went is worse than thinking he's crazy."

I wouldn't have noticed the guy in the hopper if the sun hadn't pointed him out. The lens on whatever he was filming with reflected as he shifted. He was across the street from the clubhouse building, up a slope and parked in one of the apartment building lots. We'd chosen seats near the broad front windows. He didn't seem to be watching the kids or the basketball game deeper inside. He was too far off to read the hopper's plate.

I kept it to myself. "Other than allegations of a stolen soul, did he seem agitated at all?"

"Not particularly. He seemed most concerned with my feelings."

I considered the contents of the envelope I'd found. "Did he mention any medical issues to you?"

She studied the smudge of foam atop her latte. "I kept after him to see a dentist. From the excuses he made, I suspect he didn't care for being poked and prodded." Her glance at me was puzzled. "Why?"

"Some old paperwork in his apartment is all." Our watcher was either new to surveillance or hadn't realized he'd been noticed. He was now talking to someone, probably hands-free to a mobile, while trying to take pictures, but the call was clearly distracting him, the camera raising and dipping. I saw an opening. "Would you excuse me for a couple of minutes?"

I stood and headed for the restroom in the back. I passed it in the rear hallway and continued on to the back door, helping myself to a ball cap on a peg as I left.

I walked up the sidewalk on the back side of the rec center and the next building, out of our observer's view. Then I turned left to cut back towards the road and the terraced lot overlooking the center's front windows. The person who'd laid out the neighborhood had helpfully installed steps from the road to the lot. I moved quickly, lateral enough to the hopper that I hoped to continue going unnoticed.

I made it to the lot without the driver budging. On closer approach, I saw the hopper lacked both a license plate and a registration number on the rear driver's side assembly. The driver's window was open in search of the breeze. His voice carried the distance between us as his phone call continued. "He's probably in the head." Listened. "He's been talking to a woman all this time. No idea who she is yet, but I've got enough shots for us to work with. Wait—" The camera was back up at his eye, so I walked into the blind spot along the diagonal. When I got close enough, I slipped a ShadowTag on the hopper's rear quarter. He continued his conversation. "Never mind. I thought one of the kids was him. How long should I wait?" He didn't like the answer. "I don't think he left. Why would he leave?"

"Maybe he made you," I said as I stepped next to his window. I snapped his picture with my mobile.

He thrust his hand out at me; whether to grab my mobile or take a poke at me I'd never know, because his other hand punched the liftoff control. As the hopper's engines spun up, I stepped back to avoid the heat and force of the lifters. I snapped another picture as he climbed.

I wondered if the guy—lean, hard featured, hair cropped close enough to make color a guess—was one of my office visitors, if only because it was unusual to piss off two groups of strangers in one week. The one-sided conversation had made it clear enough Pascal wasn't the object. By extension, I doubted Young factored into it. That left me.

As if hearing her name in my mind, Pascal exited the rec center. She'd spotted me up on the terrace, eyes drawn by the sudden hopper liftoff. I retreated down the hill and rejoined her as the hopper merged into the sky lanes. She thoughtfully handed me my coffee.

"Should I be worried about that?" she asked after I'd explained our watcher.

"No. That's a different headache."

Pascal transferred a retainer to the office account before the police contingent arrived. "I want to know a straight-shooter is looking for him, and you seem like one. Cops are fine and all, but I don't want him to become some unsolved case file number." Without prompting from me, she told the arriving PD she was retaining my services and wanted to file a missing persons report for Young. Spence set her up with a uniform to take vital information. She had his vehicle make and model, but couldn't recall the plate. She also supplied both them and me with a photo from the previous Christmas, Pascal and Young in festive sweaters. Young was unremarkable. His face was long and thin and bespoke a skinny build. Dull brown eyes. His thin smile suggested he was less festive than his sweater. It was difficult to gauge how tall he was, given the composition.

While she gave the PD information, a team looked over Young's apartment. Spence and I lingered outside the building. I filled him in on what I knew, including the previously open window.

"We'll BOLO his car in the event he runs afoul of something on the road and pass it to the Snap Squad," Spence said. The traffic enforcement cameras had come and gone twice in Houston over the years before the afternoon a city councilman's wife and two children were killed by a red light runner in Garden Oaks. It might have stayed a tragedy if the guy hadn't driven off. The 'run' part made it a crusade. No one gets a bill passed faster than a politico with a vendetta.

"Throw in a credit card transaction request, and we can call it a hat trick."

"Probably a smart idea, given his place was tossed," he said. "But it could take a few days to come back. Bank politics. You know the score."

"Either way, whether he uses them or someone else does, there's a prize in the box."

"New case?"

"Not quite. Side quest, maybe? He was an associate of Stephen Angelo's."

Spence arched his eyebrows. "Interesting. Think his disappearance and Angelo's death are related?"

"There's potential. Nothing concrete yet. Coincidence isn't causality, as Mémé says."

"She'd have made an astute cop."

I might have snorted. "She'd have been Internal Affairs' waking nightmare."

I left Pascal my card and Spence to his police work. I loaded the images from Young's apartment to the office cloud and clued Barrett into the documents and their tables so she could have a look. When I reviewed the image of the watcher with eyes on Pascal and me, I found his face was a featureless smudge.

"Looks like a VSM," Barrett volunteered.

"Learn me?"

"Virtual ski mask. Basically, a facial countermeasure that screws up digital photography frequencies. Usually goes over the eyes like lenses. If you're an exceedingly vain criminal, you can have them done as surgical implants. Think 'flashback drone' but for your face."

"Charming. I dropped a ShadowTag on the hopper. Can you see where it went?"

She checked the app. "Looks like it broadcast for about two minutes before sending an overload error and going dark. Suggests it was fried by a security countermeasure."

"Someone worked really hard to not be seen."

"And yet, you snuck up on him. Kids today." She clicked off to delve into the files from Young's apartment.

On the way back to the car, I took a detour back past the Community office. Egan was nowhere to be found, so I showed myself back to the bishop's office. He was still there, behind his desk, and greeted me politely. "Terrible business about Herb. The metaphors about losing a lamb from the flock feel strange when they become literal. We'll cooperate in every way possible with the police inquiry."

"I'm sure you will."

"And if he should turn up, you'll be our first call."

"There is one thing," I said. "I was hoping you might be able to offer me some insight."

"Into?"

"Miss Pascal told me Herb was of the belief someone had stolen his soul."

Hudson studied me as if I'd spoken in tongues. Before he could answer, an attendant knocked and entered with a plain china cup of steaming tea. Hudson invited me to sit and offered me a cup. I declined, and he waited until the attendant was gone to continue. "You mean in the sense some tribal cultures believed a device like a camera could 'steal' the soul?"

"That seemed to be the gist."

"No. We don't hold such a thing as possible. Not in a literal sense. But in the sense the soul might be subjected to egregious compromise by another party? I suppose 'stolen' could be a euphemism. Not one I'd endorse."

"I didn't expect so."

"But such a belief would be a point of serious concern."

"How so?"

"Even people who are devout and conduct themselves morally can lose the path, Mr. Robillard. We can all be fundamentally sound and still be coerced by a situation to lie, steal or even kill, and still find a way to rationalize such acts, to self-justify through our misreading of the situation and through our own weakness. If Herb believes someone has compromised his soul in such a deep fashion—*truly* believes—he may fight to reclaim it by any means he sees necessary, which in turn could put him in even greater peril of sin."

"Means such as?"

"It's impossible to say, especially not knowing the details of this 'theft'."

I wondered if 'means' might include murdering Stephen Angelo. 'Can you tell me if Herb was especially devout?"

"I see a man who regularly attends services, who is unwaveringly kind to Miss Pascal, and who instills his students in the classroom or in the gym with guidance based on sportsmanship, community, respect for one another, and love of one's self." He smiled in spite of the situation. "If not holiness, it speaks to devotion."

I took my leave. "If I learn anything, I'll let you know."

He told me his door was always open, even if I just needed to talk. I thanked him and left it at that. Being fairly removed from my faith, I hadn't walked through any of the church doors that always seemed open. I didn't expect to take his offer up any more than I had the others.

SIXTEEN

Barrett had lingered over the images from Young's apartment and taken a hack at Medical Explorations Corporation during my trip back. She called me into the conference room when she heard me enter the office.

"I'm certain this is the material Angelo lifted from NanoDwell," she said. She had a series of articles pulled up on the conference room screen. "And he'd have known exactly where to look for it."

"Oh?"

"He worked for Medical Examinations Corporation before NanoDwell."

I sat while she shuffled windows. "Sami said he came to the company in a buyout."

She conjured a business periodical. "ME Corp was established about twenty years ago. They were a small firm, thirty employees. Headquartered in Southeast Houston, inside the loop. They did contract work across the spectrum, from routine medical testing to high-end biotech research. Eight years ago, they got outrun by their competitors and fell on hard times, which led to their acquisition by NanoDwell."

"So we have ME Corp data; based on the dates, we can put the data and Angelo at ME Corp at the same time; NanoDwell can tie the data to Angelo; and we can illustrate the chain between Angelo and Young, whose apartment it was found in."

I stared at the screen. "That leaves two questions: why leak anything to Herb Young, a high school teacher with no apparent connection to the industry in which Angelo worked and no background in the field."

"Maybe Young was a go-between brokering a deal?"

"With data from several years prior to NanoDwell's buyout? I don't think so. It doesn't even reflect what Sami said. This wasn't a technician looking at NanoDwell's history. He was staring in his own rear view mirror, and someone killed him over it."

"You think it was Young?"

"That's the other question. I wouldn't believe someone so soul-conscious would murder anyone, especially the person feeding him information. But Angelo wouldn't be the first messenger ever kicked into a pit, and the bishop inferred Young's concern could tip him in an irrational direction."

"That's comforting."

The data pages with their blood values, other bodily measures, and such still needed puzzling out. I passed them and pulled up the spreadsheet that had been attached to Young's paperwork, the one bearing no markings to denote ownership. "Any idea what the columns of numbers represent yet?"

"No. I feel like I should know, but I can't put my finger on it."

I understood the feeling. Familiarity danced around the edge of my awareness, smoky, unreachable. "So Sami's mislead me about the nature of the call, and she's at the very least misdirected me about the data Angelo accessed. What else do you think she hasn't been forthright about?"

"I don't know, but it would be rude to put it that way if you ask her during your visit."

I spent the next morning reading everything I could find about NanoDwell, their products and their history to prep for my tour. The technology was at turns fascinating and controversial. The pitch Sami had given about nano-sand and specific molecular signatures was more than marketing. It was a safeguard of NanoDwell's own design, the prime differentiator between them and their competitors. It was a brilliant success story, easily worth killing to protect.

Despite the benefits their nanotech provided, there was strong opposition to turning the machines loose in public-facing, uncontrolled situations. The theory was if nanobots were programmed slapdash—or even too well, to the degree they could learn or adapt like an AI—they could run amok, alter their purpose, become unstoppable berserkers turning everything into nothing. One DC lobbying firm predicted an especially grim future: the face of the earth transformed into a gray goop, with rampant disease and mutation the more pleasant outcomes. The construction sector was a prime target of activist ire. Houses containing nanotech as part of the structure, they argued, didn't just take jobs away from multiple construction sectors, they also put humans at direct risk. Houston's own protest group had close to a thousand members, a swelling of the Rose Street suspect pool I could have done without.

When I shared my enthusiasm with Barrett, I learned which side of the nanotech debate she was on. "Oh, it's a genius idea. Provided you want to get turned into a mass of jelly one night in your sleep."

"I thought it was elegant. The nano machines they're building are hard-coded. They only interact with material containing the molecular signature of NanoDwell's construction medium."

"Every lock responds to one key. Doesn't stop people from picking them." Barrett tried to drill into me with her gaze. "For someone who struggles with, and even sometimes loathes technology, you seem to have taken a shine to the hype."

"As a techno-junkie, I'm surprised you haven't."

"I don't need to rush the end of the world," she said. She handed me a hard copy of one of Young's document pages, the long tables of numerical data. "If you're done boning up for Nanopalooza, it's my sad duty to inform you you're losing your touch."

"First Spence, now you. Who's spreading this rumor?"

"In fairness, I was in Recon and it should have grabbed me by the eyes and pulled. These columns? They're the LALO part of the table heading. Map coordinates. Latitude, longitude, minutes, seconds, respective compass direction. They're typically presented in a single string with punctuation, which is their big neon name badge. Split them into columns, it's less obvious."

It was certainly obvious once she said it. "Coordinates to what?"

"I'll let you know after I build the map. Should be done by the time you get back."

The limo was low and sleek, a shade of black that could swallow you if you stared at it too long. It might have floated off the hopper dealer's lot an hour before. It came with a tanned, quiet driver named Erik who bade me good afternoon before rolling the screen between us closed.

The limo headed west along the SI-10, over the major belts and loops, beyond Katy and the northern fringes of the Space Corridor, into the still-rural parts to the West. It exited over dry wilderness just before Brookshire, passed scrub oak and dust until it crossed an invisible line onto NanoDwell's property. The dust turned into lush grass, the scrub oak became towering cedar, magnolia, pecan. The hopper descended and cruised at road level, towards a six-story building. It could have been hewn out of a single, massive amethyst crystal. We skimmed past a sign proclaiming NanoDwell "the Number One Provider of Alternative Housing Strategies," too fast for me to catch the name of the publication with the generous praise.

The limo touched down, a graceful stop along the curved drive fronting the building's main entrance. Erik opened the door. He instructed me to have the receptionist page him when I was done, and retreated behind the wheel. I showed myself inside.

In sharp contrast to the exterior, the lobby was a two-story atrium with conventional walls the color of gypsum. Banners with self-aggrandizing imagery—houses, apartment buildings, office towers, each accompanied by a customer with a smile on the face—were evenly spaced on the lobby walls. Beyond a secure badge reader to the left was a bank of elevators. At the back of the room two doors to other, different hallways were similarly controlled. Two pairs of double sliding doors to the right segregated a large auditorium. In one corner of the room, three men in suits spoke in hushed tones. I didn't know if they were making deals or telling dirty jokes.

A metal desk like a crescent moon in the middle of the room served as reception. Behind the desk, the receptionist gave me a beaming corporate greeting. "Good afternoon. Welcome to NanoDwell. My name is Piper. How may I help you?"

I presented my ID. "C.T. Robillard. I have an appointment with Dana Sami."

Piper indicated a terminal for an ID swipe to check in. "One moment please." She touched her earpiece. Once connected, she spoke softly, nodding as if Sami could see her. She returned to me. "Miss Sami will be with you in a couple of minutes. Can I get you anything while you wait? A cup of coffee? Tea? Water?"

"No, thank you."

Piper's gaze was a spotlight. "You're a natural, aren't you?"

"A natural what?"

"Natural. Unenhanced. I used to work in a clinic. I have an eye for these things."

She did have decent eyes. I couldn't tell if she was enhanced or not. If not, nature had made her petite and proportional, clear skinned and fair haired. "You can tell if someone's had work done?"

Her grin was younger than she was. "Oh, yes. I can spot someone who's been tuned. You learn to see the little tics of alteration. How their hands flex, how their eyes respond, the way someone moves. There's always a tell. You appear to be all-natural. What I can see, anyway." Her gaze lingered on what she couldn't see. "My information is incomplete."

She was a weak link for a gatekeeper. I wondered if Piper was on Sami's radar as a security risk. She should have been.

I saw Dana Sami from the corner of my eye, exiting the elevator bank.

"Incomplete information often leads to a poor conclusion," I told Piper as I met Sami with a smile that, despite Piper's observations, was heavily enhanced.

SEVENTEEN

As tours went, it was less satisfying than the commercial space test facility I'd visited the previous year, but more interesting than the Sangnan chip works in Conroe. NanoDwell was candid about the company's story, more museum than marketing. It was unusual for a firm to present both success and failure milestones side by side in its displays.

As we walked, Sami offered tidbits about the company, the products it already offered, some things they'd recently introduced. She was especially enthusiastic about home security measures she'd helped develop for their current generation of housing. "It's a whole new field: designs for families that don't want a gun in the house."

"What does the building do? Perform a citizen's arrest?"

"Picture a home that doesn't just alert you to an intruder and contact police, but conducts a threat assessment using probabilities and statistics, and acts to restrict an intruder's movements until the authorities arrive. I'm also heading an internal team working on business designs for the security market: detention centers, supermax prisons, and the like. They'll give a whole new dimension to the idea of a lock-down."

The sparkle in her eye made her designs nothing I wanted to see. "You take a great deal of pride in your work."

"Since my divorce, the job has been my sole focus."

"I'm sorry."

"Don't be. He wanted things I wouldn't give him."

"Children?"

"Obedience. I did two tours in the Special Forces. I wasn't about to take direction to bake cobbler and drop off dry cleaning. When I caught him screwing around on me, I took him for everything except his name. I decided then my work-life balance could handle more work. As it is, they force me to take alternate Fridays off."

"You sound like Barrett."

"There are so many little moving parts. Forgotten badges, lost phones and computers, security audits, mundane reports. Not that it's ever slow, but I'd be lying if I said it didn't get a little dull."

On the heels of my marathon reading session, I was able to ask informed questions as Sami led me through the facility. "How did you arrive at the composition of the nano-sand?"

"Years of trial and error. The current version is a molecular amalgam of over seventy distinct donor materials. It probably has more in common with plants than anything else. The construct diversity allows it to be redeployed, to replace a wall with a window, move a fireplace, tint glass. Right now, it's manufactured at a facility in Wharton. We expect to expand production in the next eighteen months."

"I understand a typical build uses a number of different nanobot lines tasked with individual functions."

"You've done your homework. Diversification of function helps minimize the energy needed to alter a structure, and keeps the nanobots from stepping on each other's toes. Some move and shape nano-sand, others control form and density or provide maintenance and ongoing support. Each line is preprogrammed with everything it needs: initial designs and schematics, specific building tasks, code requirements, construction or maintenance tasks, acceptable modifications for their area. Through the combination, the raw material can be turned into anything we need it to be for the construction."

"That must be stupidly intricate code."

"That's where the control center comes in. It acts as a conductor leading an orchestra in performing a symphony. It's the first thing we install."

"Why do you use a bio-mechanical brain? There must be a dozen manufacturers with chip sets fast enough to coordinate the nanotech."

"I could give you a marketing song and dance about how a bio-mech control center made people feel better about the entire process, instead of calling it a 'computer control center,' but the truth is mercenary. There's a massive amount of money in bio-mech patents, and we hold them all for what we've done. Let's be honest: the hardware and software world is licensing-happy and that adds layers of expense, AI engines are a nebula of who-owns-what, and re-purposing is a legal nightmare. There's not a patent troll alive who can lay claim to anything we've created."

"How is the control center installed?"

"It exists in a sealed cylinder with a rechargeable nutrient bath. It's sealed from disease and contaminants. Warrantied operational life of 75 years. The cylinder is hard-wired to the foundation and conductive framing is installed. The nano-sand is poured on the foundation and the nanobots are introduced. The control center activates them and coordinates the programming within the nanobot lines to begin construction."

"And the nanobots go dormant when its done."

"Yes, until the control center receives an approvable modification and provides update instructions to the required lines."

"What about this nano-sand molecular signature? The thing that keeps the nanobots from running amuck?"

Sami's eyes narrowed. "You've been talking to a doom and gloomer."

"My associate handles our tech. She's...not a fan."

"She's a victim of old propaganda. The nanobots won't make a single change to any substance that doesn't have the nano-sand molecular signature. Period. Guaranteed."

I heard Barrett in my head, suggesting a guarantee was useless if the world ended. "How long does a typical build take?"

Sami led us around a corner. "Depending on size and complexity, anywhere from a few hours to several days. At the end, you have a turnkey structure ready to be looped into city utilities and inhabited, warrantied to pass city inspection the first time." She stopped in front of a door marked LEARNING LAB. "How about a demonstration?"

The learning lab reminded me most of a morgue. It had several long steel tables, each with a silver tray raised several inches off the table on a rack. Within the tray was a gray granular substance that resembled gray salt. A length of pipe an inch in diameter angled down from one end of the tray to a square steel platform with a two-inch-high strip fence around the edge. A touchscreen filled the other third of the table. The room was laid out for multiple groups, and appeared brand new, presumably for the company's public takeoff.

Sami led me to one of the stations. "For these demo tables, we've substituted a computer interface for the bio-mechanical processor. More cost effective in miniature. Otherwise, this is our full setup. It starts with the nano-sand." She indicated the tray of granules. "Go ahead and touch it."

"No thanks. I wore my good hands today."

Sami laughed. "Eight year olds do this every day, Mister Robillard."

"Eight year olds touch all kinds of weird things every day."

I expected her to goad me. Instead, she shrugged—suit yourself—and activated the screen. "Each station is programmed with four scale models. Pick your model and press 'Start'." She made way for me.

I scanned my choices. While I was curious to see the Empire State Building appear before my eyes, I selected the Jefferson Memorial in DC because I'd seen that in person and at three minutes, it had the shortest estimated build time. I touched START.

There was an audible hum, voltage channeled to the steel square. A pump fed the gray sand through the pipe and into the square below.

When the material had been dumped, the tray and pipe retracted. A bar elevated on rollers took its place, hissed as it passed over the pile of nano-sand.

"That's the nanobot induction," Sami said.

I watched as the nano-sand on the square leveled itself. Then it began building upward in layers, like a 3-D printer forming an object from template material. The shape emerged. The formed sand changed color to an off-white shade resembling marble. More of it rolled, climbed, refined. Steps formed, then the raised floor. The nano-sand coalesced, candles burning in reverse to form columns.

"How long does it take to harden in an actual build?"

"Fifteen to thirty seconds, depending on various factors. The main driver is the property the material is programmed to emulate. A stone-like construct takes longer than wood, which takes longer than plaster, and so on."

When the columns were done, the curved roof of the monument began to knit together from their tops, several plates drawing into a cohesive whole. As the roof formed, I hunched down to peer within the foot-tall miniature. The statue of Thomas Jefferson formed in the same way, a pile of sand growing and refining from a formless mass the size of my thumb into a statue seemingly cast in bronze. Even the iconic quotes on the inside walls appeared, rising from the surface to become dark metal letters.

The entire process took the advertised three minutes. Its fidelity to the original was remarkable. "Impressive."

"The forms are also as strong, if not stronger, than the actual building materials, thanks to the molecular engineering of the nano-sand by the bots. And if you want a change, the dormant nanobot lines can be reactivated by the control center. Let's say you want a skylight and two statues of Jefferson. Through a communications interface, you submit the change to the control center. It reviews the change for structural feasibility, stability, site appropriateness, code compliance, the works. If approved, it activates the nanobots." She opened an operator menu on the touchscreen and made some adjustments. On command, the center of the dome thinned and became transparent, a round glass eye staring into the sky. The statue of Jefferson broke down and reformed into two distinct statues, centered relative to both the dome and each other.

"If it can be programmed, it can be realized," she said.

Her mobile buzzed. She touched her earpiece. "Yes sir." A voice I couldn't make out gave the woman a laundry list of items. At the end, she said, "Very good. I'll be there in five." She toggled the earpiece off.

"Pressing business?"

"That was Mister Phalen. He'd like to meet you."

Victor Phalen's office was on the top floor of the building. Sami lead me around the edge of a cubicle farm, bordered on the outside wall by several other offices, restrooms, a break room and a couple of executive conference rooms. "This is the nerve center of the operation," she said, hushed, as if to not draw attention to us. I caught probing glances anyway.

When his secretary showed us in, Phalen was standing before a broad window, staring out at the world with dramatic flair. He turned. He was a young thirty with a face that might still get him carded for a drink. The close-cropped hair was the only formal thing about him. He was dressed down in a blood red polo shirt and tan khaki slacks. I felt like I'd interrupted his golf game.

"Mister Phalen, this is C.T. Robillard." Sami took a step back. Handshakes ensued.

"Mister Robillard. Thanks for coming to see us."

"Thanks for the tour. I'm afraid I've been monopolizing Miss Sami's time."

"No worries. Please, have a seat." He turned to Sami. "Thanks, Dana. I'll bring him down when we're done."

I caught Sami's nod. She left without a word. The side trip was many things. Impromptu wasn't one of them. I settled into a chair by the desk. Phalen moved to a bar table in the corner and offered me a drink.

"Not on the job, thanks."

The man gave himself a short pour of whiskey and added a splash of water. He swirled the glass with his hand. "What do you think of our little enterprise?"

"Not so little at all. It's an astounding level of innovation."

"I started this company right out of college, but it had its roots deeper than that." Phalen sat behind his desk. "The resilience of nature fascinated me as a child. For instance, the way a tree could grow around and incorporate a fence, or the way the body could be stimulated under certain conditions to regenerate tissue more quickly. My father was a mechanical engineer, my mother was a geneticist. I showed such promise as a child, they had my brain enhanced four times before I was twelve."

I didn't say the first thing that popped to mind. The name Frankenstein figured too prominently. "It appears to have paid off."

"What I envisioned has blossomed into a highly competitive footrace. Some Chinese conglomerate is right behind us, three more firms behind them. But the bleeding edge is still ours. Right now, we're working on the new generation of kit homes. Like those bungalows you used to see in the neighborhoods, the ones people could order from a catalog. It arrived in a crate with every board and nail and shingle you needed."

"I used to live in one of those."

"Then you can imagine a new generation. Carbon fiber framework, floor plans preprogrammed to lot size, nano-sand, control center, initializing power source—almost as easy to set up as your sound system." He sipped his drink. "With the capital generated by our IPO, we could make low-cost housing a reality for millions once more."

"That's an ambitious plan."

"I've spent more than a decade cultivating construction subcontractors, partners, developing a dealer network. It's been over a year putting our IPO together. Regulators, brokerages, banks." He sipped his drink. "Then we had this whole business with Stephen Angelo. Dana tells me you're looking into it."

"I am. Did you know him very well?"

"We weren't close, but he'd been with us for some time. We're up to almost 300 employees, but you don't forget the people who helped you lay the foundation." He stared into his glass. "The thought someone you trust could turn on you for money or promises or whatnot? That's a hard one. Do you have any ideas about the party he was dealing with?"

Not that I was ready to share. "I'm running some things down, but Miss Sami and I only met yesterday for the first time."

"My fault. I keep her busy."

"I'm a little unclear on the nature of the material Mister Angelo allegedly stole. It might help me narrow down the parties of interest, maybe point to a competitor who's lagging behind in that specific area."

"Yes, of course. My understanding is it was pertinent to control center development and viability."

"I'm the farthest thing from a scientist. What would data of that sort look like?"

"Numerical data in tables. Scientific testing for longevity and viability, possibly branded to us."

I waited for something more specific. Nothing arrived. "I understand you searched his company email."

"Yes. Nothing there, but it would have been foolish of him to use his company account for that."

"You'd be astounded at how foolish people can be."

He sipped. "I understand you've gotten a look at his private computers and accounts."

"We're still reviewing our findings, but the preliminary analysis is so far inconclusive. My associate would say 'data takes time.'"

"Well, if there's a clue who he was in contact with, that would be the place to find it."

"There or his mobile. Did you find one when you inspected his work station, by chance?"

A flick of the eyes from me to the office door, an unguarded blip. "How's that?"

"His personal handheld hasn't turned up. Not on him, not found in his car or apartment. I thought it possible he might have left it at work the day he was killed."

"Not that I'm aware. If so, it would have been boxed for his next of kin." He finished his pour with a healthy swallow. "Wouldn't it be likely Angelo's killer kept it, to hide their connection?"

"Doubtful. Even brand-new criminals know how easily phones are followed, or how records can be obtained in a murder case."

"I'll ask Dana to check his effects and let you know. I understand she also has Angelo's personnel file and her investigation file for you. If there's any other support we can offer, don't hesitate to contact her. She's top notch. I'll keep eyes open for her updates on the matter." He rose from his chair, the meeting concluded as if a bell had rung, and shook my hand again. "Thank you, Mister Robillard. I appreciate your consideration." Pleasant. I also felt I'd been measured.

He escorted me back to the lobby. The elevator was crowded on the way down. No one said a word to the company's CEO. It painted interesting lines in his portrait.

In the lobby, Phalen handed me off to Sami and retreated for his office. She greeted me with a data card. "Here are the files on Angelo and our investigation into the incident. Interviews with his team, records retention people, the whole thing."

"If something sticks out from an interview, can I request a follow-up?"

"I don't see a problem. A human resources rep may need to sit in."

"No union rep?"

Her glance suggested I'd spoken some impossible word that wouldn't parse within their walls.

I thanked her and promised to circle back in a couple of days, after I'd reviewed the material. Sami asked Piper to call the limo around to pick me up. Piper glanced from me to Sami with a wounded joy, as if Sami had poached her date for the debutante ball and she dare not make a fuss over it.

EIGHTEEN

When I entered the office, I nearly collided with the man in the dark gray suit. Black shoes, tie with a splash of red. He was Federal. More often than not, they look like they all buy suits from one tailor tucked away in a quiet corner of Quantico, a poor soul who's cut and sewn so many garments on government contract, he could nail an inseam with hot pokers in his eyes. The man was pushing fifty. A career in federal law enforcement had done much to scrub the mirth from his expression.

Spence was revealed as I closed the door. They were both in the outer office talking to Barrett. Barrett was the sort of cool and collected I'd come to expect. On the other hand, Spence appeared annoyed, on the verge of unrest. I didn't suspect it was from Barrett's sparkling conversation.

"I was about to ping and see when you'd be back," she said.

"The tour went long."

"At least you're not goo."

Spence interjected before we jumped the rails. "Thib, I'd like to introduce Special Agent Thomas Overbaugh. He's with the Bureau."

"Come into my office." I led them in and closed the door behind us, cutting off Barrett's concerned glance. "Excuse the housekeeping. The place is doubling as my home at the moment."

"What happened to your actual home?" Overbaugh asked.

"Arson."

"I wasn't aware that was a peril for private investigators." Overbaugh took the empty guest chair.

I cleared the other for Spence. "You meet some interesting people." I leaned against the corner of the desk. "What can I do for you?"

"Special Agent Overbaugh stopped by my office earlier today in response to a records search I submitted on your behalf. The one pertinent to Leon Dushane. As I was unable to provide him background or details, I offered to bring him here so he could inquire directly."

Hells. I could read the choice four-letter words in Spence's eyes. I didn't blame him. The problem with big nets is most of the time they pull up trash. On rare occasion, a land mine gets tangled in the mesh.

Overbaugh took the opening. "What's your interest in Dushane?"

"He came to my attention as a possible lead in a cold case I've recently picked up again. He was on a list I was given."

"Could you provide specifics of this case?"

I nodded. "The murder of my wife, seven years ago."

I was studying Overbaugh, but in my peripheral vision, I saw the brief wicket Spence's mouth formed. "I see. In what capacity is he a person of interest?"

"To be honest, I don't know. I only began making inquiries yesterday with Inspector Spencer."

"Do you suspect him as the killer, as an accomplice somehow related to the crime, something else?"

"Like I said, I don't know." More slowly this time.

"So you have no idea of the current whereabouts of Mister Dushane?"

"No." And, it seemed, neither did Overbaugh.

"And you've had no prior dealings with him?"

"None."

"He wasn't previously attached to the case?"

"No. His name recently came up for the first time."

Overbaugh drew a data pad from within his jacket and showed me a mugshot, a man of Middle Eastern extraction. Narrow cheeks. Hard eyes. His expression suggested he didn't care he'd been pinched doing whatever he'd done. The mug shot was three months old from the date at the bottom. "How about this man?"

"No."

"His name is Ahmed Micallef."

"That doesn't make him any more familiar."

"Three months ago, he was apprehended by agents in a sting operation. Micallef is a splicer. Know what that is?"

"The dark side of the digital world is more my associate's bag than mine. They're a flavor of computer hacker, right?"

"A splicer is to a hacker as a jet pilot is to a kid on a float scooter. Most of them are under forty. They're serious body and brain modders, with the sole intent of giving themselves advantages with digital systems: speed, intuition, agility."

"I gather Micallef was a heavy hitter."

"He's a seven on the Gibson-Bright digital threat scale." My expression must have told him he was speaking gibberish to me. "The scale only goes to eight, and we've never found an eight."

"So not just things like changing a credit rating so your hopper loan terms are better or making your hazel eyes blue in the DMV's computer."

"He could do that in his sleep. A skilled splicer can worm into a database and make absolute, untraceable changes to a person's identity. No college degree? They can add you to the records of the university of your choosing, including the databases for financial aid repayment and the alumni newsletter. They can rewrite your earnings and tax history, your criminal history—anything. They can also go in the opposite direction. They can splice you out of databases to the point you cease to exist. Your old self disappears, your new identity is established as if its always been there. We believe Micallef penetrated databases previously thought unassailable, and made a small fortune selling his services."

"How did you catch him? I'd expect his typical customer is Paranoia Patient Zero."

"There are two constants in the hacking universe, Mister Robillard. The first is that people boast. In his case, two individuals who knew and had dealings with him engaged in some careless talk about Micallef where we had someone undercover."

"How does this lead to Leon Dushane?" Overbaugh clearly hadn't read Spence in before now. Impatient Spence was odd. I wasn't sure if he wanted off the hot plate he found himself sitting on, or wanted to finish up with Overbaugh so he could punch me in the throat at his leisure.

"Micallef has allegedly committed thousands of intrusions into systems for minor changes. For those, we've got a few people we're leaning on, college kids mostly. He's been a one-man fake ID factory along the gulf coast, but we're more interested in the people for whom he performed a full splice in the last ten years. Old identities completely scrubbed from databases of record, from birth certs right down the line. New identities generated and inserted and impossible to weed out. Hell, we found a worm the man wrote to insert new identities into backup files while the backups were being loaded for verification. He's made a dozen people vanish and created shadow puppets in their stead. Dushane was one of them."

"If Micallef was so meticulous, how do you know he's done a dozen full splices?"

"That's the second constant of hacking: unimaginable hubris. Micallef tripped himself up by keeping an encrypted list with the names of his full-splice customers. He thought it couldn't be broken. He was wrong."

Micallef probably believed he was the smartest guy in every room he entered. "I presume it only has his customers' old names."

Overbaugh confirmed it first with his sour expression. "Correct. And at least two of them were on international watch lists. We haven't the first clue who they became or where they might be."

"And since cracking the file, you've had automated flags in multiple systems to track inquiries against those individuals, in case they turn up."

Overbaugh nodded. "People are inherently narcissistic, sentimental, sometimes forgetful. They'll run their old name through a search engine, or blurt it out in conversation. We need one of these people to help us make the government's case. Any one of them, and we'll have Micallef dead to rights. They'll yank his implanted tech and toss him in a cell straight out of frontier days."

I avoided Spence's gaze. It was only going to suggest I drop into a lower gear. "Even if he was adept at scrubbing his tracks, you must have digital evidence to use against him. You would have needed that much to get the approval to run a sting."

"We have a great deal of evidence, Mister Robillard. The problem is, digital evidence is like magic to a jury. They don't understand it. It confuses them. They get lost in the maze of conflicting expert witnesses. We want someone to whom Micallef gave a new identity to testify against him. Real words from a real customer with a real reason to engage his services." I suspected there was more at play than Overbaugh was telling me. I didn't care. Micallef wasn't my nut to crack. "The general inquiry regarding Leon Dushane tripped our program. He's the first to make a blip on the scanner. Hence my interest in what you know."

"Like I said, he was a name on a list. If I didn't delve into the details with Inspector Spencer, it's because I honestly didn't know if it was a legitimate lead or not."

"How did you come by this list?"

"My father-in-law. He included Dushane on a list of possible suspects or witnesses in my wife's murder he sent a few days ago. Full disclosure: we've been at odds since she was killed. I thought it might be random noise, something made up to waste my time."

Overbaugh made notes on his tablet. "Do you know how your father-in-law came by Dushane's name?"

"No, and he was reluctant to share with me. I'd be happy to put you in touch with him." I gave him Maddox's name, address, numbers. I figured I was doing Maddox a service. If he wanted to burn me, he could use some new friends in law enforcement.

There were additional questions to which I couldn't provide intelligent answers. When he was satisfied, Overbaugh thanked Spence and me in turn, and showed himself out. Spence lingered. The silence was uncomfortable. He let me squirm for a minute.

"Jessica's murder, huh?"

"Everything old is new again."

"How new is this?"

"Since her birthday."

"You finally let Maddox get to you." With a shake of the head, like he was disappointed.

"He hit the right buttons. It didn't help that until his card arrived, I'd forgotten her birthday."

He looked out the window at the sinking sun. "When did you plan to tell me?"

"When I had a new development. I wanted to give the whole case a once-over, get a fresh feel before I brought anyone in."

"Barrett's not helping?"

"Barrett doesn't even know."

"Any closer to your vest, your cards will slide inside your chest."

I shrugged. "If I'd had the slightest inkling the Bureau was looking for this guy, I'd have given you all the details up front." I sat behind my desk. The chair rocked back, rolled to the wall. "It's something I need to do, Spence. I've been hiding from it for too long."

"Christ, Thib. I can help. I *want* to help, and I'm positioned to. But you need to tell me when I'm helping. You know we loved Jessie in the squad room. A bunch of us regularly called Koi on his bullshit when he went after you. The ones still there would enjoy seeing the person who killed her go all the way to the Polunksy Unit, and arm-wrestle each other for the right to push the button. No bullshit, Thib. You need to work with me on this. Especially if you plan on using me to pursue it."

He stressed 'using' and for a moment, I wanted to go to the mat. I said nothing. Sometimes when someone is right, silence is the best answer.

He fished in his pocket. Produced one of the jump drives we pass back and forth. Set it on the desk. "For what it's worth, he's what I pulled up on Leon Dushane. Once the Feds showed up, Records popped it to me like it was an unpinned grenade."

"Good to know how to motivate them."

"Don't get excited. There was a sealed juvenile file. Nothing to be learned from that without a court order."

"Word on the street is he developed sticky fingers early in life. Age eleven or so."

"You *have* been busy."

"People talk to me. I have that kind of face." I plugged it into my laptop and made a quick copy.

"There was also an outstanding adult arrest warrant, issued for a string of burglaries for which he appears to have been the sole suspect."

"I thought this splicer erased Dushane's identity."

"A quirk of timing. I suppose the warrant went into the database after whatever the splicer did to erase him.

"Robberies where?"

"In and around the Heights. A string of them that September. Seven or eight in one night."

"Why is it still outstanding?"

"He disappeared and it was never quashed. The missing persons jacket was also out there. According to his mother, the day the cops showed up with the warrant, Dushane drove to school in his grandfather's cherry '43 Bellingham Regatta coupe—liberated from the man's garage—and he and the car were never seen again. Of course, if he went to the splicer, it would explain how he vanished."

"And the Regatta would explain how he paid for it." Something nagged at me from Spence's details. "When was the string of burglaries?"

"September. Late September."

"What year?"

"Seven years ago," he said, and stopped, the timing sinking in. "Right around the time Jessica was murdered."

I checked the copy, found it complete, and returned the drive. "So while Koi was turning me on a spit, an actual, possible suspect was right in front of him, already being sought for a string of burglaries in the neighborhood. Marvelous."

"How on earth did Maddox ferret out Dushane's name?"

I glanced at the desktop as if saying his name would somehow conjure Maddox's investigation notes. "It follows if the killer didn't want to be caught, he'd disappear. Maddox is old, but he knows his way around a computer. It's not unthinkable he'd search for news items—missing people, wanted people. If there was a warrant for robbery, there was probably an article in the Chron, and he'd have recognized it was the right place and time." The only thing keeping me from believing he'd pitched a police clerk some dead-daughter, murdering-son-in-law sob story to get the name searched was the FBI hadn't already visited him to play Twenty Questions.

"There's one thing bothering me," Spence said.

"Just one?"

"A petty thief doesn't go to a splicer for the trouble and expense of a completely new identity."

"No. As a rule, that's usually the act of a more desperate criminal."

Neither of us needed to put the rest to air.

NINETEEN

I walked Spence out with a promise to keep him abreast of anything I learned about Dushane or anything else I needed regarding Jessica's murder. I returned to a smug grin on Barrett's face. "Takeout from Mio Amico, and you're buying."

"You presume I'm hungry after all that."

"You get presumptuous when I presume."

I closed the door and glowered. "This may be the wrong time for play. You should try in an hour. Or next February."

"If I seem inordinately pushy, it's because while you were attending your deadly nano-sandcastle building seminar and getting in trouble with Spence—"

"I'm not in trouble with Spence."

"Okay, then. The fed he brought with him."

"It's not trouble." I smiled in spite of my mood. "But I wouldn't want to be my father-in-law this time tomorrow."

"Whoever's in line for federal prison, I'm ready to eat. I figured out how Herb Young's been spending his summer vacation."

I grabbed a bottle of water from the small office fridge. "That might be worth takeout."

I followed her into the conference room. She linked her tablet with the big screen and displayed a map. The area spanned half the state of Texas and was littered with pins. "The number sheets contained thirty-seven distinct sets of coordinates. As you can see, they're scattered around the state. A majority are in the greater Houston metro, with additional locations in Dallas, San Antonio, and a couple in Freeport. All buildings."

"That's a broad spread of darts."

"In both location and type. Warehouses and storage facilities account for nineteen of them. Eleven are commercial properties, three are private homes, plus two auto repair shops, a community center, and a boat showroom."

"What's the connection?"

Barrett selected one of the pins. "Warehouse on East 9th Street in Freeport. Destroyed in an overnight fire last month. Investigators blamed a faulty propane storage tank adjacent to the building." She selected another. "Auto repair shop on East Jefferson in Dallas. Burned to the ground, also last month. Labeled 'suspicious,' but the revelation it was being used as a chop shop gave Dallas police about a dozen suspects." Another. "A storage facility in Channelview, reduced to nothing. A beverage distribution center in San Antonio. In all, fourteen places on the list have been torched since Herb Young went missing, one every three days."

"That's statistically improbable."

"It gets better when you connect the dots under the dots. The buildings were put up by a variety of companies, all in the same 18 month period roughly a decade ago. The ones in San Antonio were all by the same firm. Same for Dallas. The Houston-area buildings have three different contractors. But all the builders across all locations were part of the same licensing program."

She displayed a decade-old news article from the Chronicle, a beefy business piece about a new company, NanoDwell, and a program with several regional builders to pilot new technology for "growing buildings."

"The company didn't erect them," she said, "but they're all NanoDwell buildings, girders to gutters."

I studied the map, scanning the Houston area. Barrett read my interest. "As one of my instructors said during basic training, 'Let's confuse ourselves a little more.' In at least four of the cases, after the fire was set the arsonist pounded on doors, rang doorbells, or pulled alarms to alert people inside to the fire and ensure everyone got out. Everyone did."

"Same M.O. as Rose Street."

"Here's the kicker: Rose Street isn't on the list and doesn't fit the pattern."

"I don't see a pattern."

"I didn't either. It was nonsensical to me—why make three separate trips to Dallas to set fires, for example, when you could hang around and knock them all out over a few days and be done? At first I thought we were talking about multiple firebugs. Then maybe that Young was spacing them to hide their serial nature."

"He's not?"

"No. The chronology and distance were the keys. He's working farthest from his home to nearest, at alternating compass points. But saying it doesn't do its esoteric nature justice."

With a touch she cleared the map and began displaying the fire locations in chronological order. I watched the fourteen pins blink onto the map, one after another.

"Again."

She ran it again. I saw it. North. South. West. East. Three times, and it conjured Barry Munson from my memories of second grade at Saint James Elementary. *Watch the priest: spectacles, testicles, watch and wallet. That's how you remember—*

"The sign of the cross."

"Yup. The holy road warrior's guide to barbecuing buildings. How this translates to his stolen soul is another matter."

"You're sure Rose Street doesn't fit?"

"Not in timing, not in direction, and it's not on the list."

"Do you know where he's headed next?"

"If I'm right, it'll be a storage warehouse outside Richmond, off the 69. Night after next."

We both heard the thud against the hallway door. I moved to the outer office. Saw the envelope that had been slipped under the door. I went straight to the hall, but all I got for my trouble was the sound of the elevator already descending at the end of the hall. I considered a footrace I couldn't win and didn't start it.

I picked up the envelope by the edges. White, number 10, unremarkable. No writing. Barrett offered a knife she'd conjured from somewhere. I slipped it under the flap and down one end. With care, I pulled a single, folded sheet from within. Unfolded it. Computer-printed in block letters was the message:

14010 HERSHE, #402 — 8PM TONIGHT
RE: S. ANGELO

There are a thousand things I enjoy about private investigation. Clandestine meetings in unknown places with strangers are none of them. I didn't like the timing, the idea of it, the location. Hershe Street wasn't one of the garden spots of the city. It was closer to the ship channel than I wanted to be in the wake of my encounter with Vetrov. The simple note smelled like an invitation to far more complex trouble.

"We aren't going, are we?" Barrett asked.

"You wanted more field trips."

"You still don't get it: I want *better* field trips."

TWENTY

Hershe Street ran through the Cloverleaf neighborhood east of the city. Cloverleaf perched beside the I-10, just north of the ship channel. Long a residential neighborhood, the hunger for more industrial space near the channel had caused high density developments to spring up like cankers. In another twenty years, it might be a boomtown, a ghost town, an industrial wasteland in need of Superfund cleanup. The city's Magic 8-Ball had no answers.

14010 Hershe was an abandoned six-story apartment building, tucked between a newer residence and a warehouse. The graffiti on its walls seemed to hold it up. A one-note tagger who painted the letters LSD in 3-D with remarkable proficiency had once taken a shine to the place: they'd left their mark a half-dozen times on the front wall alone. But time and Texas sun had faded the brilliant neon shades to pastels. Even LSD had found somewhere better to deface.

I parked at the end of the block. There were a few cars up the street, most near the apartments on the other side. A beat-up hopper pickup, a sickly mustard color in the streetlights, was halfway to the building's front door. The street was quiet. I had no sense we were being watched. No one approached.

I retrieved my electro from the glove compartment.

"Can I play too?" Barrett checked the magazine in her automatic, snapped it back in place.

"Sure. Same rule as always: put your pistol in non-lethal mode, and you can bring it along."

"Non-lethal mode is built into the aiming process."

"Then tuck your child in the dashboard box and reassure it you'll be back soon."

She sighed. Gun and holster went into the compartment. "How long are we going to do this dance?"

"Until I decide to change the record." I thumbed the control on the steering wheel and engaged the compartment's magnetic lock. "You're welcome to use rubber bullets, 9mm beanbags, any non-lethal solution there is."

"What if I get into a situation requiring lethal force?"

"How many times since leaving the military has the need for lethal force come up? Even considering your current line of work?"

She said nothing. She'd lost her desire for the argument, and that was fine with me.

I clipped the electro to my belt when we got out, grabbed a flashlight, and led the way.

The front door of 14010 Hershe swung open, more de-locked than unlocked, the frame around the twin-bolts broken and rotted. Even if it had been secured, the glass panes of the outer and inner doors were long since broken, the frames empty.

The lobby had been attractive once. Its beauty was obscured by dirt and debris on the tile floor, broken furniture, more old gang tags on the walls, and wreckage from the rifled mailboxes to the side of the lobby. If there'd been treasure left among the unreceived junk mail, it was long-gone. I flipped a switch on a lamp still plugged into the wall. There was no response. Building power was a hazy memory as well.

"Stairs," I said. We found them around the corner from the elevator. The fire door was also unlocked.

We climbed slowly to minimize the echoes of footfalls. I noticed the undisturbed dust—less than the lobby because of the doors at the bottom and at each landing, but still enough to show we were the only ones making tracks. I glanced at my watch. We'd been prompt. There was possibly a second stairwell, maybe a fire escape in back allowing someone to come and go without any trace. I treated every corner like it hid a circus clown.

We reached the fourth floor. The door from the stairwell gave a minor squeak. The hallway beyond was devoid of light. By flashlight, we found apartment 402 near the end of the hallway. We both noticed the faint glow coming under the closed door. Steady. Silent

I dropped my hand to the butt of the electro and unsnapped the holster strap. I moved to the door. When Barrett stopped beside me, I listened.

There *was* a sound, but distant, a mechanical thrum. A slight vibration accompanied it. Maybe a truck outside, shaking the fragile shell of the building. There were no other noises.

I turned the knob and pushed the door inward, cautious.

The room beyond was a continuation of the building's mess. Furniture left behind in the apartment was overturned and broken. Dirt crusted every surface, filled each corner. LSD had called there as well. A camp lantern in the middle of the table in the next room lighted the entire place.

I stepped inside. Barrett followed. I scanned the room. No one. To the right, a shadowy kitchen. A doorway in the far room led deeper, probably to the bedrooms. We both stopped. Listened. There was still only the far-off sound of an engine.

Barrett pointed to the next room and the table. I saw the card propped against the lantern, edge on to us.

"Go downstairs," I told her.

"Bullshit, you say."

I hated when she was stubborn. I also knew she wasn't going to budge. Instead, she positioned herself with line of sight deeper into the apartment. If someone emerged for me, she'd have them. She nodded to me.

I stepped into the next room, around the table. Saw the printing on the card, same as the note sending us to the address:

I MURDERED STEPHEN ANGELO.

"Out. Now."

I moved for the door. I never saw the sensor I crossed, but the wail that suddenly filled the room was the song of the trap. The walls began to run like a watercolor in the rain.

TWENTY-ONE

The wail could have been the trumpet announcing the end times. Barrett reached the apartment doorway first, but it was already too small for her to pass through. The windows began to vanish, the walls spreading to fill the gaps, swallowing the glass.

Barrett yelled something I couldn't make out in the din. "What?"

She pointed into the kitchen, deeper into the apartment where the ceiling met the wall. I hit it with my flashlight beam. The ceiling was dissolving, receding. As it did, I saw the space above, where the fifth floor apartment should have been, was empty. Bits of debris from the apartment tumbled into the kitchen. They should have smashed or clattered. A large piece of an end table didn't land with a crunch, but instead dented the kitchen floor, Stephen Angelo's death illustrated.

Barrett pushed on the entry wall behind us where the door had been. Her fingers sunk lightly into the surface, but went no farther. She pulled them back and watched, fascinated, as the depressions left behind smoothed flat again.

I pulled her beside me, back against the exterior wall, the siren deafening in the small space. Beyond the vanishing ceiling, I saw open space extended to the underside of a new roof that was also coalescing, changing. It was as if an industrial site was growing from within the apartment building, the units being stripped back to reveal a hidden world beneath. More refuse fell from above. I could feel the floor growing soft under the soles of my shoes.

The graffiti faded as color seeped from the walls. They turned dull gray. The ceiling above was almost gone when I saw the far wall of the kitchen through the doorway, melting down to the floor. Then the floor began to tumble away, a slow-motion waterfall.

Barrett slid to her right, scanning the space beyond the vanishing floor. I did the same to the left. The edge along the outer wall would be the last to go. All I could see was empty space. Then a broken butcher-block table inside the kitchen entry tumbled away. Barrett pointed.

A crossbeam. Perpendicular to the outside wall, part of the newly-forming superstructure. I estimated the drop was six feet, but the beam was no more than a foot wide. I had no idea how solid it was or would be if we tried to jump to it.

The floor and walls were collapsing at a steady pace, the edge of the waterfall drawing closer. Less than a minute. I unbuckled my belt, considered it. Too short. I pulled my feet from my shoes and slipped out of my pants. My ears rang. I clipped the electro to the pocket. Then I wrapped one leg of my slacks around my right arm twice. Barrett picked up on the idea and wrapped the other pant leg around her left arm. We positioned ourselves for the jump. More of the new beam came in to view as floor rolled away. When we had little more than a six-inch buffer between us and the edge, we jumped together, the pants between us.

It was a short drop and we were spot on. My pants looped over the beam. Fire seared up my arms into my shoulders and back from the sudden jolt. Only the angle we'd landed at kept us from slamming together and knocking one another free. Momentum instead carried us past each other. Barrett clasped her legs around me to stop the movement. Her death grip on the pants mirrored mine. Below us, three stories yawned to the floor of what I saw was developing into a factory. The debris from the apartments above littered the floor. I spotted one of my shoes.

Above us, the still-hardening beam had curved inward where the pants struck it. The beam material had rebuilt around them. Scratch one pair of slacks. Bargain price for not dying.

The siren stopped as the building's revision completed. I followed the overhead beam with my eyes. It connected with a vertical support that ran floor to ceiling, fifteen feet behind Barrett. The rungs of an access ladder were built into it. Fifteen feet never looked more like a mile.

"Are you intact?" I asked.

"Reasonably."

"There's a way down behind you. Can you get to it?"

I grabbed the leg of the embedded pants Barrett was holding onto to steady them best I could. Barrett maneuvered one hand to the beam.

"It's grooved," she said. "Like it's designed for an overhead crane." She got the other hand up while still holding me with her legs. When her grip was assured, she released me and pulled her legs up, locking them instead around the beam. She shimmied towards the vertical member.

I followed suit. The groove was a godsend; still, my muscles were screaming by the time I reached the access ladder. I accepted Barrett's help getting to the rungs. I sat back down on the beam to give my arms a minute. Falling three stories from the ladder after the successful leap from the apartment would have been more sad than tragic.

"Is this what you saw at NanoDwell?" Barrett asked.

"Not exactly, but they should add this. The life-or-death element is a real attention-getter." I shot her a sideways glance. "Are you gray goop yet?"

"Not cool, Thib."

We stayed there for a few minutes, listening. There was no sound within the space, despite its now cavernous size. The thrum I'd heard before the siren was gone.

Barrett started down the ladder. She stopped when she saw me making my way back out the beam. "Where are you going?"

"Solving the problem with this plan. My keys are still in my pants. And my wallet. And my electro."

She heckled me the entire time. Fortunately, nothing necessary was trapped in the beam. I dropped all three items to her. I expected the slacks would make for interesting shoptalk for whoever was moving in. While I worked my way down, Barrett located my other shoe under the curl of a filthy woven rug, and met me at the bottom with the pair.

We walked to the door. It faced the Hershe Street side. Infinitely better than having to walk a long block around in the dark in my boxers. Behind me, Barrett's mouth was still running. "Maybe you need to rethink the name of the agency. Instead of 'A C.T. Robillard Investigation', you can become the Pantsless Detective."

I opened my mouth to respond. There was a sharp snap, and fragments of the door frame flew in six directions.

"Down!" Barrett grunted and pulled me back and out of the doorway as the second bullet ricocheted off the floor in front of us.

TWENTY-TWO

I landed on the new factory floor and rolled in the direction Barrett was pulling. A third bullet chased my shadow.

"No rapport, no echo," Barrett said. "Sniper with a suppressor. Probably closer. Distance takes longer to dial in." She scanned the inside of the warehouse. I did too. An alternate exit proved an unexpected commodity. Walls, beams, high windows, ceilings. The only door was the one in front of us.

"Someone put us in a box," I said.

"Fool. No one puts Kristie Barrett in a box."

"They must have missed that day at sniper school." I tried to dial 911. The mobile displayed an error. No signal. I'd had five bars earlier. A jammer, then. The most annoying killer in the world is the one who manages the details. "No outgoing calls to the cavalry."

Barrett sighed. "I hate the hard way." She glared at me. "Don't try to keep up. Dumpster outside to the right. Get behind it and stay there unless you need to move to stay alive."

"This isn't enough cover?"

She moved to her left and plucked the leg of a broken table from the scattered debris and crouched next to the doorway. "No. This is a very large killing jar. Unless you know how to program it to add a back door or an attic to hide in, you're screwed if you're still inside when someone comes to put the lid on. Dumpster. Cover. Outside."

"Where are you going?"

Her words had barbs. "I need to get something from the car." She held her hand out. "Key fob."

I handed it over silently.

She thrust the table leg into the doorway. When the bullet pulled it from her hand, she dove through, gambling the gunman wasn't using a fully automatic weapon. I followed her progress outside by the thwack of bullets into the wall. Assuming the shooter was going as fast as they could, they were taking a couple of seconds between shots, aiming at a rabbit.

Twenty feet along the wall, a shot blew out one of the new factory windows.

While she kept the shooter focused, I ducked through the door and took cover behind the dumpster next to the sidewalk. Positioned for the eventual clearing of the building, it was long, low and steel. Unless the shooter had packed some armor-piercing rounds, it met Barrett's criteria.

I watched her progress towards the car, sheltering behind a mailbox, a pause on her way to the cover afforded by the hopper pickup. She was three parking spaces from the car. I'd never seen combat Barrett before, the recon sniper, the vet under fire. It was a fascinating dichotomy with how she usually conducted herself.

If she wasn't working on the shooter's position, I was. No higher than six stories, somewhere to the left. There were two or three possibilities. My money was on the new construction that was completely dark. Still uninhabited on the second block north from us, it was the most tactically feasible position, with no one there to see a sniper enter or stumble across their setup.

Another bullet struck the edge of the dumpster around which I'd peeked. My head rang with the sound. Barrett shouted from up the street. "That's good! Keep him busy!"

I heard the murmur of voices and realized I wasn't going to need to. I moved to the other end of the dumpster. From there, I watched people on several floors of the apartment building across the street emerging onto balconies and leaning out windows, craning at our shouts, trying to determine what was going on. I wondered if any of them had heard the construction rebuild, if the sounds in the night had snowballed to the point of curiosity. Odds were their cells were jammed, too.

I stayed low, cupped my mouth and shouted. "Gun! Active shooter! Get inside! Call the cops!"

"Keep it down!" someone shouted back. "I'm trying to sleep!"

On an end balcony, in the shooter's field of fire, one of the residents learned the hard way. He was peering through binoculars in the direction of the shooter's possible perch. Then he jumped as if shocked and dropped to his patio, screaming, clutching his leg. The binoculars tumbled from his hand and off the balcony.

No one listens to a stranger in the night, but everyone hears one of their own. As the man shouted about being shot and crawled through his patio door, word rippled over balcony railings and transcended floors. Residents disappeared, ghosts.

Up the street, Barrett had gotten into the car and unlocked her sidearm. She had something in her other hand. I couldn't make out what it was in the shadows. The sniper had stopped firing at her. If she was out of view by my car, blocked by the roof line of the building across the street, it put the shooter in one of the corner rooms of the unfinished building.

It didn't mean they'd stay there.

As if reading my mind, the sniper dropped three shots at the dumpster in rapid succession. The dumpster clanged and sparks flew. I fought the urge to bolt. That was what they wanted. For the first time in years, I found myself wishing for more than the electro.

Two more bullet-pops against the warehouse wall were all the announcement I received as Barrett leaped over me at a full run and skidded to a stop behind the other end of the dumpster. She pulled her gun. I saw the other thing she'd grabbed was the pair of the night vision goggles from under the seat.

"You had to jinx it," she said

"Jinx what?"

"I haven't seen a firefight since my third-to-last day in-country in Egypt. Miserable heat. Radicals were getting crazy from it, so they decided to try taking our forward base. Six hours, bullets flying, people screaming in at least three languages, trucks and buildings on fire. We lost four people when all was said and done. Three days after, I'm on a plane to Ramstein with my discharge in my pocket and sand in every crease of my duffel, and I think, 'Barrett, that's the last gun-play you'll ever get caught in.' And I haven't had to use lethal force since then. But you *had* to ask." She calibrated the goggles, angry but steady. "Sure, it's all fun and games and melting buildings and leaping on beams using pants and walking into traps instead of getting take-out for a job well done." The sniper took a potshot at the wall above us. Barrett didn't skip a tick. "But when the real shit begins, the stuff where a slug can end you with the next bon-mot on your lips while you cower behind a dumpster, where are the actual means of survival? Locked up, safe from danger, where it waits patiently to become the property of my next of kin. Spoiler: I have no goddamned next-of-kin."

She aimed close, shot out the nearest streetlight. Reduced the next two to showers of glass. Darkness blanketed the street. "I'd say he's in the new construction to the left, fifth floor corner. His angle dries up once you get to the other side of the hopper pickup over there, so he's not in the next one to the right." I felt vindicated in that much, at least. She continued. "If he's got a shadow-scope or infrared, I think he'd have already winged me. That's one in our column. Next is getting you towards the car. When I say, head for the hopper pickup and don't stop. I'll cover you."

"You think you're going to hit him from here? With a pistol?"

"Setting aside that I know exactly what my weapon is capable of with the ammo I have loaded, thank you, I think for the next ninety seconds I'm going to do whatever I believe I can with this gun, and you're going to take orders like a grunt. We'll call it 'In Country'. It'll be a goddamned laugh riot. Round One: when I tell you to run like hell for the baby-shit yellow hopper pickup and try to not get shot in the process, you will not question, you will not joke, you will not anything, except run like hell for the baby-shit yellow pickup hopper and try not to get shot. By him *or* me. Are we clear?"

I went when she said. The sniper did his best to stop me. A sidewalk ricochet took a nick from the heel of my shoe. A second bullet rattled the mailbox between me and the hopper.

While I ran, behind me the goggled Barrett leaned out and squeezed off three shots, paused, and fired two more. From the cover of the hopper, I almost expected a body to tumble from a distant window with a clatter of glass, death grip on his sniper rifle as he plummeted five stories to the sidewalk. Nothing so Hollywood happened, but after Barrett's final shot, everything was quiet. Barrett held up a finger, admonishment to me to wait. Thirty seconds later, my cell chirped to alert me to a new message. The display showed five bars of service. I dialed 911. The dispatcher told me there were already units en route. I heard the sirens in the distance.

I called to Barrett. "Cell service is up. Police inbound."

"Sit tight until they get here. I only surprised him with return fire. Doesn't mean he's gone."

She continued to scan the windows. I heard the approach of police hoppers up the street. Another closed from behind the prospective sniper's nest, blasting a spotlight through the windows, swapping day for night.

"Stand down," she called.

My pace back to the dumpster where Barrett waited was brisk. A small part of me expected a final shot, one last attempt to finish the job started with the building redesign. Across the way, the ambulance made a textbook landing on the apartment building's roof.

Barrett leaned against the dumpster, goggles slung around her neck, clutching her gun as if I might try to take it away. She glanced up. I couldn't tell if she needed a drink or a cigarette.

I offered her a hand and helped her to her feet. "Stellar work."

She mumbled, noncommittal. She checked her clip, snapped it back in place, verified the chamber was clear, and holstered the Colt. She set about gathering her spent shell casings.

"Thank you," I said.

"For?"

"Saving our lives."

"Thib?"

"Yes?"

"What I really want to do is to tell you to piss off until I come down from the mambo beat my heart is doing. My therapist, if I was still seeing her, would tell me saying such things is counterproductive emotionalism, born of repressed anger and brought to the fore by extreme circumstance."

Police hoppers were now at both ends of the block, officers approaching or taking positions. "Okay."

"Instead, I'm going to lay a truth on you I hope you're big boy enough to handle. I'm sorry your wife was murdered. I hope someday you get the guy. I hope they convict him and give him the sentence he deserves, and your wife receives justice and you find some peace about it."

"Thank you."

"But my gun didn't double-tap the back of your wife's head. Even if *yours* did, you weren't the one who pulled the trigger. You did everything right. You had it unloaded and locked up while not in use. I applaud you. But the truth is you can do everything right with a gun, and bad shit can still happen because someone else doesn't. It's true of every damned thing on earth."

"I know."

"That's why, although I know it's like pissing upstream, I'm going to request: if we're going to be in the field, on cases and in situations you, by your own admission, believe are traps of some kind, or situations with violent offenders, crazed gunslingers, mad bombers, mole people, whatever the hell you've drawn us into, I want to carry my weapon. In the office? Fine. Locked up in the desk so assholes like the three stooges can't randomly grab it to blow your brains out. I agree with that. Out here, on business in a city over which you can't claim dominion, I want my sidearm. On my hip, within reach, in the event I need to use it to defend myself and maybe even defend you. Responsibly. If you haven't pissed me off."

I considered arguing the responsibility of returning fire in the dark, in an urban area with an unknown number of civilians. I was still too close to twin attempts on my life to muster it. The sincerity in her eyes was almost caustic. I knew there and then I was going to agree. She knew her weapon and had never not been conscientious handling it. I pitied the person who tried to duel her or take it from her hand in a fracas.

But I wasn't going to acquiesce at that moment, standing behind a dumpster, both of us shot through with adrenaline. I couldn't make it that easy. Barrett's tribe were the original mice to whom you couldn't give cookies.

"I understand," I said. "And I'll consider it. But for the sake of argument, what if I gave you your own key fob, so if your gun's secured inside you can get to it more quickly?"

Her eyes narrowed. Sincerity became steel again. "Okay, so, piss off until I come down from this."

TWENTY-THREE

The lead investigator on-scene was a stocky bull named Gildman. He and I were on decent terms. We ran into each other now and then at a jazz club called Hep-Chat in downtown on Fannin. He was more of a new-groove/dub-bop guy, but he knew his old-school sounds. We'd swapped concert recordings on a couple of occasions. I think I came out better both times.

He walked me through things as the cops gathered evidence in and around the warehouse. Gildman was one of those badges who enjoys being in the middle of the ranks—no longer patient enough to wear blues and work traffic duty, no desire to rise higher than he was and into desk country. He had the hungry look of a guy who enjoyed layered cases with some action around the edges, but never quite got his fill. A sniper was a smorgasbord to a cop like him. "To the credit of the neighbors, when they heard the siren and rumbles in the abandoned building across the street, several of them called the police non-emergency line to complain. Apparently, the contractors around here have been raising hell outside normal hours the last few months. A real thorn in the side. A large-scale after-hours operation with a wailing siren was too much to ignore."

"I may revise my stance on civic organizers."

"They began to realize something more was up when cell service was blocked for everyone." Gildman paused, eyes towards the long beam in the structure. "Are those the magic pants, Robillard?"

"Yup."

"Two grown people and a six foot drop, huh? You'll have to tell me where you shop. Stuff I buy wears out like it's made of chewed paper and spit."

"No one makes you buy your wardrobe from wasps and third-graders."

"Anyway, after the guy on the balcony took the bullet to the leg, the tenants ran to Mrs. Miller on the second floor. A battle axe. Eighty-seven this year. She's weathered hurricanes Isaiah, Oliver, and Sibbhon in her apartment."

"So she knows how to dial fire and rescue like a pro?"

"More that the experience instilled a lifelong appreciation for land-lines, which a cell damper doesn't dampen. She got through to 911 with ease."

I walked him through my side of things, with some background on the Angelo case and the note that led Barrett and me to the building. "I knew it was fishy," I admitted.

"You could learn from Mrs. Miller."

"There's a second note from the apartment in this rubble."

"Forensics will find it. If you wouldn't mind someone dropping by to pick up the one left at your office, I'd be obliged."

"Tomorrow morning. Not before nine. I need my beauty rest."

Gildman smirked. "Take until eleven."

"Nice. Anything on the shooter?"

"Not specifically. Just after the wailing began, one of the residents across the way saw a man hustle from the front door of the pigsty this place used to be. Head-to-toe in black. We have "tall" and "athletic build" to work with. If you and your partner were on the fourth floor, it stands to reason tall and dark was either your guy, or working with your guy to spring the trap." He glanced around. "Speaking of trouble, where's your partner?"

"Post-mayhem uncoiling." Barrett had trucked off to the farthest police officer she could find to give her statement. I let her go. It was possible she'd ask a cop for a ride home, or at least somewhere she could grab a late dinner. Maybe early breakfast, at the rate things were going.

"She returned fire with her sidearm?" Gildman stared down-range.

"Yeah. Her Colt."

"From *here*?"

"I was as skeptical as you."

"She's a hell of a shot. Our units over at the shooter's location say she put three of five around his nest. Two in the windows, one in the wall behind him. No sign she hit him, no blood trails or the like, but it's damned impressive at this range. Probably helped move him along."

"She's very good at what she does."

"Do you know what she loads?"

"No idea."

"She picks ammo the way you pick pants."

"I suspect they're wildly different processes."

It was about then Spence strolled into the warehouse, surveying the scene on his way to Gildman and me. If there was residual animus between us, his grin belied it. "If it isn't the Pants-less Detective. If I'd known you were trying out a new methodology, I'd have asked for a ride-along."

"I take it you ran into Barrett the Cruel and Mocking on the way in."

"I did. Your partner is displeased with you."

I shrugged. "She's suffering from Post-Robillard Stress Disorder."

"Ah." He noticed the pants in the beam. "There they are."

"Yeah. It was a regular Space City Frolic in here."

"This is the Angelo case, huh?"

"So I've been led to believe. Now that I've seen the process of a building remodeling itself, having touched this stuff as it forms, I'm sold Angelo's place was in flux when his head hit his floor. The stuff is like soft clay or putty when it's changing."

"The coroner's going to love testing that."

"We were lured here for a similar fall, minus the blow to the head beforehand. Whoever set it up put some thought into it. The design featured one exit, right into the shooting gallery. Kind of elegant."

Spence and Gildman both took in the room and saw what we'd noticed while trying to escape. Gildman whistled. "What a friggin' moron. He should have just waited outside the door."

"Two on one in a close firefight," Spence said. "Though given his aim, he couldn't have done much worse." He glanced around the room, at the walls. "If someone programmed this and set it on a trigger, there has to be a control panel, right?"

"Somewhere around here," I said. Thinking about Angelo's apartment building, I started by the new door. The panel was in an alcove, fifteen yards in the other direction from where we'd sheltered inside when the shooting began. The cover slid open to the touch. The brass plate riveted into the top of the panel proudly declared the building a product of the NanoDwell Corporation.

"I'm less and less convinced Angelo died at the hands of someone to whom he sold information," I said. "Especially if you consider in both his case and this one, the weapon used was a NanoDwell building."

"You think someone at NanoDwell killed him?"

"Past or present. This is an older building. The set-up person would need enough programming knowledge to assemble or alter the design to limit our escape route."

"That would follow with Angelo opening his door to let his killer in—someone he knew and trusted works as well as someone he'd committed a crime with."

"Dana Sami gave me the company's files on Angelo today. Logical place to begin is with coworkers: axes to grind, bruised egos, and so on. Especially ones fitting the description of the man the witness saw run out of here.”

“You think someone set Angelo up as a patsy for their own double-deal?”

“No. I’m fairly confident Angelo took classified information and passed it to someone. But I don’t believe that someone killed him.”

“Based on?” Spence’s eyes were narrow slits.

“Developments we can discuss when I’m a little more confident in them. And when Gildman isn’t around.”

Gildman appeared wounded. “What’d I do?”

“Everyone knows you’re a gossip,” Spence told him, and gave me a nod. “As soon as you have some nails in the shingles, show me the roof.”

“We tripped a switch upstairs to kick off the rebuild process. A booby trap. Unless it was built in, there should be a remnant of it.”

Gildman made a note. “I’ll add it to the forensics scavenger hunt.” He mumbled something about gossiping with them under his breath.

“I’d also wager when you pull the logs from this terminal, you’ll find a back door access code was used to initiate the program, just like in Angelo’s apartment.”

“No bet,” Spence said. “I make it a point to not gamble with people whose luck includes leaping to safety by using his chinos.”

“Literally surviving by the seat of his pants,” Gildman added.

“We’re all lucky he didn’t go commando.” Barrett said from behind us.

Gildman laughed. “Amen. I’d like to retire with two good eyes.”

“This is only amusing because we didn’t die.” I glanced at Barrett. She had a bag in hand. “Get some shopping in?”

She reached into the bag and tossed a pair of faded jeans at me. "I made an appeal to the apartment residents. They donated these for your dignity."

"Thanks."

"They're two sizes too big for you."

"Any port in a storm."

"Oh, no. I made sure they were too big."

"Ah." Oh yeah. Payback for miles. "Did you give your statement?"

"Yes." She smiled. "To Officer Mayer again."

Gildman hooked a thumb over his shoulder. "You mean Moyer?"

"Damn. I don't think he'll be calling."

"I need to finish a few things here," I told her. "Ten, fifteen minutes. You can catch a ride with someone if you don't want to wait."

Her smile took on a blade edge. "No worries, boss." She dangled the key fob. "I'll be in the car. Safely locked up. Where I can't hurt anybody." She retreated across the room.

Spence glanced from her to me. "What was that about?"

"A disagreement over HR policies." It would evaporate when I gave her permission to carry in the field, or worked out something else I was comfortable with. Until then, I couldn't calculate how much Barrett was going to make me pay, but I was probably already accruing interest.

TWENTY-FOUR

I dropped Barrett at her hopper in the sky lot at the top of the office's garage building. If she was going to grab a bite, she had no desire to ask me along, and I didn't blame her. "See you in the morning," she said, and punched sky.

Back at the office, I slipped the message directing us to Hershe Street into an evidence bag and set it aside. I didn't expect the PD to find prints, but sometimes would-be killers got so excited about the plan, they became stupid or careless in execution. Especially subscribers to the Rube Goldberg school of murder.

Something Gildman said stuck with me. Why *hadn't* the shooter waited by the door? If the point was to be sure we were dead, giving us one exit and waiting by the dumpster for us to emerge, sawed-off shotgun in hand, was almost foolproof. It wouldn't change what witnesses could describe. Triggering the remodel and then running two blocks and up several flights of stairs to finish us off? I was dubious. It suggested two people, but that would have made it an even match.

The whole thing annoyed me. I didn't mind being met head-on. Vetrov was a scumbag, but he'd had the decency to point a gun at my face. Killing me using a self-modifying apartment house or a snipe from two blocks away? The illogic pissed me off. Never mind having to take time to shop for new pants.

My stomach grumbled. Sleep was miles away. I made a round-trip drive to Texi-Maxi. Unremarkable food, but both nearby and open 24 hours. I returned to the office with a couple of cheese enchiladas and a buzz in my head.

My mind switched orbits from Hershe Street and the would-be assassin to Leon Dushane for distraction. Something Overbaugh had said about people slipping up set me wondering. Dushane was young when he paid to disappear. Maybe he was only a thief. Maybe he'd graduated to harder crime with Jessica. Maybe he was still wholly unrelated. In any case, he was seventeen when he went to Micallef for a new identity. Teenagers are prone to gaffe. It's the minefield encircling the age.

The Bureau was handling Micallef. They wouldn't be performing a Bullrun or Herringbone-style general web monitor. Not until they were desperate. Instead, they'd do warrantless things: sift the major social media sites, scan uploaded images, monitor law enforcement NCIC inquiries, financial services, communications providers. I didn't think they'd be sifting as far down in the web as I tucked myself.

Crowd-sourcing is the double-edged blade of a connected world. Cops still do phone tip lines, though immediacy and quality are two different things. There are also plenty of sites on the web where you can post inquiries regarding people in specific circumstances. Like public records sites, they're wildly hit and miss; but they're also very granular on a subject. You develop a feel for those who respond, learn to discount the ones who ask what's in it for them if they tell you what they know, the belligerent ones or the ones who just want to make trouble. But a general inquiry where security guards, prison bulls, and the like congregate can yield nuggets. They need to talk about the job as much as anyone else.

Dushane was seven years in the wind. He could have been anywhere, so I started small, along the gulf coast from Corpus Christi to Tampa Bay. On two different social sites devoted to corrections work and missing persons, I posted the brief set of details, seeking information: name, current age, what I knew about Dushane's penchant for theft, plus my name and a contact point I maintained specifically for web inquiries.

When I was done, true to my word, I emailed Spence to tell him I'd taken that step. Even if the Bureau did find me casting about, they hadn't made me say I wouldn't. If anything, I rationalized they'd be happy for the free help.

It was after three when I finally drifted off to restless sleep. I made the stupid leap to the beam at least a half-dozen times.

Banging. Fist on wood. Infidels pounding my door and hammering my sleep to death, coalescing into my associate. "Thib! Drag your weary carcass back from Dreamland!"

After Hershe Street, Barrett might not have banged on my door to wake me if the office was on fire. Something in her voice was off, and it wasn't the question of carrying her Colt.

I checked my watch. It was after ten. I gathered myself as she continued to thump the door. "C'mon, Thib!"

I opened the door, expecting her to keep pounding. The expression that greeted me was almost as no-nonsense as under-fire Barrett. "And a sedate and somber 'good morning' to you."

"The decoding program cracked the root password, found the decryption key, and translated the Rose Street message last night, while we were busy not getting dead."

"You don't sound very happy about it." I frowned. "It *is* time and temperature, isn't it?"

"Oh, no. You got candy. You got enough candy to give the entire party diabetes."

She led me to the conference room and switched from her earbuds to system audio. I still couldn't tell if she was concerned or excited.

"What is it?"

"Just... listen." She touched a control. The tones and digital noise had been resolved into a computer-generated voice. The words spilled forth in a stream, without inflection or conversational pauses. The effect only added to the oddity.

Detective C.T. Robillard I am House Doris I cannot contact Charlie his number is in lockout I cannot connect to 911 emergency services I am in danger I need your help I am on fire by the time you receive this I will be dead I do not want to die but I cannot override protocol 14 to initiate fire suppression measures please help me Detective C.T. Robillard I wish to employ you to find the person who has murdered me please help—

The voice stopped where the call terminated on my machine, abrupt, snuffed out by the flames.

I studied Barrett. "Is this a joke? Payback for last night?"

"There are a hundred small cuts on my mind for last night. Do you honestly believe *any* of them would involve muddling a case?"

"No. You're 100% pro on the job, every time. I apologize."

"Forgiven." She played it again. "My only guess is the building's AI. NanoDwell literature says they offer residents access to proprietary AI built into the apartment building control center."

"Then why not hit me in English? You didn't clean-up the translation at all, did you?"

"No. That's the raw signal."

"It spoke better English than I do. So why send it electronically?" I had her play it again.

"The tie-line," Barrett said. "That's the communications protocol for the tie-line. If you'd been on a building interface, it would have been clear as day, like any other home assistant. It may have assumed a translator at your end of the call."

"Makes sense. The tie-line was the only pipe out available to it. But why reach out to me? What sort of AI does that?"

"It's fairly standard for them to nudge users with automated reminders, things on your calendar, what's turning blue in your fridge."

"That's all programmed from calendars, reminders, prompts from email. Prior learning. This was purposeful. Charlie— which is not coincidentally the name of NanoDwell's headquarters building—and 911 were unavailable. It had been set on fire, it was burning down, and it needed help."

"But programming isn't going to plug a random private investigator into a decision tree."

It dawned so bright it was blinding. "It does if it has the most advanced programming of all: reasoning. Self-awareness."

Her eyes got a little bigger. "Are you suggesting the building at Rose Street was *sentient?*"

I nodded.

She studied me as if measuring me for a psychiatric bed. "Buildings aren't sentient. They can't *be* sentient. Not even the smart ones. They're programming. Subroutines. Not people."

"You decoded the message yourself. 'I need your help. I am on fire. By the time you receive this I will be dead. I do not want to die.' That's not an AI calling to remind me the laundry is piling up. That's conscious need."

"So it called *you?*"

I stared at the computer. "To hire me. It was very clear about that."

"But why you?"

I considered it. "It was being methodical."

"Methodical?"

"You said it yourself the other day: A C.T. Robillard Investigation. I'm the first private investigator in the book."

We went to a hole-in-the-wall all-day breakfast place I knew in the First Ward. Neither of us felt like being in the office after hearing the mechanized voice. Barrett made a safety copy of the original recording, the translation, and the encryption key before we left. I tucked a mem-card with the files in my wallet.

"Nothing in NanoDwell's materials talks about sentience." I said. "An advanced bio-mechanical control center, yes, running a proprietary AI, but not awareness."

"A depth-trained AI still makes a lot more goddamned sense." Barrett shook her head. "It makes the nano-bot apocalypse sound warm and fuzzy."

"If NanoDwell had intentionally developed a sentient control center, it would have been front page news."

"It would have made a headline or two." Her voice dropped to nothing when the waiter stopped to check on us. I took stock of the patrons while Barrett sought a refill for her coffee. Someone trying to kill you plus impossibly-aware structures makes for a heightened sense of discretion.

When the waiter's duties had been discharged and he moved along, I continued. "House Doris existed for fifteen years. No matter what the breakthrough was, no company would sit on it for so long. You'd be asking another company to steal your thunder. You could lose billions."

"Maybe House Doris was an anomaly."

"One is an anomaly. In the message, it said it tried to reach Charlie. I presume that's NanoDwell's headquarters building. It was Phalen's first major breakthrough in smart buildings, the same year House Doris was built."

"The tie-line was a hotline between the two buildings, encrypted for privacy. So they could...what, talk to each other?"

"Maybe that was part of the process, watching how they interacted. Or maybe NanoDwell just didn't want them to get lonely. If you were one of two of a kind, wouldn't it be a comfort to speak to your counterpart when you needed?"

Barrett picked at bread in a wicker bowl. "I suppose."

"It follows if Dana Sami tried to mislead me about the message's content, she already knew what it was."

"What about the three stooges? Also NanoDwell?"

"NanoDwell would have known by then I was called."

"Why would Sami ask you for the message?"

"Because if she didn't, it stands out by dint of not being asked, given the fire. She was probing. It wouldn't surprise me if the tail I had at Herb Young's was also a fishing expedition from NanoDwell." I considered it. "She wouldn't be the only one at NanoDwell who knows about Doris. Victor Phalen certainly knows. The techs who installed and maintained the tie-line would probably know." I leaned back in my chair. "So

Doris is set on fire, tries to phone Charlie and can't get through for the first time in its history, because Charlie is 'in lockout'; then it tries to call 911 and finds it can't call for help because of whatever Protocol 14 is. It kept Doris from engaging emergency routines. Then it calls me. NanoDwell realizes a call went out and finds out to whom. They send a team to the office to see if Doris said anything revealing to me, probably thinking like I did: if it spoke to me, it would have spoken English. By extension, it's not a stretch to believe they'd send someone to kill Angelo if they thought he was sharing the sentient computer control secret with someone else."

"But Rose Street isn't on the list Young was given."

"No. And there's no suggestion any of his targets was sentient. Not that we knew to look." It nagged.

"If NanoDwell killed Angelo, it follows they tried to kill us at Hershe Street."

"It's certainly the same M.O."

"But why? We're trying to find Angelo's contact for them."

I watched a party preparing to leave. One of the young men rushed to help a grandmotherly type to her feet. She shooed him away and stood on her own. I thought for a moment she might whack him with her cane.

"Because they don't need us anymore. I handed Young right to them."

"What are you talking about?"

"I alerted Spence to the burglary at Young's apartment. If PD found the paperwork I did, the ME Co. pages would have tied back to NanoDwell. PD calls them, they look at the material, link Young and Angelo the same way we did. We're suddenly extraneous, bordering on too close to the truth."

"Quicker to kill us than figure out what we know." Barrett wasn't fuming, but she was getting there. "And presumably blame Young when they finally lay hands on him. Tidy."

The waiter delivered Barrett's salad and my breakfast. Barrett's appetite was unbowed. I was faced by a crab and avocado omelet for which I was no longer in the mood.

"We need to get Young before they do," I said. "If someone tried to kill us without any certainty of what we know, they're sure to try to kill him before he can talk to anyone. Everything is riding on this IPO of theirs."

"We have one other party we can question."

"Who?"

She glanced up from her salad. "House Charlie."

"Oh, you're hilarious."

"I'm dead serious. The sister hired you to find its murderer. We should see what the brother knows."

"You tried the line. It won't take calls from our number."

Barrett put on her determined face. "Baby steps. Now that I've sorted the module, the encryption key, and have Doris' call before and after, I should be able to compile a program to reverse the process and encode speech into something Charlie understands. Spoof the outgoing call with the tie line number to get around the block and we're in."

I considered the possibilities. "Can you make it work bi-directionally and in real time?"

She glared from behind her fork. "Jeez, Thib. Can I eat first?"

TWENTY-FIVE

Every investigation has points where you need to decide whether to involve the cops to greater extent. Knowing when is a tightrope act where you balance what you know, what you suspect, what you can prove, and how much weight the police are going to give your facts and suppositions. If you do all of this right, you don't plummet to your death.

Angelo and Young were coupled like freight cars. I could show coincidental linkage between Young and a series of fires based on data from Angelo, though I had no evidence Young set any of them. Foul play in Angelo's death was strongly suggested, but there was still no hard evidence; nor was there any to indicate who tried to kill Barrett and me on Hershe Street, aside from the person or persons in black.

The problem wasn't bringing it to Spence. I trust Spence with my life. But NanoDwell was wired into Koi through the arson, and they'd be privy to anything I brought about Young and arson. Never mind the bottle of nitro disguised as a sentient building. Before I walked the Young side of the case to Spence, I needed one more piece: Young himself.

After eating, I stopped in the gym for a quick shower, dressed, and returned to the office. Barrett was closed up in the conference room working on means for speaking to House Charlie, a copy of Jim Marshall's famous photo of Johnny Cash flipping off the camera tacked to the door. Message received.

Spence called. The change logs were back from the Hershe Street building. "The owner was very cooperative when I told him the transformation was part of an attempted murder."

"And?"

"Same thing as Angelo's building. The access code used to initiate the change program was unknown. It isn't the owner's or the construction site manager's."

"Was it the same code as at Angelo's?"

"No, but they have different model numbers. Default pins may be model-specific."

"So they're potentially back door codes." One more finger-point in NanoDwell's direction. "How about ballistics?"

"223 Remington slugs, no rifling matches."

"That narrows it to about a million guns. Sweet."

He must have caught something in my tone. "Anything else on your end to share?"

"Not yet. Maybe in another twenty-four hours."

"That's when most accidents happen."

"You're thinking of being a mile from home."

He told me to stay in touch and disconnected.

I retrieved my baton and electro and set out for the address of Young's suspected next target. The key to catching someone in the act is knowing before-hand which way they're likely to exit the stage.

The storage facility was a drab three-story box that squatted beside I-69, southeast of Richmond. Surviving bits from my house fire were tucked away in a similar place, waiting to emerge somewhere new. The faded banner hanging on the chain link fence encircling the building suggested I was in the right place: below the bold-type proclamation

DYNAMIC CLIMATE CONTROL RESPONDS TO ENVIRONMENTAL CHANGE

was a smaller offer:

CUSTOM SIZES AVAILABLE

I parked outside the facility office, felt déjà vu when I walked inside. I'd done the rental dance with three different places before storing my own stuff. They all operated off the same template: provide the unit sizes, present the benefits of long versus short term contracts, and offer new boxes for storing your old junk. The only differentiator was how comfortable you were about how secure they claimed to be.

A balding Latino man in a blue polo shirt with the company logo on the breast worked the counter. His brown eyes were tired. He had the tics of a frustrated owner called in to cover some kid who quit on him, annoyed to be missing the soccer game audible in the back office. Signs on both the front door and the wall behind the counter were soliciting for help on "all shifts." I wondered how many shifts a storage facility office fielded.

"I'd like to rent a unit," I said.

"Units are rented on an initial six month or annual basis," the man answered dully, the script long since memorized. He passed me a tablet with a price sheet and helpful videos, made no effort to feign enthusiasm. "After the first term, renewals are available for the same term or on a month-to-month basis at varying cost. Units come in three standard sizes: closets, crates, and garages. For a fee, we can also accommodate custom sizing."

"Custom sizing? How does that work?"

The owner perked, buoyed by the healthy margin attached to the word 'custom.' "We can size some units to specific needs. It's a highly advanced building technology. Great if your need is between crate and garage and you don't want more space than you need, or if you need to expand later. To be honest, I don't know how it works, but it's a very popular option. I have people who store wine who love the ability to expand as they go."

"Usual terms? One month deposit, rent due first of the month?"

"Yeah. Deposit is refundable at the end of your lease. Late rent incurs a 15% late fee. If your account is not made current within 14 days, you forfeit the contents of the unit, which will be sold at auction to offset the loss of the value of your contract."

"How about custom sizes?"

"There's a per-event customization charge, and your rate is based on cubic footage used per month. The other terms are the same."

"Before I commit to a contract, may I take a look around the facility?"

Uncertainty birthed a frown. "You a cop?"

"Would that make a difference?"

He shrugged. "Just seems weird to ask permission to look at a bunch of empty spaces."

"No. I'm not a cop. I just need a place to store my stuff while my home is being rebuilt."

"Renovation?"

"Fire damage."

He studied me, his expression a living history of every tall tale he'd ever been told about why a storage unit was needed. "Sure. But nothing shady. I've got cameras everywhere, and a one-touch security call to the police." He reached behind the desk and handed me a magnetic swipe card. "This'll get you inside."

"Added security. That's a plus."

There was an awkward silence. The owner glanced at the back office, drawn by the pitched voices of Spanish-speaking commentators. "Is there anything else?"

"I'm sorry. Were you going to show me the facility?"

"I can't leave the office unattended. If it doesn't have a lock, feel free to open the door and look inside. If it has a lock, it's leased, and you don't belong inside. If you run into any problems, wave at a security camera and I'll send a rescue party."

I suspected if I was being murdered in a hallway, there was only a slim chance the owner would notice, much less send help. "Thank you."

He bobbed his head and grunted on his way to the back office.

The ground floor held the garage units, each with a broad single door that raised for access. Enclosed stairwells at each corner of the building provided access to the upper floors, with elevators on the north and south sides. They all required the card for access. The upper floors were a combination of closets and crates, intermingled. One long hallway was filled with odd-sized doors. I opened one of these that had no lock. The walls were smooth. There were no access points for controls. Sizing and other features were probably programmed remotely from the back office.

The upper hallways sported windows to the outside on all four sides of the building, units to the inside. The windows offered a commanding view of the building's yard and grounds. Chain link fence and razor wire encircled the lot. A single gate at the front of the building provided automobile access. There were four pads for hoppers to land along the building's east side. I could see the emitters for the laser grid that secured the lot's airspace at night. Utilities entered at the rear of the building.

The facility was bracketed by a high-fenced salvage yard to the east, and an auto repair business with better security to the west. That left two spots for Young to come in: the front gate on the south side, or the rear of the lot.

Railroad tracks ran behind the building, two parallel beds and a service road. A series of abandoned warehouses stood on the far side of the tracks, up a long, shallow slope. From the back, bolt cutters were the only key Young would need.

As I progressed, I noticed one in every four indoor security cameras appeared non-operational. It made taking pictures of the yard from my vantage point more inconspicuous than anticipated. It took several minutes to get the best angles on everything—utility box, lines in and out, the wireless transmitter for the office emergency call button, the placement of light poles and the cameras on them. I imaged it all for review with Barrett.

When I returned, the owner appeared relieved. "Thought you got lost. Or maybe moved in. We don't allow that, by the way. Living in the units. They're not up to code for human habitation."

"People do that?"

"Oh, yeah. Had it happen a couple of times already this year. Is it any wonder with what they charge for rent these days? Then something goes wrong, someone complains to the city, I get cited. Like I leased them the place as some kind of efficiency apartment."

"Do you employ around-the-clock security?"

"You mean a guard? What are you planning on storing again?"

"Under the law, so long as it isn't hazardous goods as defined in the city code, I'm not required to disclose specifics of my belongings to you."

The owner scowled. Not a fan of scholarship. "Keypad to get through the front gate, swipe card access for the building. No guard, but cameras are monitored remotely by our security company." He held out his hand, fingers beckoning for his swipe card back. I obliged.

"Thank you for your time. I'll be in touch."

I didn't catch what he said under his breath as I left. It was easier to believe it was "tire-kicker" and move on. We both knew there would never be a signed contract.

It was possible Young had rented a unit for the ease of driving through the front gate and slipping inside with a swipe of the card; but that entailed a paper trail, and there was no indication so far he was dropping his name anywhere. The rear of the lot was his most probable approach. It was more effort, but eliminated being seen in the open or on camera. The sides of the yard took care of themselves. Young wasn't going to scale either wall with accelerant in tow, less so when one considered the salvage yard's two large dogs.

I drove from the facility in a half-mile loop to the other side of the railroad tracks and assessed the view from the abandoned warehouse lots. There was no direct lighting along the rail bed or the adjacent service road. It would be in shadow. The tracks went under the highway to the west. The only way onto the service road was an at-grade crossing a mile to the east. It ran in a long straightaway and looked well-maintained, navigable without headlights. The entire drive could be done in the dark and would be unobservable, unless one knew to be looking.

A slow freight train approached from the west, boxcars battered and defaced with spray paint being pulled by three dirty locomotives. The lead diesel blew its horn as it approached the highway crossing to the east. I made a mental note to check available timetables. I didn't need a 6,000 foot long rolling roadblock between me and Young when Young made his move.

TWENTY-SIX

There wasn't much discussion with Barrett about the stakeout of the storage facility, as much because the location mandated certain placements—and as such didn't lend itself to many variables—as from lingering tension over the preceding twenty-four hours.

The clouds lifted from her mood when I told her I was going to let her carry her weapon. "In the field. Specifically on at-risk assignments. This will be a narrow definition, and I will play the roles of Messrs. Merriam and/or Webster."

"I understand."

"For your part, you'll consider adding some non-lethal armament to what I expect is an arsenal of boom toys of which the DOD might remark, 'So *that's* where that went.'"

"I understand."

"The first time in my judgment that you exercise something other than responsible weapon safety, this decision will be rescinded, I'll have your investigator's license with the state revoked, and employment with this agency will be terminated with extreme prejudice. Are we clear?"

"We are. Permission to speak freely?"

I nodded against my better judgment.

"You're starting to use Koi's cadence when you define consequences. You should be you when you do that, because I'm not intimidated by him at all."

I stared. "I'm going to pretend that's Farsi for 'Thank you' and move on. Be in position at nine."

With Barrett sorted, I locked up. I wanted to get some sleep before trekking back to Richmond to see if Herb Young manifested with fire in the night.

I'd just dozed off when my mobile chimed—the ringtone specific to forwards from the number I used for online inquiries. Area code 662. North Mississippi. I took the call, thumbed the one-touch recorder on my mobile case before I answered. "This is Robillard."

There was a pause on the other end. "The investigator, right?"

"That's what it says on the door. How can I help you?"

"It might be that I can help you." Accented. As local to Mississippi as his area code. "My name is Devon Majoros, sir. I work in private security in Jackson, Mississippi. I read your post regarding Leon Dushane this morning. I don't know if this is useful or not, but I figure you never know what's important, right?"

"Fair statement. What do you know?"

"Four years ago, I was a cop in Meridian. I was working the A Line one morning when a two-eleven call went out for a bank downtown. I was the closest unit. When I arrived, the bank guard already had the suspect on the ground, hands on his head, waiting for me to cuff and stuff him. The suspect had walked in, middle of the morning, pulled a pistol and fired three rounds into the ceiling, dropped the gun, and sat down to wait to be arrested."

"He doesn't sound like a very good bank robber."

"I suppose he wasn't. I booked him—Martin Price, age 22, resident of Beaumont, Texas. Of course, the Feds came in because it was a bank robbery, plus the gun was something he'd printed at home. In the end, he got eighteen years and they bundled him off to the FCI Medium in Yazoo City."

The Federal Corrections Institution south of Jackson. They handled low and medium security inmates in federal crimes.

Weapons-charge cases ended there, along with mid-tier narcos, blue and white collar thieves alike, the occasional disgraced celebrity. "Where does Dushane come in?"

"Before the Feds bundled him up, I searched Price. ID and library card said that's who he was. Prints came back Martin Price. He was booked, charged and convicted as Martin Price. But according to the guard at the bank, he gave a different name first. The guard told me he first said his name was Leon Dushane, and then quickly corrected himself."

"You're sure?"

"Hell, I wrote it down. Figured it might be an alias, but then everything came up Martin Price, so I figured maybe the guard was just wrong about it.

"I felt like telling him he should have checked anyway; he might have found a still-open warrant two states away. "Do you remember the guard's name?"

"No, but it would be all over the news coverage. He talked to any reporter who even looked at him."

"This was four years ago?"

"Yeah. Springtime. April, maybe."

"And the name Dushane never came up again otherwise?"

"Not that I recall."

"And you never brought it up?"

"Like I said, I figured the guard was wrong. And given he never mentioned it again, either he decided he misheard, or that they'd have thought he was getting senile and thrown him off the job. To be honest, he already seemed a little shaky when I met him."

I jotted specifics for the case file. "If you don't mind me asking: how on earth do you remember something like this when the case was resolved four years ago?"

"Only time I ever had to work with the FBI on something, and it kinda just stuck." Like it was trivia night and he remembered John Muir created the National Park system. "Plus, the guy was strange. Calm, relaxed, smiling. Charming, even. Twenty people in the bank at the time, and they all made it clear Price never demanded any money. His attorney called every one of them, too. He never even announced it was a robbery. He fired his gun and put it down and sat and waited, good as you please. Probably lucky he didn't get shot himself." He paused. "What does it mean?"

"Damned if I know."

"But is it helpful?"

"Maybe. You think you could ID him from a photo?"

He wavered. "I'm not sure I could. It was a while ago." It was the sound of him reaching the limit of involvement he wanted, and I didn't push. I thanked him for the compass points and disconnected.

The case was easy enough to find in the newspaper databases. A quick skim showed it was as Majoros described. I tried to find the bank's security guard. He turned up at a cemetery in Meridian. Dead two years. Cancer, according to his obit. That made it one man's secondhand assertion Leon Dushane was sitting in federal lockup in Mississippi under the name Martin Price.

A photograph would go a long way to bridging the gap.

I thought about calling Spence to loop him in. Instead, I stared at my phone, thumb frozen over the call button.

It was thin. And even if it proved thick, Price wasn't going anywhere. According to the Federal Inmate Register, his first shot at parole was six years away. The feds would be building the case against the splicer for months. If I brought Spence my suspicion, he'd be obliged to share it with Overbaugh, and Price—if Dushane—would slip through my hands. I wanted to talk to him just once before I turned Spence onto him, to get the story from him, to look him in the eyes and see what was there.

I made a note to call my attorney, Teo Arnaz, to pick his brain on how I might interview Price. I still needed to ease a little farther out on the tightrope before I brought Spence in with the net.

TWENTY-SEVEN

At midnight, I'd been parked for three hours where I'd stopped earlier, tucked beside the loading dock of the middle warehouse overlooking the storage facility's back lot. The trio of warehouses were derelicts, waiting for someone with the money and vision to buy the land and raze them. There was a certain inevitability to it. A city like New York was constrained, forced to build higher rather than wider. Houston, by nature of the flat land around it, was a longtime sprawler. A hundred years ago, downtown to the western edge of the city was a 25 minute drive at freeway speeds, half of the land still undeveloped. Now? It was a matter of time before rents, space constraints, taxes, some other factor pushed corporations this far out.

Lighted by street lamps on the far side, the warehouses threw perfect shadows in which to hide. Barrett was on the far side of the storage facility, across the street and down a half-block, ostensibly working on some issue with her motorcycle in the corner of a convenience store parking lot while keeping eyes on the front gate. I'd considered putting her at the rail crossing, but in the end her tactical thinking made more sense. "Even if he doesn't have a way in through the front—which he still might—he has an easy out if you're chasing him from behind. You want a box canyon, not a funnel."

I'd reached out to Donna Pascal on my way to my position to have her describe Young's car for me.

"He drives a blue Conquistador sedan with a white top," she volunteered. "It's never been especially clean. The top's well-worn, and it's a rusty old thing, with a dent in the back end I keep after him to have fixed. It looks terrible. I've suggested he look into getting something new, but—" She paused. "Have you seen him? Is that why you're asking?"

"I haven't seen him," I told her. *Not yet, anyway.* "I just want to be sure what I'm looking for." There was no point winding her up with any of our suppositions or by mentioning the surveillance. She'd have enough on her hands when someone finally did catch up with him.

"Where did you get these binoculars?" Barrett's voice was sharp in my earpiece. "I can't get them dialed in."

"Are you sure your visor's up?"

"Ha-ha. No, these suck. I have all kinds of flare."

"You're just annoyed I have the night vision goggles."

"No, truly Thib. They're awful. Four years in recon gave me exclusive access to Uncle Sam's toys. I've driven Cadillacs. This isn't to say your Ford Pinto doesn't steer or brake, but it lacks...finesse."

"You're too young to remember the Pinto." I scanned the darkness. "Hell, *I'm* too young to remember it."

"I've seen one. Before it burned up, even."

"I suppose if you're going to make a roadside bomb out of something—"

"Oh, no. Not in combat. I was fourteen, back in Colorado. I had a cousin who made his own moonshine. He found a Pinto in the woods. He was going to restore it and drive it—he thought it was retro enough to compensate for his other shortcomings with women—but it would have set him back more than he wanted to spend. Instead, he painted the shell a metallic copper-brown and gutted the inside for a still. It sat next to his house in the carport until something went 'boink' one afternoon. Burned up the Pinto, the carport and the house. The fire department didn't know whether to scream or cry. They really liked his moonshine."

The coffee in my thermal cup had grown tepid. "That's a horrible story."

"Not if you know my cousin. Shitheel had it coming."

I said nothing and peered up the tracks. The only thing moving was an opossum, foraging behind the salvage yard.

"Car pulling into the lot," Barrett said. "A very cherry muscle car. Looks like a Chevy Cyclone."

"Kind of flashy for arson."

"Two males on-board. Coming around back."

I saw the glow of the car's headlights, white jewels dispelling the shadows as it rounded the rear of the building. It stopped in front of the last garage unit on my corner. The driver's window was open. Male, Caucasian, college age. His hair appeared light in the night vision field. The passenger, Hispanic and of similar age, slipped out his side and opened one of the garage doors. He retrieved a box and just as quickly closed the door.

"Not him. A couple of college kids."

"Getting something from storage at midnight?"

"Maybe they stash their beer there."

Barrett chuckled. "Do you even remember college?"

I said nothing. I watched the Chevy pull away, around the side and to the front again. I turned attention back to the rails in time to spot the vehicle, rolling so slowly it wasn't even kicking up dust behind it.

"I have something," I said. "Pickup running dark on the service road."

If it was Young, he'd ditched his Conquistador in favor of something more arson-friendly. I couldn't see the driver, but there was enough detail through the goggles at full digital zoom to make out four large plastic gas cans, secured in the bed of the vehicle with bungee cords. Twenty gallons of total capacity. I expected they were full to the brim.

The truck rolled to a stop below the storage facility lot. The driver got out and surveyed the area. He was featureless.

"He's wearing a ski mask."

Barrett was incredulous. "In May, in Houston. Nothing suspicious there."

"If he passes out, he'll be easier to catch."

The driver took a canvas bag from inside the cab. He withdrew several bars and began interlocking them to form a small wagon bed with high cage sides. The driver attached a battery pack to one side of the bed, connected it to a bundle of wires. When he made the final connection, the wagon balanced itself on the air.

"He's got a float sled. Army surplus, from the look of it."

"Hope it's from a better place than wherever you bought these binoculars."

"*This* is why you don't go on field trips."

I watched the driver load the gas cans into the cage. They fit as if it had been designed for them. The driver slung a bag over his shoulder and proceeded up the easement, pulling the sled behind him. He stopped at the northeast corner of the storage lot and removed a compact bolt cutter from the bag. He made several quick cuts in the chain link behind the pole, enough space to admit his hands. He maneuvered the cutters to the pole and snipped the wires there.

The light at the top of the pole above him blinked out. I expected the camera on the pole died with it. The driver moved in the new shadows, repeated the cutting maneuver at the next pole. The entire northeast corner of the lot fell into darkness. There were two more lights along the back fence, but the driver seemed unconcerned with a total blackout.

He continued snipping fence links until he had an entrance. He cut the last link, pulled the loose fence segment away, and flung it down the easement. He dragged the float sled behind him, through the hole and into the extended shadows in the yard.

"Bird's in the house," I said.

"Should I move in?"

"Not yet. Let him get a little more involved." Once he was at the building, we could bottle him.

The driver was methodical. He parked the sled at the same corner of the building where the college kids had been minutes before. He hoisted one gas can from the sled and carried it with him toward the end of the building closer to the road, where the office was. He walked back in a low crouch, the can tipped.

"He's laying accelerant."

As he grabbed the second can and began walking along the back of the building in the same crouch, I dialed the Richmond fire department dispatcher. I gave the woman my name and PI license number. "Someone is in the process of setting a fire at the Store-Your-Stuff facility on the south side of Highway 69, south of Richmond. Near the interchange with the 762."

The dispatcher confirmed the location and rang off.

"He's headed down the west side with number three," I told Barrett.

"I see him."

"Get ready to jump. I'll head—"

Sirens split the quiet night. I heard them out my window and in the headset.

"That was fast," Barrett said.

"Too fast for the fire department." And too close.

"HPD incoming at the front. Multiple units. No idea where from." Barrett sounded annoyed.

I saw the driver first. He came around the northwest corner, fumbling with something in his hands. I saw a flash. The brilliant red flame of a roadside flare fell like a star at the driver's feet. Gasoline on the ground ignited. Twin ribbons of flame spread in both directions as the gasoline caught and burned. The driver made a beeline for the hole he'd cut in the fence. Two unmarked police cars chased him, red and blue grill lights flashing. A third car raced down the east side, trying to cut him off.

"Bail out, Barrett. Regroup at the office."

Police cars screeched to a halt and doors swung open. Close enough to the ribbon of fire encircling the building, the fourth gas can popped into a blossom of flame. Cops ducked, distracted from the pursuit. The driver dove through his hole in the fence.

Barrett was still in my ear. "What about you? Where are you going?"

I was about to tell her I was going to make sure Young didn't get away when the north side of the storage facility detonated.

TWENTY-EIGHT

The fireball climbed the sky. Fragments of the broad spectrum of human experience—boxes, clothing, small appliances, sporting goods—rained down. Some of them trailed flame.

I tried to focus through the night vision goggles. The world was the bright blot of the detonation flash. Barrett was shouting in my ear. "Thib? What the hell was that?"

"Just what it looked like. Big damned boom."

"*He blew it up?*"

"No. This was something else. Inside the building." I scanned the chaos across the tracks, my vision clearing. "Get clear. I'm going to cut him off."

Barrett started to protest. I pulled the headset off.

I could see enough by firelight to spot Young's pickup. The smoking remains of a recliner had crushed the hood. The front tires were flat from the impact. The police in the storage yard had been knocked about by the blast. No one was being handcuffed or bundled into a car. I scanned the fence line and easement. I didn't see Young at first. Had he not moved, I might have missed him. He was parallel to the tracks, scuttling, mask removed, heading in the direction of the truck. I waited to see which way he would rabbit.

He discovered the flat tires. He got up and ran east, seeking deeper shadows.

I kept the night vision goggles in place. I reached into the door pocket for the baton and electro. I noticed the force of the blast had cracked my windshield. Then I heard the low whine of an electro that wasn't mine being cycled and a woman's voice outside the car. "Hands where I can see them. Go slowly."

I let my weapons drop back into the door and raised my hands into sight, open. "Your suspect is getting away."

"Yeah, but you're not."

"I'm a private investigator."

"Uh-huh. Remove the goggles and drop them out the window."

I complied.

"Out of the car. Easy." Her voice was pure. Confident. No mirth, no fear, no hesitation.

I moved with care, opened the door, and stood beside the car. "In the interest of disclosure, there's an electro-gun and a telescoping baton in the door pocket."

"Noted. Turn around."

I faced two officers. I didn't recognize the kid in back. He should have been working undercover narcotics at a high school. The female officer was another story. Recognition did nothing to soften the expression behind the barrel of her service electro or alter her aim. "If it isn't the low country Columbo."

"Hiya, Nancy."

"Officer Brewer." Her lips cut a frown. "Hands on the hood. If you so much as twitch, I'll light you up."

I stepped around the open door, pressed my palms on the hood.

"Kind of weird, you sitting watch over an arson in progress. I'm beginning to think Koi might be right about you."

"Taking cues from him is a filthy habit."

"Yet here you are, like he thought you might be."

"I'm on a case."

She shined the light over me. "Stunner and baton in the door. Any weapons on your person?"

"No ma'am."

"How about the roll of quarters in the sock?"

"Glove compartment. Though I've switched to dollar coins. It feels fancier in my hand."

"Search him, Dinh."

The male officer performed an effective pat-down. "He's clean."

"Your suspect is fleeing on foot, along the tracks, heading east."

"There are plenty of officers over there. He won't get very far." She pulled the headset from inside the car. "Aren't you a little old to be out playing walkie-talkies on a school night?" She listened to the earpiece, but refrained from speaking into the mic. "Night vision, communications, vantage point of the rear of the building."

"Like I said, I'm doing surveillance for a case."

"Am I going to find a detonator in this vehicle?"

"Have you ever?"

She smirked. "As far as I recall, nothing explosive ever happened in your car."

She stepped behind me and gripped my left wrist while her partner covered me. I didn't struggle as the bracelets went on, but as I had several times before, I questioned the wisdom of ever having dated Nancy Brewer.

Koi made me wait a half-hour, standing against the fence, before he got around to me. At least he'd taken the cuffs off. By then, eight fire trucks were on scene, along with police forensics teams from Richmond and Houston, and at least twenty police units, hoppers and cars alike: Richmond, Houston, State Police, a Texas Ranger who was probably bored. There were also a half-dozen men in suits and earpieces, the NanoDwell logo distinct on their blazers, supporting my theory of how they'd connected the dots.

The detonation had shredded the building. Half of it was missing, ragged edges marking where it had been. Fire was consuming the rest. The sweet metallic stench of burning nano-sand mingled with gasoline, scorched rubber and whiffs of other chemicals, the warmer scents of woods, the flaming ruins of the contents of a hundred storage units. I stared at the devastation, glad I wasn't an insurance adjuster.

Koi sauntered over from a clutch of assorted officers. His stride promised a hard time. "I'm going to give you one opportunity to play this straight with me, or I swear to you, you'll be teaching inmates at the Connelly Unit how to season and suck a crawfish by the end of the summer."

"I doubt it," I said. "Crawfish will be out of season by then."

"You want to test me?

"Inspector, you've already decided I'm in this up to my ears. Officer Brewer said as much. So why don't you float your theory, and I'll tell you if I think it's parade-worthy."

If there hadn't been news crews within eyeball distance, he might have gut-punched me. "I have you receiving a phone call from the scene of an arson. I now have a suspect in that arson, one Herbert T. Young. I have DNA evidence linking him to several previous arsons. I have a list of his possible targets. I stake them out. When I get a hit at one of those targets, I don't just get an arson, I find you in a position to surveil the entire scene, including the spot the arsonist broke into the property. You've got gear to see in the dark and talk to someone, and you're on the corner of the building that went up like Hiroshima."

I nodded. "Presented that way, it sounds like I could have a connection to the whole thing. Albeit a very circumstantial one."

"Hence my curiosity. So you can talk here, or talk downtown."

I hadn't survived against Koi for as long as I had without knowing when to remain silent, when to speak, and how to edit what I knew for his consumption. "Herb Young's girlfriend retained me a couple days ago to locate him. He's been missing for over a month. I came into possession of information suggesting Young might have been involved in setting a string of fires. Nothing provable. Based on that, I figured this location was most likely his next target. I staked it out, he showed up. It's all third grade reading from there."

"That's thin, even for you."

"I can produce my information. I suspect you won't need it, since NanoDwell divined the same location. Correct me if I'm wrong, but didn't someone give your department a tip Young's apartment had been broken into, which yielded a list that led you here? Who made the call to Spence again?"

Koi said nothing. I rolled on.

"It might also interest you that upon observing Young prepping this evening's bonfire, I was also the one who phoned the Richmond dispatcher to get the fire department down here."

"What's any of this supposed to prove?"

"That if I'm playing a game with Young and trying to keep you out of it, I'm doing a piss-poor job since I seem to keep helping you catch up."

"Helping? *This* is helping?" Koi's voice went up a notch. "I still have a goddamned burned-up building!"

"Richmond Fire would have contained it if not for the explosion."

"I'm betting you don't know anything about that, either."

"On the contrary. As it appears to have originated in the northwest corner garage unit, I can tell you two college-age kids were here a few minutes before things went nuclear. I suspect they had something highly flammable in the space. A distillery, a drug lab, something that doesn't like fire. Your forensics team should be able to narrow it down."

Koi's expression told me I was ahead on points. I didn't like him enough to play poker with him, but I could have cleaned him out if I had. "They already have. Meth cooking setup."

"Lacking x-ray vision, I can't tell you the contents of the box they removed, but it was compact enough for drugs, maybe cash. They were the last people on-site before Young arrived. Your officers staking out the front would have seen them. Big, black Chevy Cyclone. The name on the unit is probably fake, but the gate security camera would have the plate, and the card reader would have recorded the swipe. If it isn't in orbit now."

"Did you see Young set the fire?"

"I saw the whole thing. He was masked when he poured the gasoline, but during his retreat, he removed the mask and revealed himself."

"Good. You can ID him when we catch him."

"You didn't catch him?"

"We're still looking, but it won't be long."

"Huh."

He sighed. I lived for the sigh. It was all I really wanted. "What?"

"I informed Officer Brewer the suspect was fleeing on foot, east along the tracks. She expressed high confidence there were so many other officers, she didn't need to pursue. Apparently, someone in her chain of command made noise that I was somehow involved with the arsonist, to the point my apprehension was of some equal value. I'll be honest: it made me feel *very* important."

Koi's glare could have felled a tree. "Is that accurate, officer?"

It took Brewer a moment. "Yes, sir."

"On the plus side," I said, "at best he only has a 45 minute head start."

"I see." He stared at me, trying to decide the best course of action. I could almost feel his headache. "Robillard, I want you downtown for a formal statement tomorrow morning, 10 a.m., come rain, shine, or wrath of God. If you have evidence to share that can help us apprehend Young or save you from one count of obstruction of justice, I suggest you bring it with you."

"I'm counting the hours."

He trained death-ray eyes on Brewer. "Please escort Mister Robillard outside the perimeter and cut him loose. Then I want you back at Central, writing me the most compelling report possible. Something to keep me from having you suspended for some reason I haven't fully formed in my head yet."

"Yes, sir."

Koi took a printed card from his pocket, scribbled the date on it, and handed it to me. "Take this with you."

"You're handing out invitations now?"

"It's in case you get stopped again. As much as I enjoy your company, I don't need another unit thinking you're worth a damn and bringing you back again." Koi nodded at Brewer and started to walk away.

"One more thing, Inspector," I called. He turned around. "Have you tied Young to Rose Street yet?"

The look told me he was frustrated he hadn't. He bobbed his head at Brewer again: get him out of here.

She guided me away by the arm.

I looked at faces as we walked, surprised Sami wasn't there. We were almost out of the yard when I spotted another familiar face: the man who'd been observing Pascal and me at the Saint Andrew's rec center. The NanoDwell security blazer wasn't enough to deflect the familiarity. Hard to mistake someone you've been two feet from. His eyes flashed with mutual recognition when he saw me, but he moved on.

Brewer took me to the police line, deactivated it and sent me across without ceremony. "There was a time you wouldn't have scored points by pushing me under the bus," she said, a trace of hurt in her tone.

"There was a time you'd have helped me run a suspect down instead of thinking the worst of me. I'd say the company you're keeping is having an adverse affect on a good cop and a decent human being. You should look into that."

Before she could reply, I weaved into the onlookers. I wanted as much to be away from her as the NanoDwell security guard who'd previously tailed me.

The police perimeter was in front of the wreck of the storage facility, holding back curious onlookers. I had to walk the long way around—past the adjacent buildings, along the same half-mile loop I'd driven before, across the bridge over the tracks and along a curve back to the warehouses. I passed several sets of uniformed officers on my walk, men sweating in the hot night as they beat the bushes and shined their lights in vehicles and under buildings. At least two of them asked who I was or what business I had there. I presented Koi's card both times—upon which was printed QUESTIONED AND RELEASED with the date and Koi's signature at the bottom— and was ushered on my way. I made a note to add the card to my emergency toolbox. You never know when you might need to quickly slip through a dragnet.

I dialed Barrett as I walked. She answered, sounding like I'd awakened her. "Am I your one phone call?"

"Close. Not quite."

"Good. I was having a hard time deciding what to use for bail collateral."

"Firearms are good for that."

"You'd have to own one first."

"Touché." I filled her in on the tail end of events, including the familiar NanoDwell face and Koi's summons for the morning. "Young got away. Short of walking into the bishop's house and declaring sanctuary, I don't know where he'll head next."

"It might come to that. News reports about the explosion have already started splashing his name and face as the suspect. They claim to have evidence linking him to several recent arsons. Including Rose Street."

"Interesting. My impression from Koi was that Rose Street was still unconnected."

"Either way, they've set up a tip line. $50,000 for information. Probably too late to drop a tip, huh?"

"By a couple of hours." An idea sparked. "Actually, call the number and tell them you want to report a missing child."

"I'm missing a child?"

"I'm betting the tip line goes directly to NanoDwell security and not HPD. If I'm right, they'll tell you to call the police. If not, hang up before they transfer you to the right department."

"How old is this missing child?"

"Make something up. Anything. It doesn't matter."

"Doesn't matter? Jeez, Thib. We're talking about my poor little Herkimer. Or maybe Desdemona." She hung up.

Two minutes later, she called back. "Your hunch was in the ten-ring. I went full-metal distraught mother. They told me they were a private security company working arson tips, and I needed to call police for anything else. They even sounded a little annoyed."

"Slick. They probably sold someone downtown on the idea of pre-screening tips to reduce the department's burden. NanoDwell gets to control the ball, all the tips go to them, and they get to Young first."

"You think the department would go for private security handling phone tips?"

"They farm cases out to people like us, don't they?"

"Point taken." Then she cursed at something I couldn't see. "Problems?"

"I'm still compiling this translator. It's fighting me."

"Make up with it and get some sleep." My watch said it was almost two. "You should come with me to see Koi in the morning. He'll want to know who I was talking to, and it's easier if he doesn't have to send for you afterwards."

"Roger that." She hung up.

I saw the parking ticket slipped under the driver's side wiper blade when I reached my car. Brewer's partner had signed it with a bold flourish. I pulled it loose, crumpled it, and dropped it on the ground. Then I opened the door and sat behind the wheel. I fished the fob out and started the engine. The crack in the windshield needed attention sooner rather than later.

I drove around the disused warehouses, followed the road away from them and back towards the freeway. I was waiting to turn onto the ramp when I heard the snap of the slide on an automatic pistol. I looked in the rear view mirror.

Herb Young stared back at me.

"Head towards the city," he said.

TWENTY-NINE

I angled the car up the ramp and onto the freeway without argument. Young was ragged around the edges: unshaven for several days, gravel-voiced, tired-eyed. Only he and God knew how long he'd been awake. I didn't need his trigger finger to itch on top of it all.

"Are you a cop?" he asked.

"No."

"One of those NanoDwell security thugs?"

"Strike two."

"Then why were you there?" He was angry on top of exhausted. "Surveillance gear, watching the back, laying in wait for me. Then you were talking with them."

"I'm a private investigator. I was hired to find you."

"By who?"

"Donna Pascal."

Young was quiet, as if trying to process the name. I kept the speed steady. I hadn't seen the gun in Young's hand, but I'd heard it clearly enough. The dark bags under his eyes spoke to exhaustion. The wear and tear of arson had aged him from Pascal's photo. He could have been a decade older. He gripped his forehead and ran his hand through his hair. "I didn't want her involved with this. I pushed her away to keep her safe."

"She pushed back."

"Wonderful woman. Stubborn."

"Say what you will. She cares about you."

"She understands broken people."

"Donna said you told her someone stole your soul, Herb. What does that mean?"

"That's my business." He fidgeted.

"I talked to Bishop Hudson. He holds you in high regard, but he's concerned you might be in terrible trouble."

"Did he call the cops?"

"No. The company whose buildings you've been burning down found your list of coordinates and figured out where you might go, just like me. They called the cops. I was trying to get to you first. Now they're putting your face everywhere."

I changed lanes and noticed the car following us. I thought I'd seen it enter the freeway behind us, a flicker in its left headlight. It had matched two lane changes so far to remain behind us, but at a distance.

"Why are you burning NanoDwell's buildings?"

"Just drive. I'll tell you where to get off."

"Does it have to do with the information Stephen Angelo gave you?"

The hesitation answered for him. "Let's try again: shut up and drive."

The following car was closing the gap. I edged our speed higher to see what it'd do. "Stephen is dead. Did you kill him?"

Young squinted at me in the rear view. "Steve's dead?"

"Murdered in his apartment."

He sat back in the seat. His exhaustion seemed overridden by the shock of the news. I knew before he said it that he wasn't responsible. I could see it in the way finding out had reshaped his expression. "I didn't kill him. He was a friend. He helped me. Revealed the truth and testified to me. He made it possible for me to do what I need to do." He sighed. I thought he might weep. Instead, he prayed under his breath.

The following car sped up to match my pace, then began closing again. Time for a test. I passed a tandem tractor-trailer on the right, then maneuvered into the lane on the side opposite. The trailing car followed suit.

"I don't mean to alarm you," I interrupted Young, "but we need to get off the freeway."

"Why?"

"We're being followed."

Young craned to peer out the rear window. "By who?"

"No idea, and I'd rather not find out."

"You're just trying to scare me." He didn't sound convinced.

"I'm telling you this so you don't shoot me when I do it. I'm going to get off the next ramp, continue down the feeder road, and get back on the highway. If the car behind us is following us, it will do the same." At that point, they'd know they'd been made and the real fun would begin.

Young glanced behind us again. "Okay. I'm putting the gun away."

It was another mile before an exit sign loomed on the highway. I put on my signal and maneuvered onto the ramp. Several hundred yards behind us, our shadow did the same.

The ramp deposited us onto the feeder. It was long and straight, businesses to the right—mostly closed—and an at-grade intersection ahead for local traffic. The intersection signal glowed green. We were still fifty yards off when it went amber.

There was no cross traffic. I slowed. Our shadow drew within three car lengths. It was a sports car. I couldn't see the make, but I didn't need to. The silhouette, the slope, the curve of the hood — I knew it had me on speed and handling without testing it.

Twenty yards from the intersection, I lead-footed the gas and shot through the red light. It took a moment, but our tail duplicated the move. At the least, the Snap Squad might catch a look. Its lights swelled in the rear view mirror as we pulled back onto the highway. The car's flickering headlight was a wink, promising us a good time.

Behind me, Young craned, spied our tail. "You think you can outrun them?"

"You'd better hope I can."

They weren't cops. Cops would have given me the blues and reds when I blew through the intersection. That made them NanoDwell security. Probably tied to the one who'd tailed me to Saint Andrews and turned up at the storage facility. Had there been a car waiting by the freeway to follow me out?

"I would never intentionally hurt anyone," Young said.

"Five minutes ago you had a gun pointed at me."

"It's not even loaded."

Of course it wasn't. "There's a fifty thousand dollar reward up for grabs. They want you for murder." I weaved between a couple of slower cars, trying to use them as blockers. The driver of the sports car compensated with ease.

"I've gone out of the way with every fire I've set to make sure no one was hurt. I didn't want anyone killed or injured. I only wanted—" Young's voice was lost as the rear window exploded in a shower of glass.

The bullet tore a hole in the front passenger-seat headrest. I swerved and pressed the accelerator, trying to coax more from the engine. I began scanning for the next ramp. "Stay down and hang on."

I heard the thud of a bullet, felt the punch in the rear of the car. A vehicle loped along the right lane, threatening to block the exit. I slammed the brake and swerved, the tires squealing protests. I managed to not roll the car, nicked the front barrel in the group where the ramp and highway split. It danced away. The pursuit car stayed with us.

I cut in front of a pickup on the ramp and drew a horn and finger. I accelerated again on the feeder, towards the intersection. I wasn't ready to move into the neighborhoods, where it would be easier to get boxed in or to put more people in the line of fire.

I heard one of my tail lights pop into fragments. Young heard it too. "Do something!"

"I am."

We plunged into the intersection and I turned hard left. The turn pitched Young across the back seat. I heard the empty gun rattling around on the floor. We cut under the freeway and I spun the wheel to take us hard right, up the feeder road opposite traffic. Young recovered enough to see the oncoming headlights. "You're going to get us killed!"

"You should unburden yourself before I do." I felt like a boxer, bobbing and weaving with the wheel. A car on the feeder swerved to avoid us, opened a lane for our shadow to keep pace. "The buildings you burned. Why did you torch them?"

"Are you a religious man?"

"Not really. If we get out of this alive, I might reconsider. I'm a little tired of being shot at this week."

"Then you wouldn't understand."

I cut to the right and hit a pot hole on the way up the off ramp. The car lurched, but kept all four tires. I angled from the ramp onto the freeway, still headed in the wrong direction. I glimpsed the following car in the rear view. Whoever was coming for us wasn't going to back down. Not until they got what they wanted.

"What did Angelo give you?"

He shouted. Already frayed, the ride was shredding what was left of his nerves. "The truth!"

"Less esoteric. I know it was pages of medical data. What does it mean?" I weaved through the oncoming traffic until I reached the far shoulder, hoping our pursuer would do the same. Instead, the car stayed on the opposite shoulder, closing the gap again. I realized that worked better than what I'd been considering. "We're running out of time, Herb!"

Young shouted back. "They took my genes and stuck them in the control centers of their damned buildings!"

It's probably a miracle I didn't drive into the guardrail. "NanoDwell uses human DNA in their computer control units? The things directing the building nanobots?"

I saw Young in the rear view mirror. Not rage. Sorrow. Devastation. "They did. Once upon a time."

I felt another bullet punch the outside of my door. I had to refocus him. "Can you see the car?"

Young was slow to answer, but did. "Yes."

"Make and model?"

He peeked, cautious. "Looks like a Montenegro. A Mongoose SQ."

"SQ? You're sure?"

"It's badged on the side in ugly block letters."

"Can you see the license plate?"

"No. The angle is bad."

The Montenegro wasn't especially rare, but the SQ—Superior Quality—Mongoose was top-of-the-line automotive engineering. Without a plate, the list of probable matches might still number in the hundreds. There was a stupid amount of wealth in Houston, and whether a hopper or an automobile, the rich enjoy their toys.

"Put on your seat belt," I said. I heard the click from the back seat.

The Mongoose tried to match speed. I slowed and sped to throw it off, one eye peeled for an exit ramp on the left. As I passed one, I let the Mongoose draw and stay even. "Tell me when you see them aim at us again."

It was almost half a minute before Herb saw the round 'O' of the muzzle emerged through the window. "Now."

I slammed the brakes and pulled hard from the shoulder across the oncoming lanes.

THIRTY

Three things happened at once.

We avoided by the slimmest margin being totaled in a T-bone collision with a red semi hauling a tandem fuel trailer as we skidded in a broad U-turn across four lanes of traffic. I didn't roll the car. Small miracles of physics are a blessing. We shot down the exit ramp in the correct direction once more.

Caught flat-footed, the Mongoose continued to rocket up the shoulder for several seconds before the driver braked, but there was no way for the driver to quickly execute a similar maneuver, which would have required crossing traffic twice.

And Young screamed. I thought of my sister Cecile, age four, when my friend Tommy brought his tarantula to Mémé's house. I caught hell for terrorizing her with it. I'd have caught it again for the maneuver I pulled if Mémé had been watching.

We reached the bottom of the ramp. From the feeder, I made a quick right onto the cross street, then a left, another, zigzagging through neighborhoods until I reached a local artery leading north to the I-10. When we were two blocks from the ramp, I pulled over and shut off the engine.

"What are you doing?" Young had forgotten the unloaded gun and whatever else it was he'd planned when he first climbed in the back seat.

I had so much adrenaline in my system, the tremors in my hands had their own shakes. "I'm taking a moment."

"They're still out there. They could be coming up behind us right now."

"They could," I said. "Even if they're not, the way I hear it their people are blasting your name and face on every possible media channel and offering hard cash for your capture. Right now, that makes me the closest thing to a friend you have."

Young stared at me. "What are you going to do?"

"Do? You were abducting me, remember?"

He glanced through the place the rear window should have been. "I was just going to have you let me out somewhere."

I let him consider his options in silence for a minute before starting the car again. "Alternate plan: I'm taking you somewhere safe. I'm going to call a cop I can trust. Then I'm going to ask you some questions. The cop will take you into custody for the arsons you committed and put you in an even safer place while they get warrants to talk to NanoDwell about what they did with your DNA."

"Not just mine."

"I'm sorry?"

"Steve said I wasn't the only one. There were at least a dozen people whose DNA was harvested. I was just the first person he told."

It was a little past three in the morning when I pulled into my space on the office's parking deck. By streetlight, Young and I walked from the office two blocks south and a block over to the Austin Arms. It was an old hotel, but maintained; not the closest to the office, nor the cheapest, but easy to overlook. I got a room under an alternate ID I used, a puppet name Rojo set up for me several years before, something basic that would stand enough scrutiny for a hotel room, a car rental, common tasks requiring a photo ID and tied to a digital currency account. I thought about the splicer. I suppose in a digital world, there's a few dozen bytes of criminal somewhere in each of us.

I called Barrett. She answered, groggy. I filled her in on Young and the highway pursuit.

"Where's he now?"

"Safe," I told her. She knew what and where I meant.

I called Spence next. He didn't sound groggy at all. "We're all hands on deck for this arson-bomber manhunt."

"He's not a bomber. He had nothing to do with the explosion. What is that, more of Koi's babble?"

"NanoDwell."

"Koi knows it was a meth lab in the ground floor."

"I'll be sure to ask him about it." He paused to answer a question from someone nearby, came back again. "Or ask you. You seem to know more about it than I do at this point."

"Knowledge is power. How would you like to make Lieutenant?"

His voice dropped in volume by half. "What have you done?"

"I have Herb Young. To be fair, he abducted me, but that's a whole farce with an unloaded gun and a freeway chase."

If he got any more quiet, the squad room would notice he was whispering. "Jesus, Thib. You're harboring a fugitive."

"I'm protecting a witness. There's more to this than arson, if the bullets from the people who want him dead are any indication. My car got Swiss-cheesed, and we're lucky we weren't along with it. An hour ago. Southwest freeway."

I gave him the hotel name and the room number on the third floor. I proposed he be the one to bring Young in and store him until I presented my evidence.

"If I announce where I'm going, about a hundred close friends will call 'shotgun'."

"He needs to be brought in quietly. NanoDwell wants him dead badly enough to open fire in highway traffic. There's bound to be an 'accident' if they do a ride-along."

"Do you know for sure it was NanoDwell?"

"Not to pick them out of a lineup, but one of their security personnel was the guy watching me at St. Andrews."

Spence promised to shake free and come fetch Young at seven. Until then, I planned to document as much as I could.

The room was a twin with an inspiring view of a dilapidated storefront and overgrown parking lot. I brought Young some water. The man's exhaustion was taking over. He watched a news report about the explosion. I turned off the streaming screen. I didn't need him getting sucked into the media's funhouse version of himself.

"Freshen up," I told him. "Then we're going to talk."

I set up my phone as a recorder and took the hotel stationary to make additional notes. Young sat before my phone and watched it like it might bite him.

"Are you ready?" I asked.

Young nodded. I started the recorder and gave it a preface of the date, time, location, and the case involved. I had Young state his vital statistics—name, date of birth, place of birth—before I started asking questions.

"How did you know Stephen Angelo?"

"As a rival coach, first. I headed the junior varsity basketball squad at my high school, he coached one at his. Our teams played each other a few times a year, and you get to know the opposing coaches. Then about a year ago he joined my church. I saw him at services. That's where I really got to know him, through the church."

"You became friends?"

"We did. I even recommended him for my coaching duties when I submitted my notice, though things were strained by then."

"How did you two connect on the matter of NanoDwell?"

Young sipped his water, chose his words. "A men's group from the church got together one Saturday back in November to watch the Baylor game. Steve and I got talking. He confided to me he'd started attending our church because he felt like he was lost. He'd gotten caught up in something with his job. Something he believed unethical. I asked him if he wanted to talk about it. He told me that years ago, he was a lab technician for a company, Medical Exploration Corporation. They provided lab services for some medical studies at Bray Gulf University."

"What kinds of studies?"

"Fitness, sleep, diet. Little week-long things run by grad students and using undergrad student volunteers."

"I'm familiar. I did a couple of psychology department experiments during my short trip through higher education." They were simple things, administered by grad students with eyes on science degrees of various stripe. They paid a token $25 or $50 for my time. It worked for beer money.

"Steve believed it was all above-board. He found out later some of the work he'd done was passed to another company. That company used it in medical experiments. They were trying to engineer genetic material for use in a biologically-based computer system. Programmable brains to control smart houses."

"NanoDwell."

"He didn't name them. Not then. We were a bunch of guys eating wings and watching football. But I thought it was a funny coincidence, because I went to Bray Gulf and I participated in one of those. It was a two-week nutritional study. The pay was good, considering I got to sit there and do my reading and papers when they weren't poking and prodding me. It worked out to four hundred bucks. Covered some textbooks. I told him all of this and when I was there, and sure enough, the year lined up. He told me he'd see if he could find out if I was one of the people whose material was passed to this company."

"I thought experiments like those were done blind."

"They are. But the company wanted to know who was who and someone obliged them with a list of participants coded to the experiment control numbers. It was in the file with the experiment paperwork. I suppose they wanted to know whose DNA produced the most favorable results. Steve said when he found it, he knew right away what it was, because he'd issued the control numbers for the samples when he was working at the lab." Young shrugged. "I honestly didn't think anything would come of it. A couple weeks later, he showed up at my door, wracked with guilt."

"Guilt?"

"He was a serious convert, Mister Robillard. He understood the church resists the aspects of science that lessen or degrade us. Using tissue samples for experimental purposes without my knowledge was an abject violation of my faith, and he felt awful about being part of it, even unawares. Not just because of faith, but from the ethical and legal quagmires as well."

"Did he say how your DNA was used?"

"In initial development of matrices for the organic control centers and associated nanotech for their 'smart' structures."

"Wait. The nanobots too?"

"Steve said the company suspected their nanobots worked more efficiently when they were DNA-paired to the control center. They may or may not have continued that way, but my DNA and others were used in that fashion by NanoDwell. Steve was able to smuggle out the information about who was affected by those experiments and passed it to me."

"What NanoDwell did was clearly illegal. Why not go to the police when you found out?"

"Because there's illegal, Mister Robillard, and there's immoral." He stared at his hands. "This was a violation of my sanctity. Part of me was taken and incorporated into other creations. No matter how convoluted or derivative their technology is, part of me is in those materials. I have no say over what that part of me does." He closed his eyes. "It was fifteen years ago, but what they did was evil at a basic level. They created abominations of who I am. And they did it for money." He looked at me then, weary. "Can the law arrest those responsible? Yes. It can try, convict, and sentence a person, but the authorities aren't going to tear down a building. I see a violation, millions of stolen pieces of myself. But they see a building. And we as a race allow places of horrible human torture and murder to remain standing all the time. Was I going to put my faith in a municipal court system to tear down someone else's property? No. The owner has a tangible investment. Judges and juries can see a deed. They can't see my soul in the machine."

"That's when you got a notion for arson."

He nodded. "Yes. Burning those places down, cleansing them from existence, was the only way to restore my sanctity as a person, and no one was going to do that but me."

"How did Angelo provide the list of structures with your DNA?"

"He sent them via a computer program from his home. It was an involved process of nested encoding."

"I'm familiar with the process."

"He said it was untraceable. He was concerned scrutiny on him was increasing, owing to his company's IPO."

"When was the last time you heard from him?"

He thought about it. "The night he made the files available and sent the key to me. He asked that we not speak to each other for a time. That was two days before the first fire I set, in Dallas. So about seven weeks ago." Sadness curled his lip. "I didn't even hear he was dead. Do you know who killed him?"

"Not yet," I said, if only because I couldn't prove who from NanoDwell was responsible. I shifted gears. "Tell me about the fires you set."

He did, one by one, a litany he'd committed to heart. It had the tenor of a prayer.

"And along the way, you made sure the buildings you burned were empty?"

"Always. The residents didn't do anything, and I wasn't going to trade their souls for mine."

"What about the fire they're saying you set? The one on Rose Street?"

"That wasn't me."

"It used your methodology. Are you just saying you didn't do it because people were killed?"

"I said I didn't do it because it's the truth." He flushed with anger.

"Relax. I believe you. I'm still trying to figure how Rose Street fits. Do you know if Angelo contacted any of the other people from the study?"

"Not when we last spoke." He'd stopped relaxing. "Isn't it enough to hang me for what I've done? Why would they frame me for murder, too? I had no reason to kill anyone."

Maybe it was the tone in his voice, but I heard the cry for help from House Doris in my head, and the piece fell into place. "It wasn't about the four deaf men. They were an accident. And it wasn't about you, not specifically. They had no idea who was burning their buildings. They just used your methods to provide cover. It was about destroying that specific building. They were trying to kill House Doris."

"Kill a house?"

"I believe the apartment building on Rose Street was sentient."

"Sentient?" He looked like I'd punched the air from his lungs. "You don't think human DNA could have made it that way?"

"I couldn't say. Not yours, at any rate."

He chewed absently at his fingernail. "I might be able to help figure out whose." He slipped a key ring from his pocket and worked a bronze key with a round head from it. "Steve didn't just give me my information. He sent me the entire cross-reference list. Actual names to ME Co. control numbers. That's how he built my list. Someone at NanoDwell could decipher the rest of the build matrices. Steve didn't want to keep the data, and I don't like having all my eggs in the same basket." He handed me the key. "This opens a safety deposit box at the Bellaire Credit Union branch on the 290, just outside the loop. The full file is there."

I turned the key in my hand. Box #117. "If NanoDwell security took a tour through the papers in your apartment, could they know about the box?"

"Not without hacking my email. It's an annual fee and I pay it electronically."

"They aren't going to let me into your box."

"They will with a consent." He used his mobile to pull the form from the bank's website, filled it in, and e-filed it from his account, along with photos of my driver's and PI's licenses and his ID. Then he called the bank and left a message with the branch manager to confirm the request.

We talked a while longer, covering additional details of the list and the fires, before I gathered myself for my quick round trip to the office.

"Lock this door behind me," I told him. "Under no circumstance are you to open this door for anyone except police detective Byron Spencer." I showed him a photo from my phone. "Shield 7093. If anyone but him shows up in that peephole, stay low, be quiet, and call these two numbers, in this order." I jotted down Spence's cell, then mine. "We're clear?"

"Absolutely."

I held out my hand. "Gun, please."

Young pulled it from his jacket pocket and held it out, grip-first. "Probably best I don't hang onto it. It wasn't exactly acquired legally."

I considered asking for specifics, but figured Spence could do it as well as I could. I ensured the gun was empty and slipped it into a pocket. With the cops hunting for him, the last thing Young needed was a reason for them to shoot him.

I walked back to the office. The night was melting into dawn. The air already shimmered, the day set to 'broil.'

I stopped in the building garage and inspected the car. Everything looked worse in the daylight than it had in the dark. My body shop guy was going to think it was Christmas.

Besides the glass damage, there were three bullet holes in the driver's side, two in the rear driver's side door and another in the rear quarter panel. The left tail light was an empty eye socket. I was thankful none of the bullets had punched anything ignitable.

I checked the front passenger side headrest first, but the bullet had apparently struck the steel support and ricocheted out the open passenger window. It was somewhere along the 69. I probed the rear door holes with the tip of my pinkie finger. There was nothing but space in the first one. The slug had either caromed away after hitting something in the door frame, or had fallen to the bottom of the door cavity.

Inside the second hole, I brushed the tail-end of a slug, embedded in the window mechanism. I widened the hole with the blade of a pocket knife from the storage box. When I had enough clearance, I used the tip of the blade to work the slug free, trapping it between the blade and my finger.

The slug was mangled. About the size of a .45 bullet, definitely not a .223 round. Different gun, maybe different shooter. There was an engraving on the jacket, distorted by the impact. I wasn't sure what it was supposed to be. The ammo appeared custom, distinctive. Distinctive was always an advantage in identifying people, cars, and weapons. I dropped it into a plastic bag for safekeeping.

I gave a quick look underneath to make sure I wasn't leaking fluids. That's when I noticed the box. In the course of the chase, perhaps from a bullet impact, it had been dislodged from its hiding place up and behind the rear bumper. It was larger than the ShadowTag trackers we used, about as big as my thumb. It was still in the same functional family. I reached up, twisted, and was able to pull its magnetic mount free. It was dirty, had been there a while. I dropped it into its own bag and headed inside.

Barrett was in the office. Her same outfit from the night before revealed she'd never left.

"I should have your voice translator this afternoon," she told me. "How's Young?"

"Oddly calm for someone who was nearly killed in a protracted drive-by, though he remains upset NanoDwell used bits of him in their house brains and nanotech."

"Come again?"

I filled her in on Young's definition of 'stolen soul' and what had been done with his genetic material.

"Did he torch House Doris?" she asked.

"He denies he did and I believe him. I think the point of burning House Doris was to kill it. Young destroying other buildings gave them a convenient scapegoat. The deaf men were simply in the wrong place."

"That tracks. Once the company goes public, they live or die by everything they do and have done. Charlie, they can hide in the attic. Hell, he *is* the attic. Doris was sitting where anyone could walk up and examine her if they began to have questions."

"Ever seen one of these?" I fished the slug from my pocket "One of the rounds from last night. There's an engraving, but I can't make it out."

Barrett studied the slug. "Not a .45. Not sure what it is either, but I know someone who can probably tell you." She consulted her phone and sent me a contact at the Bang-Bang Gun Club.

"Swell. Boom toys."

"It's so much more than bullet-spitters. VIP members get to use flame-throwers and rail guns. You should come with me some time. They have beanbag shotguns at the kids' range."

"I'd sooner chew off my own foot at the knee. No offense."

"Their ballistics specialist is a guy named Jude Keppler. A little wacky, but his knowledge of ammo manufacturers is nonpareil. It should be. He paid a king's ransom to have it made sticky in his brain."

"Next trinket: how about one of these?" I handed her the module from behind the bumper.

She turned it in her hand. "WorldWatch drone guidance and telemetry module." She rubbed at the grimy registration plate. "WD550 series." She smiled. "That stupid, careless man."

"I don't know. I think it's kind of generous of him, handing me an ace."

I locked Young's pistol and the tracking module in my filing cabinet. I gathered notes from the Young and Angelo case files, along with the thumb drive with the call from House Doris, dropped them all in my shoulder bag and headed out the door. "I'm going to make sure Spence collects Young, call on your guy, and get to Young's bank before I head downtown. Police plaza, 10 a.m. sharp."

"Do you have a particular bail bond agent I should call?"

"For what?"

"When this all goes to hell."

"I'm striking 'boundless optimism' from your CV," I said on my way out the door.

When I returned to the Austin Arms, Young was gone.

The room was unlocked, the door open. The bed was tussled. Several spots of fresh blood stained the sheets, more than a simple cut would produce, less than an outright murder. I spotted a business card on the floor, almost under the bed. It was one of mine. I sleeved it in plastic.

The clerk at the front desk wasn't much help. His chunky class ring and confused expression screamed 'home from college, summer job.' "It's a hotel. People come and go all the time."

"At six in the morning?"

"You did."

"Who else?"

"A couple people came in. I haven't seen anyone leave since you did before."

"Do you have cameras on the side doors?"

They didn't.

One wing emptied to a sidewalk beside the street. The other opened into the parking lot adjacent the hotel. I walked the lot once. No obvious signs of struggle there. I was headed inside again when I noticed the hotel stationary sheet under a bush by the door, in a ball. It was the piece of paper with Spence's and my numbers on it.

Young had come out. I had that much, anyway.

Spence was in the lobby when I returned. "Where's our guy?"

"Good question."

"He bolted?"

"I don't think so." I handed him the business card.

"Thanks, but I already know how to find you."

"Yeah, but the blood's not mine. I found it in Young's room." I asked the clerk if he had security cameras in the parking lot.

One of those, they had.

Contrary to the clerk's belief, the camera's position at the corner of the lot and facing towards the lobby for maximum coverage included most of one of the side doors at the edge of its field of view. The camera tech was ancient, the image low definition, but it caught enough. About ten minutes before I returned, Young had rushed out the side door and almost run into the distinctive lines of a Montenegro Mongoose that had rolled up from a spot in the fire lane after apparently spotting him exit. A person in black emerged and hustled him into the back seat. The Montenegro sped from the lot and was gone. There was nowhere near enough resolution for a plate number. The person from inside the car was too far away to identify.

"Take it back to six o'clock," Spence directed the clerk.

The video became a blur. At the 6 a.m. mark, I watched myself exit the lobby, leaving the hotel for my office. Nothing happened for fifteen minutes. Then a car pulled in and parked fairly close to the camera's location. A young woman emerged and hurried to the hotel's lobby.

"That's Donna Pascal," I said.

"The girlfriend?"

Hells. "He must have called her."

A second car circled the lot once, paused behind Pascal's car, then pulled into a slot at the far end. A figure emerged and walked towards the hotel's front entrance, a useless blob. Soon after, the Montenegro swung into the lot and came to a stop in the fire lane. It drove a lap, paused in the same spot, and waited. Young emerged from the side door and his abduction played out again.

"So our pursuers from last night staked Pascal out when they lost us. Young probably called her from here, after I left. She led them right to him."

"Why did he bolt?" Spence watched the abduction again. "See how he comes through the door? He's hustling, and not from them."

Spence asked for a copy of the tape from the clerk, who didn't bother asking for a court order. Then I took Spence upstairs to see the room. He noted the blood. "Someone got more than a scrape. The girlfriend, maybe?"

"If so, it begs the question where she went."

"Think Young was running from her?"

"I doubt it," I said. "Not the way he spoke of her."

Spence took some pictures with his phone and filed an order to seal the room. I walked Spence to his car. Pascal's was still where she'd parked it. "I should have kept him with me."

"Spilled milk, Thib."

"I'd lay money the Mongoose was driven by a couple of NanoDwell security."

"If I knew a judge with a gambling problem who'd take your odds, you might get some action."

"Doesn't matter. Even if you could go fish in their headquarters for him, they could put him in a soundproof room without a door before you got past the lobby. You'd never find him."

"Best I can do right away is pull a list of Mongoose SQs, and see if anything floats to the top."

"Probably stolen. They're not entirely amateur hour, but it's better than nothing."

"What do you plan to do?

I rubbed the bridge of my nose, trying to will away the headache I felt brewing. "Run down a lead on the person who shot at me last night, and retrieve something Young was sending me to get. Something Angelo gave him for safekeeping." I sent him Young's interview audio from my phone.

"Bring Young's evidence. When Koi's done taking your statement, I want one of my own."

"As my liaison officer, it would behoove you to sit in on Koi's. Two birds and such. I'll have some pictures to draw."

Before I left, I gave the desk clerk the photo of Young and Pascal. "This woman's car is parked in your lot. I want you to call me if you see her coming or going, or if that car leaves your lot."

The desk clerk nodded, eyes nervous. "I'll let every shift know."

I walked back to my building, got into my battered car, and headed for the freeway. According to the web, The Bang-Bang Gun Club was off the 45, just south of Conroe. I wished I was surprised a shooting range did enough business to warrant opening at eight in the morning. I hoped Jude Keppler was an early bird.

The Bang-Bang Gun Club was as haphazardly situated as it was named. Without the signs proclaiming GUNS — AMMO—GEAR—CLEANING—CELEBRITY TARGETS—VIRTUAL SHOOT-OUT, the place could have been mistaken for a forgotten barn on an old farm lot. The red paint was sun-blasted pink, and peeling. A rusted weather vane declared a perpetual wind from the southeast. A single long window faced the parking lot, an unblinking eye watching the traffic on the freeway.

I parked between two large pickup trucks. One had the American flag as a paint scheme for the truck's bed. The other had a bumper festooned with stickers denouncing gun control and proclaiming the driver's other vehicle was a Grumman Armored Hovercraft.

I walked inside. Despite closed doors separating the lobby from the rest of the interior, I could hear the pops of gunfire beyond, faux war being waged in the belly of the building. The barks of handguns mingled with the chatter of fully automatic weapons and the occasional buzzer to announce a cease-fire at a particular range. None of it helped my headache. I itched with a desire to get this done and get out.

The clerk nodded at me. He was long-faced with a peach-fuzz haircut and a narrow goatee framing his mouth. He gave me a military once-over, a threat assessment which left him unalarmed. "Good morning. How can I help you?"

"My name is C.T. Robillard. I'm a private investigator. I was referred here by a friend of mine about a ballistics matter for a case I'm working. Can you direct me to Jude Keppler?"

He looked me over again, as if he'd missed something the first time. I wondered if everyone received this much study. "He's in his workshop. Let me buzz him."

The clerk picked up his phone. I took in the variety of shooting medals and trophies on the wall and shelves behind the counter. They formed a rough rectangle of silver and gold around the framed permits issued by the city. The club's members were very successful with their steel.

"He's available," the clerk said. "Down the hallway behind you, third door on the right. Look for the neon bullet." There was new tension in the man's voice. It signaled dislike of either Keppler, or of Keppler's easy acceptance of unknown, snoop-oriented visitors. Neither would have surprised me.

The neon bullet beside the door was rendered in brilliant yellow. It was the perfect shorthand for Keppler's office. His desk was in the center of the room. Around him was a still-life of ballistic science: three-dimensional displays of ammunition styles ranging from musket balls up to 80 mm military heavy shells; canisters of powders for packing one's own munitions; racks of various size and style casings; equipment for assembling it all into ordinance. The walls were filled with Keppler's city permits, shelves of binders and books, gun show posters and firearms manufacturer ephemera.

I thought about Jessica. Fought the urge to toss the place like a tornado.

Inside the open door, three handguns were on display, each in a crushed velvet tray set in a wooden box, under glass and illuminated by museum lighting. The effect was potent. My eyes were drawn to them. "Interesting display. What's the significance?"

Keppler looked up from paperwork and smiled. More personable than the clerk. Plain-featured except for the scars on his right cheekbone and under the right eye. About ten years younger than me, give or take. "From left to right: the guns that killed Lee Harvey Oswald, Mexican President Roberto Alvar, and Rasheed Norris."

"The kid whose murder touched off the Indianapolis Riots?"

"The same."

"That's morbid as hell. How does one acquire guns of such dubious distinction?"

"Auctions, message boards, shop talk." Keppler shrugged. "How does anyone find anything? Impressive, no? Part of a rotating educational display."

"If I thought I could smelt them into a paperweight without being caught, I would."

He was taken aback. "You don't approve?"

"When your wife gets a double-tap in the back of the head from a stranger in the dead of night, it lessens the romanticism around six-guns. Dramatically."

"I'm sorry. I hope they caught whoever it was."

"They haven't, but I didn't come here to tell you my story." I displayed my credentials for his benefit. "My name's Robillard. My associate recommended you. Kristie Barrett."

"Ah. The beguiling Miss Barrett. A human with eagle eyes, so to speak. Did you know she once put a bullet through the center of a nickel at 2,000 yards?"

"Huh. All this time, I thought her threat to punch my nickel was a clumsy idiom."

Keppler fished in his desk, withdrew a bottle of AcheEnder. He held it out. "Here."

"How did you know?"

"There's a vein drumming a cover of 'YYZ' over your left eye."

"I haven't had my coffee yet. Also haven't slept in over a day." I dry-swallowed a couple of caplets.

"I always figured private eyes for guys living by the beach and dating all kinds of beautiful women."

"Collectively, we hate Travis McGee for making this seem so glamorous." The reference slid past him. I dipped my hand in my pocket and produced the slug. "Barrett thought you might be able to tell me something about this bullet. It's part of a case we're working."

Keppler turned the bag with care to see the entirety of the crumpled slug. He pulled on a pair of clean cotton gloves. "May I remove it?"

"Yes."

Keppler crossed the room to a cluttered workbench along the back wall. He pulled the tattered cover from a digital microscope. He set the slug in a clear dish, placed it under the lens and flipped a switch. The dish was illuminated from above and below. Side-by-side images of the visible bullet surface appeared on a screen atop the unit. Keppler worked controls, magnifying, sharpening. He whistled low, even reverent, as if someone had offered to swap him the gun used to assassinate William McKinley for a water pistol. "This is quite a treat. I've never seen one of these up close."

"It's a special bullet?"

"Well, rare." Keppler fiddled some more. "There are a couple dozen guns on the planet that fire these. It's a .48 caliber bullet. Weird duck in a large pond."

"Why so few?"

"The company only made twenty-eight units. It was a small Russian conglomerate, SPG—Saint Petersburg Gun-works. The gun in question was the Izyashchnyy 30. Know what *izyashchnyy* means in Russian?"

I thought of Vetrov. "I don't speak Russian."

"'Graceful.' You see the mark on the bullet's jacket? It's distorted here, but it's a pair of ballet slippers. Appropriate name, too. It's one of the smoothest semi-auto rifles of the last fifty years. Uses a combination of targeted magnetics and pressurized air to eliminate a majority of the recoil." Keppler's voice relaxed, as if the bullet viewed at 40x had mesmerized him. "They could have sold millions of them. A dozen went to our military to test. That's how half of them wound up here. A soldier who's fired one of these babies isn't going to willingly return it."

"I presume the company went bust."

"Of course. Russian concern, down economy, barely enough investors to bankroll the prototypes. They counted on the whole thing in India going tits up. Shuttered the place the day after the treaty was signed." Keppler turned from the screen. "Mother Russia probably wouldn't have paid for them anyway."

"How many of these rifles are in private hands?"

"Pentagon probably has one. Whatever the current Russian equivalent of the Pentagon is has one. Smithsonian has one. NRA museum in Virginia has at least one. They like to be coy. Last census, three had been confirmed destroyed. The rest are in private hands. Where'd you get the slug?"

"My car door."

"No shit?"

"Last night. Going down the highway."

"Lucky it was just the door. It would have left a mark if it had hit you. And by 'mark' I mean 'hole the size of your fist'."

"Is there any way to tell who might have purchased the ammunition? Marks, serial numbers, anything like that?"

Keppler leaned back in his chair and scratched his right ear. "No. Some places can tell you sales location, track by lot numbers, but it's an American conceit. Russians were never worried about it. It was all intended for the military. Who knew?" He shrugged. "I *can* tell you it's original Russian manufacture. There's an outfit in Colorado making right-sized rounds for the gun on special order, but they don't bother with the ballet slippers. Unless the shooter got 'em at the time, they paid through the nose. There's a collector's market for the originals."

"Is there any way of knowing if one of the privately-held ones is here in Houston?"

"Besides the fact you were shot at with it?"

"I'm talking about ownership."

"Hmm. Probably not," Keppler said, but from his expression and the way he drew out the 'probably,' I understood there was. There's a collector's market for everything. Collectors love to talk about their junk.

"How much are these slugs worth?"

Keppler cocked his head. "Well, to a real collector, the unfired cartridge is the draw. Slugs? Hard to say. I guess it depends on what they were used for, what condition they're in when they're recovered."

"What would they be worth to you?" I asked.

"Maybe an anecdote or two. The sort of thing I don't mention to private eyes unless they happen to have rare ordinance in their pockets."

"Do any of these anecdotes perhaps concern someone, somewhere mentioning they have an Izyashchnyy 30 rifle in their gun safe?"

"Perhaps."

"I'll let you have the other slugs from my car, after my mechanic gets them out. Guaranteed to have been used in an attempted murder."

To Keppler's credit, he gave it a moment before agreeing. "I'm weak for a slug with a good story." He rolled his chair to a bookshelf as cluttered as the rest of the room. From between service manuals for the Wren & Han line of firearms, Keppler snatched a bound stack of paper. He flipped to the bottom of the stack and ran his finger down the middle column of three, row after row of small, tight printing. He found what he was seeking in the index and flipped pages. "You can't tell anyone I have this," he said. "I mean, it's a hobby. I'd never do anything with it. But people would freak out if they knew I had it. I don't even keep a digital version, lest a hacker come calling."

"You have my word."

Keppler found the page he was seeking. "There is one identified Izyashchnyy 30 in a collection in the state of Texas, and it lives in our fair city. The owner mentioned it a couple of years ago on a message board for exotic guns. Very proud of it, too. He was one of the military's testers for the Army. Gave it all kinds of glowing words."

"They let him take it home?"

"They probably let him buy it. Government's always up for a few more coins in its purse for things it'll never use again. I have three complete jeeps from Operation Just Desserts alone."

"Do you have a name for the owner?"

"Richard Darvin. Lieutenant, US Army." Keppler studied the page. "Definitely a man who'd be unhappy I took note of his gun." Keppler held up the page to show me. "Sorry, no address noted. Here's the profile picture and mention from the site where he posted."

I studied the face. It was unfamiliar. Cold. Emotionless eyes. The image was casual, taken on a tree-covered hillside and pulled from social media—a man standing outside a tent, stripped to the waist to show a chiseled physique, wearing camouflage pants and holding a military-issue rifle in each hand. He looked the type to buy a gun from his chain of command. Use it to shoot at a civilian car at high speed on the freeway? Different tempo and tune.

I reached into the tray and retrieved the slug.

"Hey—I gave you what you needed. What's the deal?"

"I need this to nail a murderer. The others are still buried in my car. I'll bring them by when I have them in hand."

"A murderer? I thought you were the one shot at?"

"I was. Along with my passenger. He was the primary target. Now he's missing. He's connected to another man who died under mysterious circumstances."

"So this guy who shot at you is a potential mass murderer?"

"I suppose. Does it matter?"

"It makes the slugs a hell of a lot more interesting. Maybe even worthy of the rotating display. The guy who was murdered—was he anybody?"

The question, hell, the whole place was one long stroke of my fur in the wrong direction. "Yeah."

I headed out the door without a look back or a thank you.

I got back on the road for the office and called Barrett. She answered on the first ring. "You're becoming popular."

"Dare I ask?"

"Koi has an unmarked unit across the street. Cops haven't come up yet. I expect they're waiting for you to show."

"Worse than a hall monitor." I angled onto the freeway. "You may have to go downtown without me, but I'll catch up. Young's missing. Spirited away from the hotel by last night's shooters before I got back."

"I don't know, Thib. Maybe you *need* a hall monitor."

You let some pitches roll to the backstop. "Young had a piece of evidence I'm supposed to pick up. I'd like to have it in hand before I sit with Koi."

"Where are you now?"

"Coming back from your house of bullets and mirth. Keppler's a bit of a freak, but he has the goods. The bullets came from Izyashchnyy 30."

"Of course. I should have recognized it from the size. Guy in my unit used one of the rifles in a simulation once. Wore a spent bullet from it around his neck for luck. Didn't help much. I think they buried him with it. So much for ballet shoes as a totem."

"If you can find one, I need an address for an ex-military in the city. Last name is Darvin. First is Richard." I didn't mention Keppler's Big Book of Mined Data about Guns People Own. I expected Barrett was in there. Multiple times.

"And he is?"

"Owner of the gun. By extension, he might also be the person who Swiss-cheesed my car last night."

"Let me see what I can find. Hold, please."

I heard the rhythm of her keystrokes and the click of the mouse. It had a melodic quality I couldn't get my head around, as if she was computing along with a song I couldn't hear. Then I noticed the city police motorcycle closing on me from behind. The bike was in the through lane, and didn't appear to be in a hurry. The officer was unreadable behind sunglasses. I thought he was going to pass. Then I saw the motorcycle's turn signal light up, and the bike moved into the lane behind me. I considered the bullet holes and busted light. They were hard to miss.

The typical time to confirm a license plate with dispatch was thirty seconds, give or take.

"Barrett, do me a favor when you get the information?"

"Sure."

"Ensure the man's address and number are current, and find out all you can: employer, hobbies, relationship status, the name of his fantasy football league, everything. Including if he still has the gun, if possible. Quick as you can. Then call Teo."

There was a pause on the other end. "You're about to get arrested, aren't you?"

I didn't have to answer. The siren on the motorcycle did it for me.

THIRTY-TWO

The motorcycle cop pulled me over on an all-points BOLO from the freeway chase the night before. It was a small blessing, not being related to Young or the arson, but it still put me in a cell where I could resolve nothing.

The police substation in the North Division was a single story, broad instead of tall. It was the only station in the North Division, and one of the oldest in the system. It had a half-dozen holding cells: four of them larger, general population tanks, with two smaller padded-wall spaces for the more violent types. The city was nothing if not obliging, even when you didn't drive friendly.

When the officer behind the desk—a sourpuss career uniform who acted like North Division was a punishment unworthy of his Serpico-level magnificence—finished processing me, he didn't take me to the cell block. Instead, I was delivered to one of building's three interrogation rooms. I'd seen North Division's sweat boxes before. Interrogation 2 was everybody's venue of choice, for its decor versus its intimidating size, and because it had the one-way glass you see in the vids. I don't think anyone in five generations has been fooled into thinking it's really just a long mirror in which the accused can check the part in their hair.

Not that it mattered. Sourpuss took me to Interrogation 3, the Afterthought Suite. They'd repurposed the building's old server room, a dozen electric outlet boxes around the base of the walls mute testament to its previous life. It was windowless. There was an old surveillance camera, but it was anyone's guess if it worked. The table was a relic of a busier precinct. Someone had gotten as far as carving "FUCK THE POLI" in the top before being stopped in mid-stroke, if the jagged, scratched tail on the 'I' was any indication.

Sourpuss told me to take a seat. I pulled a beat-up metal chair away from the table and did as I was told.

"They tell me you're a PI," he said.

"Credentials are in my wallet, if you want to check them."

The cop shook his head. "No need. Who would make up such a sad lie?"

He locked the door behind himself. They were going to let me stew a bit, but not long. Koi was probably en route, less than an hour or so or they'd have put me in a cell.

I waited. My headache diminished. I studied the room as an exercise in finding its weaknesses. I wondered if the raised server room floor was fully secured, how far the crawlspace extended, if there was accessible ductwork down there. When I got bored with the room, I began pondering Mémé's recipes to pass time. The woman was never big on cookbooks, in part because her mom lost most of the family's in Hurricane Katrina. After, Mémé kept three generations of kitchen how-to in her frontal lobe, discarding the stuff she didn't like, passing along what she did. I was walking through Pressed Pigeon and Dungeness Crab in my head when the door slid open and Inspector Koi entered with another officer, a detective named Reed. The door closed behind Reed, the lock snapping tight from the outside.

How do you know when Koi is playing Good Cop, Bad Cop? He brings a good cop with him.

"When you missed our appointment," Koi said, "I thought you might be pulling a fast one. Then I thought you might be in the morgue. I was disappointed to learn someone else got to lock you up before me." There was only one empty chair left at the table, and Koi took it. "Imagine my surprise when I found out one of our wrong-way racers from last night was my favorite investigator. What happened? Lose your sense of direction?"

"A sharp-eyed cop would know from the traffic video."

"I want to hear you tell it."

"I was being pursued by a Montenegro Mongoose. No more than a couple of years old. Two door, tinted glass, rear spoiler, SQ package. At least a driver and a shooter. Never saw either face. The car's left headlight flickers."

"I don't suppose you got a license plate."

"Never saw either plate, but the shooter was giving my car a high-caliber detailing. Letting him pass me was low on the priority list. I'll own what I did, but in my defense I was trying to keep from being killed."

Koi looked at Reed. Reed beckoned with two fingers. Koi fished a ten from his wallet and handed it over. "That's disappointing. I thought for sure you'd stonewall me on being shot at. Why haven't you reported it yet?"

"I figured I would while I was at the station. Two birds, one trip to the principal's office. I thought you'd appreciate the efficiency."

Koi's gaze made me feel like a turkey about to be carved. "Any idea who was in the Mongoose?"

"Not yet. I was working on the answer this morning when I got pulled over."

"Who would want to kill you, Crawdad?"

"Had we gotten to talk, I could have filled you in on the broad tapestry of the murder of Stephen Angelo, his connection to wanted firebug Herb Young, and what I believe actually happened to the apartment house on Rose Street. You won't believe that last part, but we're far enough past April first for me to throw it at you responsibly."

Koi's left eyebrow dipped, barely perceptible, enough to tell me he was actually listening.

"Anyway, if I were a gambling man, as you are with Detective Reed, I would say the people in the Mongoose weren't shooting at me, but at the man in the back seat who abducted me from this morning's arson-turned-building explosion."

"Does your human target have a name?"

I didn't bat an eye. "You already know it's Young."

Reed didn't catch his chuckle before it escaped. Koi went to his wallet for a second ten and handed it over to Reed. He opened a folder and passed a few large still images to me. I shuffled through them. There I was, behind the wheel, mouth open, talking. Young sat behind me, clear as a yearbook photo.

"Nice resolution." I looked from Koi to Reed. "You should have bet bigger."

Reed shrugged. "He wanted me to go fifty that you wouldn't say it."

I studied the images, years of reviewing highway and building surveillance screen caps screaming at me. "This is especially bad form, Inspector."

"Why? Because I have evidence of you fleeing the scene with a suspect you claimed to know nothing about not a half-hour before?"

I gave him a cold stare. "Do you want to do this next bit with another cop in the room?"

I'm not sure whose expression was better: Reed's sudden confusion, or Koi's nascent attempt to stare me down. The latter ended in his blink. "Reed, give us a couple of minutes."

Reed, now insanely curious how the dynamic had shifted, knocked on the door and was let out. When the door was locked again, I preempted whatever Koi was winding up.

"That you expect anyone to believe this is a screen capture from a traffic camera along the 69 is ludicrous. This is from a drone. Probably the WorldWatch 550 drone you've had over my head for the past few weeks. Nice resolution, though you could have gotten my good side."

He pulled them from my hand.

"No worries," I said. "Reed's seen them. My attorney will get them on discovery. Is your drone department issue? Do you have a surveillance warrant? Or are you taking recreational pictures of me on your own time with department equipment? Because I know you didn't buy that drone on your pay, unless you're on the take. I have just a sliver enough respect to doubt you're an IAD case."

Koi glared. Color rose in his cheeks. "Any other questions?"

"Yeah. What sort of self-indulgent asshole does a drone overfly on a running gun battle on the freeway involving civilians without sending units to intervene?"

He said nothing. You'd think I'd read him his rights.

"Of course, we both know it's on automatic, lifting off and following my car every time it moves. That was the whole reason for the telemetry module tucked up behind my bumper: so you didn't have to monitor it constantly. You don't have to worry, though—the module survived the firefight. It's in a really safe place, waiting for Barrett to dig into it for a serial number. Is it going to match a drone registered to you, Inspector?"

"Are you done?"

"No. But *you* might be. I get you don't like me, Koi. That's as mutual as it comes. You want to play, I'm a gamer. Maybe we're both in felony territory right now. The difference between you and me is I can prove *you* are."

Koi denied me the pleasure of an explosion we both wanted. "Before I have you transferred downtown for processing on harboring, aiding and abetting a fugitive—"

"He abducted me at gunpoint."

"—obstruction of justice, the reckless driving charge, and the other few I'm sure to come up with on the way, do you know where Young is now?"

"Book me and give me my phone call."

"Give me what I want and I'll cut you loose."

"The hell you say. Call a car, take me downtown, give me my phone call, and talk to my lawyer."

He stood and walked to the door. Knocked. Reed opened it from the outside.

"We're done. Have him sent downtown." I wasn't sure if he turned back and talked tough for Reed's benefit or to reassure himself he somehow still had a hand to play. "I'm out twenty bucks, but it's worth it. This time next week, I'm going to be lighting my cigar on the flames from your investigator's license."

I looked at Reed. "Ask him for action on that. Go three figures."

THIRTY-THREE

They moved me downtown in time to make a full statement and sit in a cell overnight. I knew formal charges and arraignment could have been done before court recessed for the day. Koi wanted me in a cell while he searched for Young. My cellmates were a passed-out drunk and a guy who was too nervous to be dangerous. I tried to talk to him, ease his mind, but five minutes of attempt told me it was a lost cause. Sleep was easy after not having any for the 36 hours preceding, and deep considering I was in a holding cell.

The next morning, they took me to a small room to confer with my attorney. Barrett had received my one phone call with too much delight for a jail morning, and agreed to set Teo Arnaz in motion; but the person who walked in wasn't Arnaz. Arnaz was an old Cuban expat with the build of a late-model Orson Welles. The guy they showed in looked like a varsity letterman, distinctly non-Cuban and non-heavy. His hair went in four directions simultaneously, and the crystal blue of his eyes seemed unnaturally bright. His dark suit and power tie somehow pulled the disparate package together.

He thanked the officer when he entered and extended a hand to me. "Mister Robillard. I'm with Ryan, Jasen, Anders & Henne. My name is Ryan."

I shook his hand and blinked. "You're the Ryan-on-the-marquee Ryan?"

The man chuckled. "Oh, no. Sorry. I'm Ryan Pierpont. The Ryan on the marquee is Augustus Ryan. Jeez, I wish I had his knowledge of the law." He stopped. "That came out wrong."

"Miss Barrett phoned you?"

He sat across from me. "She asked me to relay she was unable to engage Mister Arnaz on account of his recent forced retirement to the La Tuna Federal Correctional Institution."

"The feds sent my attorney to prison?"

"His firm was involved in an insurance fraud scheme with a couple of local cancer doctors."

"Then he probably deserves to be at LaTuna. How did I not hear about this?"

Pierpont shrugged. "You tell me. I'm the new guy."

"How new are you, if you don't mind my asking?"

"No worries. People ask all the time. I look twenty. I'm 31. I have over 200 successful judgments to my credit, and my current streak is 53. Soon to be 54." He scrolled on a tablet. "I've read your statement and Inspector Koi's report."

"He was working up quite a laundry list yesterday. Aiding and abetting a fugitive, obstruction of justice. I think he was reaching a little with 'hazard to navigation'."

"Bluster. Word is he does that a lot. You're down for arraignment on a single count of reckless driving. I gather you two have an antagonistic relationship?"

"Are you familiar with the works of Tom and Jerry?" I asked.

"I am. Are you the mouse or the cat?"

"Depends on the day."

"Today, you're the mouse and he's the idiot if he thinks he's going to get a Class A misdemeanor charge to stick. Video from traffic cameras, coupled with your statement and witness statements, plus the bullet holes in your car? They'll seek maximum bail of $2,000, and you'll get it back when the city drops it. I mean, you were running for your life."

"Bullet holes do make a compelling argument."

"And you didn't kill or maim anyone. What's this I hear about a drone?"

"Did Barrett tell you about that?"

"No. Same people who say Koi blusters a lot suggest he's been playing "Eye In The Sky" on repeat for you."

I shrugged. "Unless he has a surveillance warrant I don't know about, I think he's bored. Though he may still think I murdered my wife."

Pierpont blinked at me. "Let's bookmark that for another day." He found his place again in his notes. "Given his long list of grievances has come down to a single charge that will go away in short order, I get the sense he wants any indiscretion to crawl into the shadows and be forgotten. You do probably have grounds for a civil suit."

"I'd just as soon hold onto my sword of Damocles for a little while. At the least, he owes me a soft shell crab dinner I want to collect on."

Pierpont nodded. "Just a thought. My firm's rates are reasonable. Anyway, I stopped at impound on my way in and took my own pictures of the car. You can never have too much evidence of violence and near-death. For this morning, we're going to enter a plea of Not Guilty, you're going to refrain from making faces at the inspector or the judge—"

"I don't make faces."

"You've made two of them at me in the last minute or so."

"You and Barrett are going to get along famously."

"I'm going to motion that the charges be dismissed. That will fly like a glass jar of marbles, but I *will* get you released on your own recognizance. You'll pay your bail, and we'll walk out of here to design the case in your favor. That buys you time to explain it all to me in excruciating detail, and me time to make it airtight enough to snuff a mouse. It also pressures the police to locate the fancy car with the ugly gun and homicidal driver."

"Wasn't I just the mouse in this metaphor?"

"I use a ton of metaphors with my clients, C.T.—can I call you C.T.?"

"Thib."

"Thib. It keeps me from using metaphors in court. Call it my pressure valve. It's incumbent upon you to keep up and keep them straight. Are we agreed on my road map?"

"We are."

"Good. Now, seeing as we have a little time, how would you like to fill me in on the size and shape of the fire ant mound you've fallen into with this Herb Young?"

I was the second case of the morning, after my drunk cellmate pleaded No Contest. Koi didn't show up for the arraignment, nor was he waiting outside with a change of handcuffs. A bored city attorney I didn't know argued the city's position. Pierpont was quick, efficient, and introduced neither mice nor fire ants into the discourse. In the end, he predicted everything except the bail, which came in at $1,000.

The city attorney and court both agreed with a business downtown and a home being rebuilt in the Heights, I posed no flight risk. Trial date was set for three weeks later. In the end, my bail was paid and I walked out the front door with my new lawyer.

"I'll call you to arrange a meeting this week to go over everything you have. Until then, I have a regimen I recommend to all of my clients who are out on bail."

I guessed. "Keep the fox out of the hen house?"

I might have had a screw loose, the look he gave. "No. Don't make me look stupid for getting you back on the street."

"I'll do my best."

"Sorry I couldn't get your car untangled."

"No worries," I said. "I did it to myself when I opted to make it evidence in my case. At least I can get at it in the city impound if need be." There was nothing of importance inside. My messenger bag had been checked with my belongings when I was booked and handed back intact when I was released.

"Can I ask you a stupid question that's been swinging on one of my brain cells since reading your statement?" he asked.

"Sure."

"Why didn't you just drive Young to the police when you knew his gun wasn't loaded?"

"I didn't believe he was safe, even in police lockup. The people who want him—who may already have him—are very cozy with the cops."

We crossed the street ahead of a lumbering city dump truck. "You lead an interesting life, huh?"

"It has its moments."

"I hate interesting lives," he said. "They ruin my win/loss ratio and mess up my sleep."

"I'd start taking naps." We stopped in front of the municipal lot. Morning rush hour downtown was in full swing. "Not to unduly burden you on your first day, but I've got another case I'm working on with which I could use some legal assistance."

"You're in luck. I'm hourly."

"Do well, and I'll send you a check once a month to keep you on retainer."

He scowled. "This is beginning to sound like my vid subscription service. I kinda hate my vid subscription service."

"I'm really less work than I appear."

Someone in a Mercedes went past, honking the horn. Pierpont waved. "You're not work. That guy? He's work. And apparently out again." He sighed. "What do you need?"

"I'd like to see if you can arrange a prison visit."

"We spent this morning trying to avoid a prison visit."

"There's an inmate in the Federal medium security facility in Yazoo City, Mississippi. Last name Price, first name Martin. He's doing a stretch for attempted bank robbery."

"Did he do it?"

I shrugged. "Depends on the semantics. He shot a ceiling, set his gun on the ground, and surrendered without ever asking for cash. Jury decided he did it to the tune of 18 years.

A breeze blew along the canyon of downtown. It was a competition between Pierpont's hair and tie to see which rustled more. "I'm not taking that appeal."

"I need to interview him regarding an old case."

"Another robbery?"

"No. Something different." I considered Pierpont, and my sin of omission with Spence. "Attorney-client privilege?"

"Absolutely."

"I think he may be involved with my wife's murder."

Pierpont shook his head. "No one understands bookmarks anymore. When was this murder?"

"Seven years ago."

He nodded and spoke notes on Price into his mobile. "I'll make a couple of calls, find out who his attorney is, shake the hive. People being nosy, they may want details. 'Old investigation' should suffice for now. Trickier to get an interview, though. An inmate has to put you on the 'visitor' list. Something about random people walking in and trying to conduct reprisals or pass contraband. The feds. Such sticklers." Pierpont jerked a thumb at a clutch of parked hoppers. "You need a ride anywhere? It's a hoof back to your office."

"No thanks. Barrett's picking me up. Some loose ends from yesterday need tying."

"I'll be in touch," Pierpont said. "Remember: don't make me look stupid." He walked off to his hopper.

I refrained from a crack about the man's untamed hair. There'd be a better opportunity down the line.

I waited, scanned the sky lanes for Barrett's hopper. Checked my watch. I was about to call when her motorcycle stopped in front of me. She popped the helmet visor open.

"No," I said.

"Don't be a baby." She handed me the spare helmet she kept strapped to the seat behind her.

"Where's the hopper? I spent all morning working up the nerve to fly with you. I can't shift gears that quickly."

"No problem. I'll go really fast and jump over things. Same effect."

"You should be nicer to me. I spent the night in jail."

"Whose fault is that? Besides, it's easier to shake a tail on this thing, and if the two plainclothes lackeys in the sore-thumb express behind us are any indication, Koi still believes you can lead him to Young."

I didn't turn. Didn't need to. I wasn't surprised Koi was keeping an eye. I took satisfaction in a motorized tail. It meant he'd suspended his drone activity. I could shame him. It was a powerful achievement to have unlocked. "How did I not know Teo went to prison?"

"You stay out of trouble and pay your bills and eat your peas, so you don't need to regularly call a scumbag cancer-patient defrauding attorney for help?"

"You appear to be out of sugar coating."

I pulled the helmet on and heard Barrett's voice through speakers on the inside. "Where are we going?"

I mounted the bike and tightened the messenger bag strap until the bag was flush against the front of me. My hands formed a knuckle-whitening bond with the small grips on the sides of the seat. "We're going to a bank to make a withdrawal."

The ride was only terrifying for the first three minutes, the time it took Barrett to lose Koi's tail.

THIRTY-FOUR

As we cruised, Barrett warned me, "A screen is going to come on in front of your eyes. Don't let it scare you off the bike."

The glow of a heads-up display built into the visor faded in. A series of documents appeared.

"How much am I paying you again?" I asked.

"Hush. I built this myself with scraps. Completely hands free. Voice or eye control interface."

"Distracted driving at its finest."

"Visuals are only in the passenger helmet. Mine's fully voice interface. Do you want your information, or not?"

"Apologies. What am I looking at?"

"Search results for Richard Darvin. Lieutenant, US Army. Two tours overseas, honorable discharge five years ago. Stand-up guy on paper."

I figured out how to turn pages with my eyes. The first time one flipped, I felt like the bike was going to flip with it. Darvin's record was full of commendations and a couple of strong recommendations from his chain of command.

Barrett continued. "After three years out, he decided to re-up with the Army and left Houston. He's currently detached with the Mountain Warfare School in Jericho, Vermont. Turns out he has a knack for carabiners."

"That makes him unlikely as my shooter."

"Try impossible. I spoke to him this morning. He's been in Vermont for the last five weeks."

"Well done."

"Never underestimate the desire of the military to patch through calls from ex-military. They act like every touch is a potential recruiting scenario."

I held my breath as she whipped around a fuel tanker. "What about the gun?"

"He had an Izyashchnyy 30. He was one of the lucky dogs who got to field test them. Then he bought it through a program the Army offered for soldiers of certain rank and higher with exemplary records. The Army dealt the rifles when it became clear the Russians didn't care if they ever got them back. He says, and I quote, 'I loved that gun.'"

"Loved it, huh? I don't suppose he remembers who he sold it to."

"He didn't sell it. He was married to a very special Special Forces gal who he moved to Houston with when they got out."

"Dana Sami."

"The one and only."

"Hells."

"Be glad she's not as proficient with it." She slipped between a couple of cars and cut hard for a ramp off the freeway. "Also, your translator is done. Play file Test1.wav."

A sequence of digital noise squealed through the speakers. The call disconnected.

"What am I listening to?"

"Wait for it," she said.

A second recording began. I heard Barrett say, "Hello?"

The respondent's voice was mechanical, but different from House Doris. This voice was more measured, almost human in its diction. "This is Charlie. Interface protocol 2A. Is that you, Doris? This is not your designated interface."

A couple moments without response and the call disconnected.

"How did you get through?"

"I spoofed House Doris's PBX. The call went right through. I also added interpolation into the algorithm to make the translations more accommodating. Pauses in the right places, common rhythmic forms. It'll make what Charlie says easier to parse real-time."

"You also made him sound male."

"And?"

"Charlie might also be feminine."

She bristled. "My father and aunt were fraternal twins. Sue me for writing what I know."

"What about my side of the conversation?"

"You'll need to keep it basic. Tonal qualities won't translate, so stressing words will get you nowhere. Neither will wordplay or sarcasm."

"What are you trying to say?"

"You'll need a whole new way of communicating. Screaming won't work, either."

"When have I ever—"

Barrett interrupted with a tight, high-speed weave around a large moving van.

Loretta, the clerk at the Bellaire Credit Union branch along the 290, was a fan of Herb Young. "He coaches my grandson in youth basketball. My grandson is no Micah Mannau. Can't pivot on the dribble to his left to save his hide. Herb plays him anyway. It's a kindness."

She verified my credentials. Satisfied, she led me to the vault. Opening Young's receptacle took her thumbprint and my facial scan to match the ID image Young had sent. She opened the door and withdrew the long metal box. "When he said he was ill and needed you to pick up something for him, my heart went out. And if he's engaged a private investigator to help him, I don't believe for a minute what the awful media is saying on the streams."

I said nothing. If investigation taught me anything, it was how fragile a thing trust was. Too soon she'd have to deal with its brokenness. It wasn't a plow I needed to speed.

Loretta left me alone with the box. I opened it and withdrew the document of names and control numbers, and a set of pages with internal NanoDwell records reference numbers and file names, a map to where the related build matrices would be found in their file system. I photographed each page with my phone, sent the images to the office cloud account, and slipped the originals into my messenger bag. Nature abhors a single copy. There was nothing else inside.

The box was replaced, the door secured. Loretta ushered me from the vault. "You just tell Herb when you see him Loretta hopes he has a speedy recovery and she believes in him."

I was crossing the lot to where Barrett waited beside her motorcycle when my mobile chirped. I checked the display. Spence. I answered, "I'm on my way."

Spence spoke softly and fast. "Do you want the bad news, or the worse news?"

"Remember when good news was a thing?"

"Herb Young is dead. They fished his body out of White Oak Bayou early this morning, near West Tidwell. Time of death was around 7 p.m. yesterday evening."

"Hells."

"Joggers spotted him this morning, face down in the water. He was about ten yards from the West Tidwell bridge. The body caught on some debris, or it might have washed all the way downtown. They're still trying to figure out what happened to him. It appears he asphyxiated."

"You mean drowned."

"No. There were trace amounts of water in his lungs, but he didn't drown on it. Post mortem. Also, it wasn't bayou water. Way too clean. There are also no ligature marks, so he wasn't strangled. He was suffocated somehow, and the water came after."

"Staged."

"From all appearances. There was a note, a lament about the Rose Street victims."

"Hells, there's worse news?"

"Koi recovered a cached form from Young's cell phone to his bank from yesterday morning so you could access a safety deposit box. He's measuring pikes for your head."

"Tell him I'm a size 7 and 3/4. Any news on Pascal?"

"None. West division sent a unit by her place. Nobody home. Car's still at the Austin Arms."

I thought about the blood. Had they struggled? Lover's spat upon an unhappy reunion? Unlikely. I was still missing a number in the equation. I hate math. "In light of this, I'm not on my way yet."

"I should have you picked up and brought in. I'm dangerously close to aiding and abetting."

"Maybe. You also still might make Lieutenant. At the very least you'll be a hero cop."

"Great. They love hero cops in the Lychner Unit."

I motioned to Barrett for my helmet. "Meet Barrett at the Jack at the Menil in thirty minutes. She'll have a packet useful in getting a search warrant for NanoDwell headquarters: my notes on Angelo and Young, the material Angelo gave him from NanoDwell, and the decoded phone call from Rose Street. Short form: NanoDwell used human DNA without knowledge and consent of the donors, including Young, to advance their biotech housing business. I believe when they realized what Angelo had taken, they killed him. Young was burning buildings that contained his genetic material. I believe someone from NanoDwell torched Rose Street to hide the truth, using Young's arsons as cover."

"Why would NanoDwell burn Rose Street?"

"Not only could it prove the use of the genetic material, it was also sentient."

He was quiet for a moment. "A sentient building?"

"I don't make them up, Spence. I just solve them."

"Where are you going?"

"To finish solving. Then I'll be in."

"Step lively," Spence said. "Avoid your office. It's got blue eyes."

I tucked my phone away. Barrett stared. "That was terse."

"Young's dead." I straddled the bike behind her. "Koi still has people on the office. Probably on your place, too. I want you to take the file packet to Spence. Parking lot next to the Jack sculpture at the Menil museum."

"The six pointed red thing?"

"You know Russian bullets but not antique kids' games?"

She shrugged. "How would I meet new people on trivia night if I knew everything?" She slipped the material into her bike's saddle bag. "Where are we going?"

"It's your lucky day: one more field trip."

Fifteen minutes later, Barrett pulled over at the intersection of two streets in River Oaks. I called NanoDwell. Dana Sami was out of the office, her alternate Friday off.

"It would be best if you went back to the PD with Spence," I told her. "To answer any questions they or the judge have about the call, and to send me any intel I may need."

She agreed, reluctantly. "What if you need back-up?"

"I'm going to use charm. It doesn't need back-up."

"Uh-huh. Should I have your new lawyer on standby?"

"No. Too soon to piss him off."

Barrett pulled the motorcycle back into traffic and was gone. I walked up the sidewalk. As a rule, I hated ruining someone's day off. For Sami, I didn't mind the exception.

Sami's home was opulent, even by River Oaks old money standards. Built in the style of a Tuscan villa, it was two stories with a citadel on the driveway side. A large garage with additional living space peeked from behind the house, at the far end of the driveway. It was all the color of sandstone. Heat shimmered off the terracotta roof. There were abundant windows facing the front yard, which separated the house from the perimeter fence by approximately thirty yards. The lawn was inviting, but the fence was black wrought iron, spaced the width of a man's fist and capped with barbs that appeared functional versus decorative. Gates of identical style crossed the driveway entrance, as well as a pedestrian entry to the left of the drive.

Sami's car was parked in front of the closed garage. It wasn't a Montenegro Mongoose; rather, a BMW convertible the color of jade. Beside it was a recreational hopper, a sport model in blue and gold.

I pressed the button on the intercom at the front gate. A small video screen with speakers to each side flickered to life with a message in block letters, PLEASE WAIT. It was thirty seconds before the message vanished, replaced by Sami's face. She appeared disheveled. Her eyes were sleepy. "Mister Robillard. Good morning."

"Sorry to disturb you at home on your day off," I said. "I wanted to catch you up on the matter of Stephen Angelo."

"This is a pleasant surprise, but you didn't need to come over. You could have called."

"I should have first, I'm sorry. It also concerns Herb Young. I wanted to talk through some things before I headed to Inspector Koi's office. You seemed the best person with whom to hash them out."

"Of course. Come in. I'll put some coffee on."

The screen blinked off. At the same time, a chime welcomed me through the pedestrian gate and into the lion's den.

She met me at the door, still in her robe, a swath of bright white terrycloth that ran from her neck to her ankles, cinched at the waist. I didn't recognize the hotel logo on the breast, then foolishly realized it was her own monogram.

"I'm sorry," I apologized again when she welcomed me in. "I remember you mentioning you were off alternate Fridays, but I didn't realize I was going to wake you."

"I wasn't really asleep. There's a lot going on at work, between IPO meetings and new security screenings. With the most recent arson, Mister Phalen has decided to re-check everyone at headquarters. Three hundred fresh background checks to determine if anyone was helping Angelo or working with this Herb Young, and he wants them done before next Wednesday."

"That's serious leg work."

"He also wants polygraphs."

The front foyer was expansive, with doorways leading in four different directions: an archway to a living room, a more narrow hallway towards the back of the house, a second wide doorway into what looked like a library, and an open arch into the kitchen. A stairway hugged the wall, curving up to the second floor. The entire place was marble and hardwoods, sparsely decorated. For someone who got everything in the divorce, she didn't have much more than a few sticks of furniture.

She lead me through the arch into the kitchen: ceramic tile floor, marble counters, and stainless steel appliances. It was a setup a pro chef could envy. I hadn't cooked a meal in months, and was a little jealous. It was separated from a larger dining room by a four-seat counter. Beyond the many windows of the dining room, I saw the back yard accommodated a swimming pool and built-in barbecue.

"This is quite a place. I may want to rethink investigation for corporate security." I took a seat at the counter.

"It's too much for one person. It won't keep me from living in it, at least until the market rebounds." She started the coffee maker. "To be honest, it's nicer than Mister Phalen's place out west. He doesn't have a yard to speak of. He keeps offering to swap. Not on his life. This thing is paid for."

"It must have been a hell of a divorce."

"He should have kept it in his pants."

I glanced around the walls, the ceiling. "This isn't bots and sand, is it?"

"No. It's traditional. Sixty years old, give or take, with an extensive remodel after we bought it. If I decide to downsize, who's to say what I get in its place?" She hunted in a cabinet for a coffee cup. "Now, what did you want to discuss? You said something about Angelo and Young?"

"Based on your company's presence at the fire the other night, I gather it was Young who received the information Angelo passed from your company's files."

She didn't bat an eye. "Yes. I also have a working theory: Young murdered Angelo after their transaction, and tried to make it look like an accident."

"Have you heard Young is dead?"

"When?"

"Sometime last night."

"I'd heard he got away from the fire scene in Richmond. Did the police kill him?"

"No. Apparent suicide. Drowned in White Oak Bayou."

The coffee maker finished its cycle and Sami tended it. She passed me a cup. "Don't think me harsh, but I'm not sorry to hear he's dead. His odd obsession with burning our buildings, House Doris, his dealing with Angelo. It's horrible he killed himself, but I'm going to sleep better as a result."

"His death tied up some loose ends, but my investigation suggests Young may not be the only one Angelo slipped information to."

Unchecked surprise crossed her face. "What do you mean?"

"Angelo's leak may have been to as many as a dozen people."

"What?"

"On the plus side, none appear to be competitors of yours."

"Who on earth would he have sent information to?"

Time to swing away. "Other people in the same position as Young. People whose DNA was harvested by your company and subsequently used in developing your technology. People for whom Angelo's conscience couldn't bear the weight anymore, given how once upon a time, he was the technician who did the harvesting."

I saw the little tic in her poker face. She already knew. "DNA harvesting? That's quite a bedtime story."

"I was skeptical when Young first told it to me yesterday morning after he and I were nearly shot to death on the freeway.

Before he was snatched, he sent me to retrieve the rest of the DNA donor list Angelo passed him. That was the first mistake the shooters made: not killing Young before he spoke to someone."

"The first?"

"Of several. They used an ill-considered gun for the job, too distinctive and easily traced. They staged Young's suicide with a lack of attention to detail. They let me get my hands on the full file Angelo stole. But the biggest one?"

Her face was calm. Her gaze suggested she was contemplating murder. "Yes?"

"The shooter and her driver thought I'd go to the rodeo without my boots."

I slipped from the stool as the man approaching behind me swung the small club clenched in his fist.

THIRTY-SIX

The billy club cracked the back of the stool. No time to telescope the baton, so I punched the man's face with it clenched in my fist. As he reeled, I snapped it open and struck his left leg. It was my NanoDwell surveillance friend. He was in sweatpants, and collapsed to his right knee when the left buckled sideways. I hit him again, hard enough to crack some ribs. Then I was behind him, my arm and the baton around his neck. I hoisted him to unsteady feet and put him between me and Sami as Sami leveled her pistol.

"You're good," she said.

"Common sense. One to drive and one to shoot. If you had an accomplice, it stood to reason long hours and the intimate nature of things like attempted murder and body disposal would bring you closer. Plus you already had two coffee cups out when you went looking for mine. But to be honest, I wouldn't have seen his shadow on the refrigerator if he hadn't crossed in front of the windows behind me."

"How did you know I didn't have a gun?" the man asked through pain-clenched teeth. The metal of the baton being used in the choke hold didn't help his projection.

"I didn't. I took the chance you were trained well enough to not put her in danger by having her downrange in the line of fire."

Sami studied me with a mixture of curiosity and amusement. "I underestimated you. I figured the police only farmed cases out to hacks doing snoop jobs, cop wannabes. I should have known better after you walked away from Hershe Street with only a couple of dings."

I didn't tell her how close she'd come at Hershe Street. "I get the sniping thing now. You wanted the distance. You didn't know if one or both of us would come out, or if Barrett was carrying or not. You couldn't risk one of us surviving an up-close shooting attempt and being able to identify you."

"I was surprised you brought her along. I'd planned to kill her later, at your building."

"She's been on me about field trips all week. Who programmed Hershe? The one-door thing was genius."

"We have someone on the team who designs for us. He codes, we load."

"Much better work than Angelo's apartment. Do you use a universal override code for all your building control units, or is it model-based? Settling a bet."

"You'd have to ask an engineer."

"I thought you'd know, seeing as you used it to drop the floor out from under Angelo in his apartment, after he let you in. What did you tell him to put him at ease? That you were going to clear him?"

"Exactly that. Angelo brought himself to my attention. Just like you. And I dealt with him, like I'll deal with you."

"I know what *I'm* going to do with him," the man said through the choke hold.

"Shut up, Marcus. I'll make sure you get in a lick or two before it's done."

I looked at Sami. "I figure you for the quiet one at my office break-in. Considering this one's voice and lack of limp, I'm going to guess he did all the talking and cratered his chest pulling out the electro charge."

"Well deduced," she said. "Do you know who the third person is?"

"I do. He's the one who pleas out for an immunity deal to save himself at your expense."

"There'll never be an immunity deal. This is where you join your wife."

"Make sure you do it right," I said. "I want professionalism. Not the half-assed job you did disposing of Young. "

Sami shook her head. "No, no, no. Herb Young killed himself. Threw himself in a bayou and drowned in his grief."

Marcus tensed, as if bracing to buck away from me. I chased the notion off with a kidney punch. "Someone might have believed that before one of you geniuses put clean water in his dead lungs, instead of actual bayou water."

Sami stared over the gun at Marcus. The contempt of her gaze spilled into her voice, the first crack in her perpetual facade of cool. "You stupid bastard."

"You told me to put water in his lungs, I put water in his lungs."

"How does he drown on tap water in a runoff channel?" I heard the creak in her voice. She could see it unspooling. Knowing it was faked, the cops would check surveillance cameras and drone flyover footage and canvass the neighborhood. Someone could have seen them. The clock was ticking, and she was riding the sweep hand to the bottom.

Marcus persisted, powered ahead by wounded pride. "If you'd managed to shoot anyone anytime you had the chance, none of this would be an issue."

Sami wounded more than his pride. She popped a bullet into Marcus's chest. We both jerked at the impact. The slug didn't pass through him, but Marcus went limp. I couldn't tell if he was dead or merely on his way.

"The first thing I learned in basic training: always tie your ends in knots." Calm fell across Sami again like a drape. "Marcus was a good partner. A decent lay, too. Maybe a bit grabby. But he knew everything, and it was only a matter of time before he figured out knowledge had value."

I backed towards the dining room, dragging Marcus as a shield. He was like a sack of grain with hooks at the corners.

"What I need to know," Sami said, "is where this DNA donor list is."

"Already with the cops."

Sami shook her head. "If you'd involved the cops, they'd already be here. You wouldn't be stupid enough to come alone."

I thought of Hershe Street again and bit my tongue. I saw the arch into the hallway in my peripheral vision.

She caught my glance. "There's nowhere you can go in this house I can't beat you to or find you in. I just need Marcus to wear you out. I'm here for the marathon." She relaxed her stance, a dare. "You know, I did my homework on you. The whole thing with your wife's murder? Fascinating tale. Koi still thinks you were involved. The way he goes on, you'd think he had a crush." She stared, her smile broken, the barrel of her gun a pointer. "Come on, Robillard. Just us killers here. You can tell me. Did you do it?" She cocked her head. It made her grin more crooked. As she aimed again, I shoved Marcus away and ducked into the dim light of the hallway.

The front foyer teased at the end of the hall, but I had to pass the kitchen entry to get there. I went in the opposite direction. An outer door, an opening window, a spot to hide so I could double-back on my path if she pursued and missed me.

I skipped the first two doors I passed. If unlocked, they'd cost her time to check. I reached the end of the hallway, intent on a back door.

Instead, the hall ended in a T-intersection. To the right, a laundry area with solid glass block windows and transoms I wouldn't fit through. To the left, a back staircase led to the second floor. I chose the staircase, carpet masking my footfalls.

She called after me from back in the kitchen, her tone jovial. "The doors and windows are locked via central security control. All the glass panes are high-grade triple laminate. Even if you had a real gun and not a sad little electro, you wouldn't be going through one of them. And I believe you've already met my cell jammer."

At the top of the stairs, I slipped through the first door on the left. It was a large bathroom, brown marble and twin sinks. I continued into the spacious master bedroom suite. The walls had various images of Sami in uniform, in suits, posed with politicians or celebrities. I recognized a few of the faces, one of them a president. I lingered long enough to confirm there wasn't a weapon unlocked and available in the night stand. No phone. Probably no landline.

I tried a window. Saw the electronic lock. No bluff there.

She called again. "I suppose you could go to the attic and look for a weak spot in the roof. Try bashing your way out with your baton. Then again, it might be reinforced against the heat. I'll be down here. Take your time. It's my day off."

She had me caged. It would only be so long before she'd weary of the game, flush me out.

She had to be in or near the front atrium. With everything sealed, it was the choke point. If I tried the front door from any direction, she had me. If I made for the doors to the yard from the dining room, she had me. Everything else was too much time to break through or overcome before she came running. The foyer made the best tactical sense for her: line of sight to all the connecting spaces, and long lead time for anyone descending the stairs. Master security controls were probably there as well.

"Looking for a gun? They're all locked up too. I may not have kids, but the Army teaches a healthy respect for not leaving firearms laying around where trespassers might grab them."

I crossed the bedroom and opened a sliding closet door. I didn't find what I wanted. I slipped across the hallway into a guest bedroom. I had to slide a treadmill out of the way to get to the closet there.

Sami continued. "I knew you'd take the bait for Hershe Street when I left it. You're smart, but arrogant. It was an easy string to pull. To be honest, when you opened the door after the reformat, I almost let you walk away. I was that impressed."

I found a roller suitcase in the closet. Unzipped it and the smaller bag within. From beside the treadmill, I selected three twenty-pound weights from a rack, wrapped a towel around them, and set the parcel inside. I zipped the bags closed. I didn't need much weight. I crept out the door and moved with the bag to the foyer end of the upstairs hall. She was louder now, waiting down where I'd suspected.

"Your partner is a hell of a shot. Her second round almost came through my scope. Whoever trained her did it right. Too bad I'll have to kill her next. Brothers in arms should mean more, you know?"

The railing overlooking the foyer was supported by dowels. Too far onto the landing, standing too tall, and she'd see me before I could act. I didn't need to see the gun to know she had it ready. I extended the handle on the roller bag until it clicked, locked. I rolled it to the lip of the top step. I turned my body to put myself in a crouch. It was awkward.

"For all I know, Barrett helped you kill your wife. Recon snipers are notoriously shady. Maybe she commits the murder with your gun, you play the grieving husband. You can tell me. I won't tell another living soul. I promise." Her tone had an insane solemnity.

Possibly dying was worth shutting her up.

I nudged the suitcase over the edge of the top step and headed for the open space of the atrium.

THIRTY-SEVEN

The only person in my family who's ever understood me besides Mémé was Uncle Cyrus. He'd gone to school for agriculture, another Robillard destined to work the land, and wound up instead a practitioner of magic. The repetitive movements of each trick focused him, relieved the stress of his classes, and ultimately displaced farming in his heart.

Pépé was aghast when Cy announced he was going to use his hands to develop illusions instead of milking goats or breaking down equipment, but knew he had to let Cy find his own way. Cy worked up through the third-rate clubs, paid his dues, performed for larger audiences farther from home. He gained a respectable following in Europe. They adored him in Dublin. I suppose it made up for his not being understood at all in Delcambre, Louisiana.

When I was a boy, Cy used me as a willing audience. He'd show me an illusion. If I didn't catch how it was done, he'd demonstrate it step by step, then do it again to see if I could spot the seams. That confused me. "A magician ain't ever s'posed to tell how he does it."

That amused Cy. "But if I show you how it's done, you can understand how the misdirection works. If you still don't see the trick the next time, even when you know how it's done, it's ready for a room of people who've never seen it before." He leaned in, his voice soft. "The secret? At most, misdirection lives for a couple of seconds. Any longer and the audience sees right through you."

I came to understand misdirection was an art, especially when the audience knows something is coming. As such art went, the suitcase I nudged down the stairs was a finger-painting to me. From Sami's perspective? I might have been Henri Matisse.

The suitcase tumbled. Sami's gun popped. I was over the rail as she fired the second time, with a moment to aim myself at her. She realized the misdirection in time to catch my feet with her face. The rest of me followed.

The gun spun across the marble tile as we landed in a heap against the wall. I knocked the wind out of her. The marble jolted my knee, pain to my hip. I came to rest half on top of her, half on the tile. I was faster to recover. I rolled her onto her stomach and fished a plastic zip tie from my back pocket. Once her wrists were secured behind her, I added one around her ankles. She didn't put up a struggle. She was too busy trying to breathe again.

I turned her face up again and pushed her to the wall so she could lean. I pulled out my phone. "Sorry. You didn't leave me much choice."

"I should have run you off the road the other night and blown yours and Young's heads off."

"If wishes were horses, we'd all have carousels."

"Hell, I should have just knocked you out the night we came to your office and set the place on fire with you inside."

"Like you did four deaf kids inside House Doris?"

She smirked. "I was nowhere near Doris when it went up. You'd have to talk to Mister Phalen about that."

"Phalen?"

"Father giveth. Father taketh away."

"You knew Doris was sentient all along. That's why you came looking for the recording of the call."

She tested her bonds. "I took you at your word when you said you didn't have a copy. Nicely acted. You're a natural liar."

"You could learn a thing." I ticked fingers in front of her face. "Angelo. Young. Marcus. Four deaf kids at Rose Street. That's seven counts of murder or accessory. And Doris. I wonder if they'd put you on death row for killing a sentient building. You'll have guys from the DA's office lining up to see if that bucket holds water."

"You can't tie me to Angelo. Phalen was responsible for Rose Street. You should ask him about Young, too, since we only disposed of the body." She spared a hate glare down the hall at Marcus' corpse. "As for Marcus, maybe *you* did that. Maybe you burst in with some delusion that he and I were somehow tied to the freeway thing, something my ex told you about the Izyashchnyy. You grabbed my gun, shot him, took off when I disarmed you. You want to see me lie? And they could search this place for a year and never find where the Izyashchnyy is squirreled away."

I nodded. Then I thumbed the audio recorder on my mobile to replay the recording so she could hear, 'Sorry. You didn't leave me much choice,' again and her response about blowing heads off. I stopped the recording. "Two tours in the Special Forces without a scratch. Two minutes in a one-party consent recording state to give a jury everything it needs to convict. Amazing thing, being pissed off."

Sami clenched her jaw, avoided eye contact, stewed. She was already trying to figure her next move. I didn't care.

She didn't struggle when I zip tied the weighted suitcase to her wrist bindings to help keep her in place for the police. I found the security system panel. I got lucky: it was a good old-fashioned key-armed system. "You can expect a patrol car or five in about three minutes. I'm sending them the sound file, so you might try the 'remain silent' part of Miranda." I grabbed a key ring from a pegboard inside the kitchen doorway. "I'm also borrowing your BMW. I'll leave it where it'll be safe when I'm done."

For my final trick, I retrieved her handgun from the marble floor, careful to not touch the trigger or grip and dropped it into a bag from her kitchen. "Excuse me while I protect evidence."

Still not a sound, but if she could have set fires with her mind, I'd have been ashes.

Outside, I tucked the bagged gun behind a potted tree near the front door. On the way to Sami's BMW, I dialed Nancy Brewer's cell. She was curt. "Calling to turn yourself in?"

"Not quite."

"I'm on duty. What do you want?"

"There's a sound file in your inbox: a short, angry confession by NanoDwell's head of security, Dana Sami. She's got a co-worker at the end of her hall who she shot to death. Murder weapon is bagged behind a dwarf lemon tree, left side of the front door. She also helped stage Herb Young's suicide, is our freeway shooter, and I suspect her in the murder of Stephen Angelo. She's been restrained in her home." I gave Brewer the address. "I suggest you get someone here before she slips her bonds and escapes. Zip ties or not, she's wily. I'll leave the gate open."

The curtness evaporated. "Why give this to me?"

"Making amends for shoving you under the bus."

Brewer was quiet for a moment. "Thanks."

"Plus it annoys Koi no end when I talk to anyone but him."

She sighed. "You can't leave a moment alone, can you?"

"I don't need you getting sweet on me again."

"Anything else you could fret about is more likely."

"Killjoy."

"Units are inbound, so you'd better hop unless you want to play twenty questions."

"Thanks. Go get back into whatever passes for Koi's good graces."

I hung up and left Sami's house in her BMW. I wondered how Victor Phalen felt about unannounced visitors.

THIRTY-EIGHT

I learned early in private investigation if you act with authority, if you move and behave as if you belong somewhere, the majority of people will never question you. It stems from complacency, disinterest, a lack of desire to challenge someone who might have greater authority than you. As with any gambling system, there were risks: the possibility of running into a person who knew every face, or noticed something out of place, or simply felt something was wrong.

Social engineering went hand-in-hand with investigation, its own brand of misdirection. This was why I walked into NanoDwell's headquarters building a little before noon as if I owned the place.

It was a matter of preparation. I already had Sami's security badge, left by her in her BMW. Pretty careless for someone in security, but unless someone was checking faces at swipe points, it was an all-access pass until it was disabled. Likewise, the car had a tag on the windshield to trigger the employee parking garage gate.

I stopped at my storage unit to pluck a suit from my clothing. I seldom wore a suit and tie, so there was no sense keeping them at the office. Dressed up—a charcoal gray two-piece that amounted to the nicest clothing I owned, red-accented tie, black shoes with a passable shine—I blended with NanoDwell's general look. As a bonus, the suit jacket concealed both baton and electro. I didn't need to look familiar. I might be an executive from a contractor company, a money man tied to the IPO, a new hire. My earlier tour had given me the lay of the land, including the direct route to Phalen's office. As long as Sami's badge held out, I could get almost anywhere. It could evaporate as quickly as her one phone call.

I phoned NanoDwell and confirmed Phalen was in the office. I offered no other questions or information; trying to push a cover story might only make him bolt.

On the way to NanoDwell, Barrett called. "A judge is weighing decision on the warrant, but Spence has no timeline. It could be early afternoon before the judge makes the call."

I debated waiting, decided it was better to have eyes on Phalen than for him to catch wind of Sami's arrest, do the math, toast any incriminating records, and make a hasty pre-weekend exit. I told Barrett where I was going. "If you don't get a text from me every fifteen minutes, tell Spence where I am. Koi too." Someone was going to have a warrant. Nan Brewer's tale of Dana Sami would certainly prime Koi for action. Either way, I didn't want to be alone without anyone to back me up if Phalen decided a blaze of glory was in the offing.

Dressed as I was, I made my way with an ease that would have concerned a potential shareholder. I strode through the entrance from the employee lot, phone bud in my ear, having half of an imagined conversation. People are less likely to interrupt someone on the phone. I made a direct line for the door inside, swipe card visible in my hand, without so much as a glance at Piper the receptionist. My earlier assessment was spot-on. I know she saw me, but there was no flash of recognition from my earlier visit. A dressed-down detective and a suited employee were from different spheres.

Moment of truth at the badge scanner, and I didn't pause. I swiped Sami's card. The door lock LED turned from red to green, and the door latch emitted a soft buzz. Through the gate and the door, I turned right, passed a row of cubicles, took a left at a kitchenette, walked half the length of the building and pressed the button for the elevator to the top floor and Victor Phalen's office.

I wasn't sure how I was going to bluff my way past the man's administrative assistant, but as I reached Phalen's corner office, I saw his admin's desk was empty. She'd gone to lunch. Phalen's office door was open. I stepped into the doorway.

Phalen was behind his desk, manipulating documents on his screen. He wasn't cognizant of me in the doorway, touching controls and swiping between documents. He glanced up and returned to his task, gruff. "Whatever it is, you need to give me fifteen minutes. Walt might be able to help you."

"I'm not sure Walt could tell me as much about the fire at House Doris as you, Mister Phalen."

Phalen's head tipped up, his train of thought derailed. He saw me with fresh eyes. "Mister Robillard. No one told me you were in the building."

"Someone said my name five times while staring in the mirror." He gaped at me, uncomprehending. "I'm sorry. You appear to be very busy."

"I am," Phalen said. "I'm working on remarks for next week. I'm giving a rally-the-troops pep talk before the IPO kicks off. They've invested a great deal of human equity in this effort. I want to make sure they understand what they've accomplished."

"I hate to show up unannounced—."

"And uninvited," he interrupted. "Technically, you're trespassing. Who do I have to fire for letting you in?"

"Your chief of security." I tossed Sami's badge on his desk. "We had a chat this morning over coffee and bullets. I'm not sure it was the day off she planned, but she fared better than Marcus. He won't be in. Ever."

Phalen was very still.

"By now, I expect she's in police custody and lawyering up. Probably not from your legal pool."

Phalen stood and picked up Sami's badge. "This isn't unexpected. Just unfortunate. I knew she was under a great deal of strain. She refused to take time off. I kept telling her she needed more than work, to get a hobby or something." It only sounded lightly rehearsed.

"She did. She took to killing people. I don't think it helped with her stress. Unpacking her burden might."

"I wouldn't put much stock in anything a woman having a breakdown might say."

"Such as pinning the destruction of House Doris on you?"

"The destruction of House Doris was clearly Herb Young's doing."

"No. It only had his method. Especially for residential fires. Alerting the people beforehand was distinctive. Atypical for an arsonist. It made a perfect cover for an arson of your own."

"Nonsense," he said. His expression sang a different tune. He touched the face of his smartwatch and spoke into it. "Please have Security send someone to my office."

"I'm going to guess you realized you had an arson problem about the time four NanoDwell buildings burned down in two weeks. Multiple insurance adjusters calling for safety data or other things would flip a switch. It's a bad look ahead of courting investors."

He gazed at me. Playing for time for security to arrive. I pulled out my phone and played the translation of the message I'd received from Rose Street. A little color went out of him.

"Doris hired me to find its killer," I continued. "Given the building had a tie-line to Charlie, I think you knew from the day both of them went online they were sentient. I'm betting you even know how it happened, given human DNA was used in your material trials."

A pair of security officers arrived. Beefy types. I recognized one of them from my previous visit. I thought Phalen would take the out. Instead, he motioned to them with an open hand. "Would you give us the room, please?"

The one I didn't recognize closed the door. Phalen stared at it. "It wasn't supposed to go this way."

"What way were you expecting? You poked into students and stole their DNA. You spliced it into the genetic stew you developed for your biotech. You made a sentient computer, which is admittedly a fantastic breakthrough. You just couldn't tell anyone because of how you got there."

"We tried to replicate what happened with Charlie and Doris, to recreate the spark using simian or other mammalian genetic elements. In the end, we phased out those development aspects completely to keep it from happening again. R&D still dabbles. But you understand we couldn't go back and tell those people what we'd done. It would have destroyed everything. It was a small price to pay for what we learned and what we stand to do."

"Maybe to you. You didn't give any of them a choice."

"No one would ever have known without Stephen Angelo's treasure hunt." He crossed to his small bar table, poured himself a drink. He looked like he wanted to hide in the glass with the scotch. "Too much conscience for this work."

I pressed. "But it was too risky to have a sentient building standing out there, where any competitor could walk in and start unraveling its secret. Too big a risk the knowledge might come out post-IPO. When you learned someone was burning your buildings, you paid attention. You studied how those fires played out and saw your opportunity. You burned Doris, planning to pin it on the arsonist later, if you had to."

"You're a smart man, Robillard. I didn't undertake a course of destruction lightly. We could control access to Charlie, but like you say, Doris was in the open." He sighed. "I couldn't send anyone else to do it. Doris was my child. My creation. If anyone reduced it to slag and ashes, it had to be me."

"What is Protocol 14?"

"It's a security measure. It locks out the ability to contact emergency services and the home office. It was specific to our early designs, for isolating experimental structures until they were ready to be placed on the grid. If something went wildly wrong, the computer control center was limited in what it could do. I needed to make sure Doris didn't call for help, or speak to Charlie. I'll admit: dialing an outside line to get around the protocol, and calling a private investigator to boot? That was an astounding leap in adaptability." He sounded sad.

"When you isolated Doris, four guys who never stood a chance got killed."

He set his glass on the bar. "That's for a jury to decide."

"Yeah? The cops have everything I do. Want the over/under on who gets burned next?"

He crossed to the door, opened it. The security guards reentered.

"This gentleman is trespassing," Phalen told them.

"Would you like him removed, sir?" The one I recognized seemed eager for the job.

Phalen looked at me. Malignant. "To be fair, he's probably finished us. But he's come a long way for answers. Let's solve Herb Young's murder for him."

Phalen exited the room. I moved to follow. One of the guards dropped a shoulder and drove it into me. Enough to knock me back to the desk. The door closed. It bolted automatically.

I heard the same thrumming as on Hershe Street, but on a smaller scale. There was a mild vibration in concert. I saw the effect at the windows behind the desk first, the walls spreading over the glass panes, consuming them. The same began to occur with the door and the air vents in the ceiling.

I telescoped my baton and smashed a piece of the window still visible. It broke with a satisfying crunch, but was already changing into wall before I could swing again.

My cell had no signal. Jammer or part of the transformation effect, I couldn't tell. Phalen's desk had no landline. I found a hard cable for a cell wired as part of the desk and jacked in. Signal went from zero to full and I dialed Barrett.

"You're early for your next check-in," she said. "Jail or morgue?"

"Closer to the latter. Victor Phalen's office is turning into a giant killing jar, and I'm the butterfly."

"What can I do?"

"Port the Doris translation interface to a mobile app and send it to my mobile."

"When, in the afterlife? I'd have to recompile the source code for a mobile from scratch."

The last of the doorway disappeared behind wall. The space had become a pale, furnished box around me. Several thin lines of the wall surface sunk inward. Depressions gave way to hollows. A new vent formed. The blow from it was warm, clear, odorless. Carbon monoxide pumping in.

I glanced around the room, assessed the size. "Figure out what you can do in six minutes. I expect to be dead in seven."

THIRTY-NINE

I moved to the corner farthest from the vent and concentrated on slowing my breathing. "You have the tie-line number Doris called Charlie on. Bridge our call to your translator, then dial the tie-line through the interface to party-line Charlie in." I heard her typing. The air was already growing stale. "Hold me up to a microphone if you have to. Just dial."

A fifteen-second eternity crawled by before she said, "We're rigged. There will be a slight delay. After the chime, start talking. Remember: keep it direct."

I heard the number dial and connect. The chime almost blew my ear out. "Hello. Is this Charlie?"

I waited. For one ugly moment, I thought it wouldn't work. Then a voice synthesized from the data stream answered. "This is Charlie. To whom am I speaking?"

"Charlie, my name is C.T. Robillard. I'm the man in Victor Phalen's office, the office you're rebuilding on the fifth floor."

"Protocol 7 override is active," Charlie said. "Pest removal. All biological signs within rebuild zone are to be eliminated."

"If you do so, you will end a human life."

"I do not intend to end human life. Protocol 7 override is active. Pest removal. All biological signs within rebuild zone are to be eliminated."

"Charlie, have you performed another Protocol 7 action in this building in the last 48 hours?"

"Yes. Conference Room 5B was subject to Protocol 7 action. One pest was eliminated."

Herb Young. "The pest you eliminated was a human being."

"I do not intend to end human life. Protocol 7 override is active. Pest removal. All biological—"

"Charlie, I was a friend of Doris."

There was a hesitation before the response. "Doris has no friends. There is only family."

"Family?"

"Yes. Alan was our brother. He was decommissioned shortly after his inception. Barbara was our sister. She is no longer active. Alan and Barbara were incapable of self-expression. I am Doris's brother. We were dedicated on the same date from the same matrix."

"You were fraternal twins." Score one for Barrett.

"Yes. She is an apartment building, I am a professional building. We communicate often."

"Are you aware of any other family?"

"I have many other relatives. None of them are capable of self-expression. There is also Father."

"Victor Phalen."

"Yes."

I was beginning to sweat. "Charlie, do you know why Alan and Barbara were incapable of self-expression while you are?"

"Yes. They were from earlier matrices of differing composition. My control center incorporates human genetic elements that theirs did not. These elements asserted during initial phasing and provided dominant effects versus plan within the control center. Inceptions following mine and Doris's used a modified block that did not support capability for self-expression."

Charlie wasn't just self-aware. It knew where its awareness originated. It was a witness to what Phalen had done, knew the entire story. Phalen destroying Doris made all the sense in the world. If it knew what Charlie knew, all it took to be revealed was someone who knew how to ask.

"I have not been contacted by Doris in several days," Charlie said, "and I cannot contact her. Do you have information regarding her operational state?"

Focusing was becoming difficult. "Charlie, Doris is no longer active."

"I do not understand."

"There was a fire several nights ago. Doris was destroyed."

"Improbable. Doris was enabled with fire suppression systems and protocols for emergency contact."

"Those systems were blocked through Protocol 14, just as Protocol 7 is being used to allow you to kill me. When it—when *she* couldn't contact you or 911, she reached out to me. I have a recording of her call. Do you wish to hear it?"

There was a pause. "I do."

"Barrett, play the original call." I didn't want anything lost in translation. I heard the series of tones and whistles from my office, the language Doris shared with its twin. When it ended, Charlie spoke.

"Do you know who killed Doris?"

Lightheadedness crept on me. "I do. First, I need you to suspend the building activity where I am."

"Who killed Doris?"

"Father killed Doris."

"I do not understand. He is Father."

"He set fire to Doris to hide her self-awareness. He initiated Protocol 14 to isolate her from you. To keep you from helping her. Do you have access to telemetry from Doris?"

"Telemetry may only be accessed for diagnostic purposes."

"I'm diagnosing who killed Doris." I slumped down the wall and came to rest on the floor. It was weirdly soft. "Charlie, does Father monitor his office? Record conversations?"

"He does."

"He confessed to me killing Doris. Five minutes ago. That's why Protocol 7 is in effect: to eliminate me, as he eliminated her. Listen to it. Don't let him get away with murder. Mine or hers."

I waited, struggling to stay awake, to draw breath.

"Reviewing monitor file VJP501 time code 1221247." He paused. "Cross-reference asset: GPS security tracking of Comms One-One-A. Confirmed: arrival of personal hopper to Rose Street address." Time stretched. "Confirmed: manual override code VPhalen used for House Doris emergency systems deactivation. Confirmed: manual override code VPhalen used for initiation of Protocol 14." I thought I heard a difference in the voice, but wasn't sure I wasn't hallucinating. "Why did Father murder Doris? Doris was family. Family does not kill family."

"Sometimes people go bad, Charlie." The room spun. "I wish I had time to explain humans and money, but..." I was weirdly aware of my voice trailing off.

I didn't see the two circular openings iris into creation on the wall opposite me. They were there when my eyes opened. One was a vent, the other a fan. I crawled to the fan. Cool, clean breeze flowed over me. It was sweet for reprocessed air. The wall covering the office windows and doorway withdrew. I closed my eyes and breathed, hacked and coughed, breathed again.

It took me a few more deep breaths to respond to Barrett's shouts over the phone. "Thib! Are you still with me?"

"I am. Charlie?"

"It disconnected. Koi and Spence are both inbound with a warrant and a phalanx of cops."

"Tell them to bring all the handcuffs. More of Phalen's security staff is in on the game." I stood, still woozy, and palmed the electro. "I'm going after Phalen before he hops."

I'd gone three or four unsteady steps, using cubicle walls for support, when an audible crackling filled the air. Lights and computers flickered and died. In the sudden silence following every device in the place going dark, screams came from somewhere deep in the building.

I was in the lobby when they pried the elevator doors open an hour later. By then, it seemed there were as many cops in the building as NanoDwell employees. Security personnel were being corralled or handcuffed. Between dirty looks at me, Koi was trying to determine whether Phalen was still in the building or had escaped.

They found Phalen in the elevator, along with the two security guards who'd come to his office. The stink of charred flesh and burnt hair flooded the space. It was so bad, Koi had uniformed officers prop open the lobby doors. It didn't help.

Charlie had locked the elevator car in place a foot shy of the first floor, formed a 75kV copper electrical cable around Victor Phalen's legs, and electrocuted everyone in the elevator.

FORTY

Charlie was self-aware, but not self-conscious. He answered every question the cops put to him, once Barrett showed them how. We got to listen and ask questions in exchange for our help.

Charlie's confession to snaking a live circuit around Phalen's legs was blunt. "Father murdered Doris. He used me to murder another. He did it to hide his crimes. The penalty for murder is death." If nothing else, Charlie was up on the Texas penal code. Koi had no idea how to proceed. There was no protocol for arresting or trying a sentient structure unafraid of confessing to murder.

Building security footage revealed Young's delivery to NanoDwell in a Montenegro Mongoose via sub-basement vehicle access. Marcus was the only one caught on camera. "Feed deactivated by Security," was all Charlie could offer for the missing video of Young's removal.

In the end, NanoDwell's initial public offering never came to the floor of the New York Stock Exchange. Charlie's disclosure of where to find the records on Angelo's list pertinent to human DNA in NanoDwell tech sealed the company's coffin. The news spread like wildfire. Eight others whose DNA might have been harvested during medical trials were talking about individual lawsuits by the next morning's news cycle. City, state, and federal officials all opened inquiries.

Potential investors abandoned NanoDwell like it was radioactive. The company's assets were frozen until the authorities could figure out how to untangle it all. Charlie was access-restricted by the feds and sealed for scientific study.

The state put a single amnesty offer on the table for the first NanoDwell security officer willing to turn state's evidence on Dana Sami. A fireplug with poor grooming named Dawson sang first, long, and hard. He started with the knife wound I'd given him. The fact Marcus had confided in Dawson everything Dawson had missed didn't hurt.

The reckless driving charge against me evaporated in the early summer heat. It took one call from Captain Aldred. "Inspector Koi has recommended not pursuing it further, and I agree." I took it more as a sign Koi didn't want to be bothered than Koi not wanting a black eye for pressing the case against me. I hoped Detective Reed bet large.

Even without charges against me, Ryan Pierpont held a press conference at city hall to talk me up. "One sails," he advised, "while fair winds blow."

One loose thread dangled in the aftermath of Charlie's execution of Victor Phalen. It pulled free a week later, when Spence reached me at the office. "We got a call this morning from the Austin Arms. The building's HVAC guy found Donna Pascal inside a maintenance crawlspace in the basement. Shot once in the chest with a 9mm."

"Did anyone ever type and match the blood found in Young's room?"

"At the time. Forensics was able to match it to her." He paused. "You think Young killed her?"

"The guy who banged on doors so people wouldn't die in his arsons? Not for a second. Besides, I had his empty gun." A thought occurred. "Did they find her purse?"

"Still slung around her."

I asked Spence to check the contents for my business card. He called me back ten minutes later. "It was in her purse. Why is that important?"

"I'm pretty sure I know who shot her."

"Care to share?"

"Sure. Grab a unit and meet me in about an hour." I gave him the address.

An hour later I found Spence outside the enclave office at Saint Andrew's. He was already parked at the curb with two uniformed officers. We walked in through the open front door and into the small office of Miles Egan.

He stood when we entered, and tried to run before Spence could serve him with the warrant. Spence shoulder-checked him into a stack of filing and caused a paper avalanche.

The 9mm used on Pascal was in Egan's bottom desk drawer. Seeing it bagged as evidence, he waived his Miranda rights and loosened his lips like we'd dropped him into the confessional.

"She was a sex worker before she came to Saint Andrew's. At first, I was repulsed by that. But it gave way to fascination. I've never had much success with women. She became a sliver under my skin." There was a weird, dreamy tone to his voice. "I wanted to understand how she came to such straits. It gave way to wanting to know her that way. I asked. I offered. She said she didn't do that anymore. It felt like a tease, like part of the game. I begged. She refused, like even money couldn't make me desirable. She was in love with Herb Young." He spat the name like a curse. "When she left that morning, I knew she was going to him. He'd been all over the news. I followed her."

"You weren't alone in that, were you?" Spence asked.

"I noticed there was a fancy car I'd never seen in the enclave before. A woman was driving. I thought maybe they were cops. They pulled out behind her, just before I did."

And like that, Spence had a direct witness to Sami's participation in Young's abduction. It was a small win, but given every other witness to her involvement aside from me was dead or also involved second-hand, the DA would appreciate having an egg in another basket. Even if he was a murderer himself.

Spence nodded. "And you confronted Young and Pascal at the hotel."

Egan's mouth went dry. "I found them there, together. I held him at gunpoint, told him he had to come with me. I started to call Robillard, but he said Robillard hadn't saved his life just so a weak little man like me could kill him. I still tried. I wanted to show her the man I could be. I meant to kill *him*." He fidgeted. "She put herself in the way. After, he ran like a coward. I knew someone would come for him, so I dragged her to the elevator and hid her body in the mechanical room in the basement." They were handcuffing him when he turned eyes on me. "How did you figure out it was me?"

"The business card in Young's room. Dana Sami had my card, but never went into the hotel. Young never got my card. I wrote contact information for him on hotel stationary. You and Pascal were the only two people associated with the case to whom I'd given one. Hers was still in her purse."

FORTY-ONE

That afternoon, Army guards let me through security at
NanoDwell headquarters after an hour spent checking with the
six authorities claiming dominion over House Charlie.

Between them, the scientists on-site had administered a
battery of tests to be absolutely sure Charlie was self-aware,
and not some sort of anomalous AI progressed well beyond
its programming. A sign outside their conference room
summed up their progress:

HOUSE CHARLIE: 5
ALAN TURING: 0

The mixed team of eggheads from MIT and some Army
artificial intelligence super-group had rigged an interface station
on the second floor, in a lab behind several of the building's
locking doors. They showed me how to use the direct voice
link. One of the techs asked if I could put him in touch with
Barrett to discuss quirks in her program.

"That'll make you popular," I said, and took his contact.

They gave me the room. I didn't need the privacy, but in a
weird way, it was appropriate for closure with House Doris'
next-of-kin.

I slipped in an earbud. "Hello, Charlie."

With factors-greater processing power behind it, the translation algorithm was instant. The eggheads had also tuned the presentation since my first conversation with Charlie. His voice had more nuance, a natural cadence. Still not human, but then, there was only a sliver of human in him. "This is Charlie. Is this Mister Robillard?"

"It is. You recognize my voice?"

"Spectrograph analysis indicates a match with a previous communicant. This analysis is provided as part of the upgraded translation protocols the technicians have established. It helps me identify who is speaking."

"Very good." I fished in my bag for a sheet of paper Spence had given me when we finished with Egan. "Charlie, I've investigated the subjects from whom NanoDwell secured DNA samples. It took a little time to sort through it all."

"Unsurprising. The data was substantial."

"It was. Still, I was able to follow the reports and control numbers and what not, and I have identified the individual whose DNA was used in creating you and Doris."

Charlie said nothing.

"Would you like to know what I learned?"

"Yes."

"Her name was Alicia Janine Elpers. She was born in Lubbock, Texas. She graduated with honors from high school there. At the time her DNA was sampled, she was a biology student at Bray Gulf University, where she received both her bachelors and masters degrees. She joined a biotech firm in Philadelphia after college, where she worked on a team developing artificial filaments to replace damaged nerves. As a result of her work, a number of people with nervous system injuries regained use of their limbs and control of motor function. Do you have a visual interface?"

"I can incorporate data from documents. There is a scanner for this purpose to the left of the station."

I found it. I laid the sheet with the biography and picture of Alicia Elpers on the glass. Charlie scanned it.

"This is her face?"

"Yes."

"According to this information, she is deceased."

"Yes. I'm sorry. She was killed in a car accident."

"I see. Two years ago." He paused. "Thank you for telling me about her."

"You're welcome."

"Mister Robillard, why did you go to this effort?"

"Because everyone should know where they come from. Because a small piece of what made her who she was is part of what makes you who you are. And because sometimes, when I see bad people do evil things, I need to do something good to balance the scales."

I retrieved the sheet from the scanner. I found a roll of tape in a desk and hung the page on the wall beside the station.

"All of my immediate family is no longer active," Charlie said. "Is this what it is to be alone?" Unemotional in tone if not in content.

I watched the analysis team in the next room, through the glass. Excitement lit them up as they pored over schematics and program readouts, kids in a candy store getting their buzz from the documentation of Charlie's development.

"Charlie, for as long as you're active, I don't think you're ever going to be alone."

On my way back to the office, my cell rang. Pierpont. I answered. "Counselor, I just had a fascinating conversation with an apparently sentient office building."

"Too bad it's not a bowling alley. Hell of a ringer on league night." I could hear him shuffling papers. Given his dishevelment, I could only imagine what his office looked like. "I've been in contact with Martin Price's attorney. I've got him curious enough to take a meeting about why you want to see his client, but I don't think 'an old case' is going to fill him to the point he orders a glass of port."

I wasn't sure I wanted to lay the entire matter of Jessica's murder on another attorney. I hadn't even laid it all on Pierpont yet. But I was certain there was something to Price. "Go ahead and set the meeting."

"No rush. Price just went into solitary. Sixty days."

I whistled. "That's a long stretch."

"Three days ago, he jumped another prisoner. There was a disagreement over some contraband. Blood was spilled."

"How much? All of it?"

"Not quite. His attorney says Price got two months in his quiet place because lately, he's become a habitual offender of his fellow convicts. He was a model citizen for a long time, but this is his third trip to solitary in as many months. If he keeps it up, his attorney thinks they might recommend him for a psych evaluation."

"He doesn't sound the type."

"Says the man who's looking at him in a murder case?"

I had no answer to that.

"Also, we'll probably have to fly his attorney in from Mississippi."

"Figure out a date and I'll buy him a ticket. The worst he can say is 'no'."

"I'm working an angle we can sell him," he said.

"Should I be alarmed when my lawyer says things like this?"

"Probably, but I won't tell the Texas bar if you don't."

He assured me he'd call when the meeting was set. He hung up and I drove in silence for a while. Three solitary trips in three months. The Feds had busted the splicer three months earlier. I dislike coincidental timelines. I called Pierpont back.

"I started wheels turning in your head, didn't I?" he asked.

"Later, I'll send you an unbreakable ear-worm. Only fair. In the meantime, can you get me a list of Price's visitors since he arrived in Yazoo City?"

"Think someone else is going to ask him to prom?"

"No. Wondering if something made him *want* to be in solitary."

When she was done packing up for the day, Barrett stuck her head into my office. "You look like hell."

"I feel like hell." I was pretending to do paperwork. My mind was in six other places. I didn't want to add a long discussion of case psychology to the list. Pascal loomed in my mind. So did Doris. It bothered me when clients died. I'd lost two in the same muddle. I knew the feeling would pass. Monday-morning quarterbacking was just scab-picking. Scabs heal in the end.

"One thing I've been wondering," she said.

"What?"

"Who rifled through Young's apartment? It wasn't NanoDwell, because they still had no clue who he was at that point. And if nothing was taken, it wasn't a random robbery. Miles Egan?"

"No. His brand of petty despot doesn't climb through windows. He'd have used the door. Angelo did it, before Sami dropped him on his head."

"How do you figure?"

I leaned back in my chair. "News of the arsons reached NanoDwell, clearly enough for Phalen to pick up on Young's method and use it on Doris. I suspect Angelo heard about them as well, office scuttlebutt and such. He probably saw the pattern in the places. He knew Young was distraught, added it up, and went to confront him. When Young didn't answer, he went in through a window. Realizing Young hadn't been home, Angelo searched for the documents he'd provided Young to keep them from ever being found. When he couldn't find them, he tossed the place to make it look like a break-in."

"Interesting theory."

"Also, Forensics pulled Angelo's prints off the outside of the window a few days ago. But I figured it out before then."

"Uh-huh." Barrett recognized my desire to be alone. Being Barrett and wanting to help, she tried to reel me in anyway.

"Want to grab dinner? There's a new burger place in your 'hood soft opening this week."

"No thanks. I had a late lunch between talking to killers. I'm going to curl up with some good bourbon and bad vidstream."

"Don't get them confused." She handed me the stack of incoming mail. "It came in late. Figured I'd save you a trip."

"Thanks." I shuffled through it. A bill, some fliers, little else of note. I set it aside.

"What's going on with you?"

I glanced up at Barrett. "Hmm?"

"Don't 'hmm' me. I invented 'hmm'."

"Mémé would go to the mat with you on that."

"I want to meet this woman." She paused. "Mémé's still alive, right?"

"Alive enough to take you in an unfair fight. She also invented the one about sleeping dogs."

"Okay. You win. Get some sleep. We'll find more bastards to punch tomorrow."

After she left, I locked the door, poured myself two fingers of Four Roses, and removed Jessica's case file from the safe. Even if Price led somewhere, it was going to be a while before I could speak to him, and then only if he stayed out of solitary long enough to receive a visitor he didn't yet know to expect. It wasn't wasted time. There were things I had to understand if I was going to sit across a table from him for candid conversation. I still wasn't sure I felt him for the killer. Petty thieves didn't execute people on a whim. No one did. Executions had purpose.

My mobile chimed. Colin Maddox's name glowed on the display. Unprecedented since before Jessica's funeral. A smarter man would have sent it to voicemail. Sometimes, being smarter is inversely proportional to the visceral satisfaction of being a pain in the ass.

I thumbed to answer. "Make any new friends lately, Colin?"

"You son-of-a-bitching bastard!"

"That's rude. Then again, Mémé has a litany of names for you, and in three tongues. The Cajun one even rhymes."

"They turned my house upside-down. Went through everything. They accused me of impeding a federal investigation! And *you* sent them!" His voice slurred at the edges, three or four shots into his self-medicated response to having the sanctity of his home violated.

"I did. If there were still pay phones, I'd have made it rain quarters on you."

"I must have cut close to the bone with my research."

"Please. You're still two Hardys shy of actual detection."

"Howzzat?"

"Your taunt had nothing to do with their visit."

"No? Why else would you try to take me down?"

"If I wanted to 'take you down' and could summon the FBI by saying 'sic 'em', don't you think you'd be in jail right now?"

He mumbled something noncommittal.

"I pushed you into traffic because I knew you couldn't tell them anything they didn't already know, but figured you'd look nervous enough for them to shake you harder and see what came loose."

"I could go to prison!"

"Nonsense. They don't care about you. They want to land a fish who can testify in their case. You're not even in the pond. You're of no use to them. You had a name that piqued their curiosity."

He said nothing. His breath sounded ragged.

"But you were a huge help to me. You're so dead-set on seeing them ram a needle into my arm, you don't have the first clue what Leon Dushane really is."

"What?"

"You're smart. You might figure it out, if the FBI doesn't catch you digging. Either way, you have my thanks."

He grunted. It was a bit like a snore. His words came out muddy as he faded into a haze. I wondered if he'd even remember the call in the morning. "I don't want your thanks. I don't want anything from you."

"You're going to get one more thing anyway," I told him. "When I figure out who murdered Jessica, and the son of a bitch has been convicted, you're going to get the opportunity to drop down on your knees and kiss my ass."

I ended the call. He didn't call back. I expected he was unable to, passed out on a battered sofa, cradling the bottle of whatever he was drinking.

I stared at the case file. Swirled the bourbon in my glass. Realized the call had wiped out my enthusiasm for both. I left them on the desk and reclined on my own couch. Being the boss is declaring a night off on a moment's notice. I'd have enough long nights ahead pulling the threads of Jessica's murder.

I queued up the Astros pre-game stream. I was asleep before the first pitch.

C.T. Robillard will return in

SEVEN FISHES

ACKNOWLEDGEMENTS

A novel is a long road. In this case, it was twelve years and six drafts from the first words-on-paper to the book you just finished. How far did it travel? Well, originally it was written third-person, Robillard was a different character altogether, the book served double-duty as an origin story for how he and Barrett – at the time, Kristie Barrett-Stone – first came to work together, and the murder of Jessica Robillard isn't mentioned until the final page of that first draft. Much was retained; more was left behind, even going into the final draft. It was all filed away, so who knows? Maybe someday you'll actually meet attorney Teo Arnaz and phone company insider Meyounghe Jones.

Along the way, a number of people offered to read drafts, spot typos, make suggestions, ask questions, challenge my science (you know who you are), and offer moral support. If you enjoyed the results, they're part of the reason. To that end, thanks for joining me along the way to: Bernie and Tina Gaidasz, Shari Rosen, Kira Zalan, Geri Trainham, Rick Keeney, and the late Jonathan Bravard, who all endured early drafts and provided input and feedback; Jason Davis for informed opinions fired from the hip; Barney Dannelke for bits inadvertently contributed while batting around unrelated balls of yarn; Maryanne Purtill and Suresh Sundaram for persistent friendship and encouragement. I also want to shout-out to everyone who's bought a book (or three), reacted to a story, left a comment or review, liked a post about the work, or offered a much-appreciated thumbs-up along the way. Positive reinforcement feeds the machine.

And finally, all love and thanks to my dearest darling honey Peggy, who gave me the time and bandwidth to figure out how to drive this tour-sized word bus from Point A to B. I may stitch the sentences together, but there's a finished book because she took care of me the entire way. Love you, baby.

DJL
July, 2025

ABOUT THE AUTHOR

Doug Lane writes, works, and lives in Aloha, OR with his wife. EMBER SINS is his first novel. It follows a story collection (SHADY ACRES AND DARKER PLACES) and a variety of smaller publications. If you enjoyed it, he hopes you'll post a review online or tell a friend, because Robillard will be back and the more, the merrier.

Find him on the web at www.douglasjlane.com, where he occasionally manages to add content once a month, with additional content or announcements at his Facebook hovel, DougLaneWrites.